HUNTED

THE DHAMPYR SERIES
BOOK ONE

V. M. NELSON

Published by VMNelson Books LLC
www.virginiamnelson.com
Developmental Edit by Courtney Andersson
Copy Edit by Lara Kennedy
Proofread by Liz Gilbeau
Cover Art by Stefanie Saw at SeventhStar Art Services

COPYRIGHT © 2022 VMNELSON BOOKS LLC

All rights reserved. No part of this book may be reproduced, distributed, or transmitted in any form or by any means, without written permission from the author, except for the use of brief quotations in an article or book review.

Thank you to everyone who has purchased this book and for respecting the hard work of the author.

All characters and events depicted in this book are fictitious. Any similarity to real persons, living or dead, is purely coincidental.

ISBN Ebook: 978-1-958280-00-3

ISBN Paperback: 978-1-958280-01-0

ISBN Hardback: 978-1-958280-02-7

❦ Created with Vellum

DEDICATION

Thank you to my partner-in-crime, Jon, and my sister, Evelyn, for always supporting me. Without your support, this would only be a dream.

1

What started out as a routine task to find blood turned into an onslaught of pain. I rubbed my eyes, allowing the darkness that filled my head to fizzle away. My hands, tender from scraping against the gravel, grasped at the cold metal fence. I flinched as my cuts burned against the steel. I'd done this to myself. The thumping under my skin and my lack of balance were all a result of ignoring my need to feed.

Now here I sat, watching my blood as it dripped down my leg and pooled onto the sidewalk. A tingling sensation ran through me as I flicked out the tiny shards that had embedded themselves in my skin. My body helped to push them out in an effort to heal itself. This was not part of tonight's plan. I stared back up at the fence—my nemesis. Razor-sharp wire wrapped itself around the top of the rusty, twelve-foot-high chain-link barricade.

Take the shortcut, Tasi. It'll be quicker and safer, Tasi. What a stupid idea.

Under normal circumstances, I could dart up the fence, hop over the barbed wire, and gracefully land on my feet. My overall dexterity might have won me a gold medal in gymnastics, but that was so not happening in my current condition.

An ache thundered through my body as I reached for the fence again. I hoisted myself up for the first time since tumbling off. With one last labored breath, I ran my hands down my pants, dislodging the remaining rocks from my newly healed skin. Nearby, a rustling sound echoed through the alley. My breath caught. The metal garbage cans clanked together as if they were being tossed around. If I were human, I wouldn't think twice about the commotion. Lucky for me, I knew better. It was probably setting up to kill its next victim. There were a few shady-looking dive bars and run-down nightclubs in this area. The repetitive pounding of music stemming from different directions would drown out all screams. This was a perfect feeding ground.

Over the past few months, these creatures had become my reality. Since I was thirteen, I'd known of their existence, but only recently had I been in the same vicinity as them. And when they were around, you didn't want to be, so it was time to go.

With a quick pivot in the opposite direction, I ran. I didn't get farther than a few feet before my shoelace caught in the grate and my chin scraped against the ground. More blood dripped from my body.

Tasi, seriously—what else can go wrong?

Wrapping the shoelace around my fingers, I yanked until it released itself. By the time I tucked it into my shoe, it was too late. *It* had heard me. The pounding in my ears was no longer from the nightclubs but the pavement, and it was getting louder. I'd piqued its interest. Rather, my blood had piqued its interest.

I'd run away enough times in the past that I knew I'd be able to shake the monster. I mustered up as much energy as I could and took off running, snaking through run-down buildings, dodging cars, and running across baseball fields until I thought I had gone far enough. I listened for feet thumping steadily on the sidewalk, but I couldn't hear my pursuer anymore—good for me; bad for someone else. My weakened state was taking a toll on my body, and I needed to get back to the hole I currently called home. I was just glad I didn't have to fight for my life tonight. I'm not sure I would have won this round.

When I turned the corner, I saw safety within my reach. The gaudy lights of the motel shone brighter than ever. As I approached the building, a low hum electrified the surrounding air, and the mildewed smells burned in my nose. The grunts and noises that came from each room crawled over my skin. This was not at all a place we should be staying.

When I reached the room, I looked around before opening the door. The glow of the soda machine lit up the silhouette of a couple arguing nearby. On the opposite side, a man wearing boxers and a dirty white tee stood in the doorway, a cigarette hung from his mouth. When our eyes met, he forced a grin, showing his stained teeth. I fumbled with the keys. This week, I had not been careful. Instead, I'd been lazy and hadn't made smart decisions. This trip could've killed me. More importantly, it could've killed Emily.

As I passed by her bed, I glanced over to make sure she was still sleeping. If she had woken up and seen I wasn't there, I don't know what she would've done. There was so much I still needed to tell her. I placed my backpack on the bed before going into the bathroom to clean up.

There was nothing in the world that made me feel more at home than a hot shower, and this was a good one. Warmth wrapped itself around me, giving me a much-needed hug. I watched my feet as the water took all the horrid parts of the night and pulled them down the drain. Reluctant to end such a perfect shower, I shut off the water and stepped out of the tub. A shiver at the quick temperature change made me think getting out was the wrong decision, and I pulled the towel tighter around myself.

I wiped away the thick steam covering the mirror, and there the truth stared back at me. The shower had cleaned up the blood and dirt, but what remained was still unrecognizable. My eyes were bloodshot, and the shadows building underneath them made me appear sick. I looked deeper, hoping to find a glimmer of my old self, maybe a speck of my greenish-blue eyes or just a shimmer of my dark silky hair. Even my freckles, which had been scattered across my face, no longer existed. Nothing was there that reassured me I was still Tasi. I ran my fingers along my pale skin, pulling at it, hoping it would fall off and reveal what used to be. Instead, dark gray eyes stared back at me.

I studied the rest of my face, looking for familiarity—something I did often. I looked well beyond eighteen and seemed to have aged years in only a few months. I braced my hands on the edge of the sink, dropping my head as if it suddenly weighed a hundred pounds.

How in the world was I ever going to get myself together the way I should for Emily? She was counting on me, and I kept making stupid mistakes.

I took one last deep breath, threw on some sweatpants and a long-sleeved T-shirt, then flipped off the light switch in the bathroom. Making my way into the main room, I sat on the edge of the bed. I knew it was time to move on from this seedy motel that had become our home for the past few weeks. The real world scared me, and I was afraid of making the wrong choices.

Sometimes I couldn't help getting mad at having been raised in such a sheltered environment. Maybe it wouldn't have been so bad if I had given up a normal life by choice, but that wasn't the case. I'd had to give up friends, parties, and all the other things that come with being a regular teenager, all for the people I loved—the same people who had ended up lying to me. Now look at what my life had become: I was on the run with my thirteen-year-old sister from someone or something that wanted us dead.

A lump formed in my throat. I crept over to the small table and turned on the lamp. Emily fussed, but her breathing steadied. Turning back to the desk, I stared at the drink I'd made with my newly acquired supplies. It was okay when I put the blood in coffee, but today I'd diluted it with juice. The thought made my skin prickle. I plugged my nose and downed the vile concoction, knowing I had to build my strength again. I couldn't have any more nights like tonight.

Our aunt, Eva, used to make my drinks. Not knowing what was in my special shakes—as she called them—or how she got the supplies had made drinking it much simpler. I rubbed my forehead to alleviate some of the throbs that appeared whenever I thought of Eva.

She'd raised us because our parents died when Emily was one. Sometimes, I think Emily was lucky not to remember them. There were times we would be in the supermarket or taking a walk, and I'd see someone with long tousled blonde hair. In that instant, I always hoped it would be my mother. But it was always a stranger's face.

One memory stood out among the rest. My father and our long night walks. I would hold his hand and always ask him why his were so cold. He would laugh and say, "My heart holds all the warmth in the world, leaving the rest of me hard and cold." I never knew what that meant until I was older.

Reaching into my backpack, I pulled out a beat-up manila envelope. Emily stirred as I searched for a specific paper. It was a letter that had frayed at the edges. A single tear fell onto the page. I wiped it away, smearing the ink. It wasn't the first smudge, and it wouldn't be the last.

My Dearest Antanasia,

If you are reading this, we aren't alive anymore, and you have to take Emily and go. I'm sorry we lied about being dead all these years, but please understand it was safer this way. If Eva doesn't make it, you must leave Maine. You need to take the money I left you and seek Sonya Bourne in New York City. She will be able to help. Again, I'm sorry, and I love you both very much. Believe me when I say I thought you were safe.

Love always,

Mom

I stared at the paper, running my fingers across my lips. *Who are you, Sonya Bourne?* How was I supposed to trust someone else after everything that had happened? My parents and Eva had lied to us. They said it was to keep us safe, but even if that was true, my parents had been alive all these years.

I had to remind myself to stop judging what they did because I was doing something very similar to Emily. Since their deaths, Emily and I had moved from motel to motel. At night, I kept Emily in the room for two reasons. First, that's when the bloodsucking creatures came out to play, and I wouldn't let them find her. Second, she didn't know what we were. So I snuck out when I needed to only after she fell asleep. I could imagine the look on her face if I said, "Sorry, Em, I have to stop off at the hospital and pick up blood for lunch."

Luckily, we were currently in Portland, Maine, and it wasn't a big enough city to house a large population of monsters, like Boston or New York City. It was just big enough to keep me busy. Tonight was a prime example of why I needed to take care of myself.

I folded the letter back up, shoved everything back into the envelope, and bound it before placing it into the bottom of my backpack once again. I tiptoed over to my bed and pulled back the sheets, and the musty scent filled my nose. I hoped sleep would come instantly, but that was never the case. My nights were often filled with tossing and turning, reliving what used to be. When I was younger, all I'd wanted was adventure, and to see the world. If this was the world and my future, all I wanted now was to go back to being locked up in a house where it was safe.

2

"Run, Tasi—don't just sit there!" Eva yelled. "Did you hear me? Get Emily and the backpacks. Now!"

The day had started like any other. That was, until Eva's phone rang while we were making dinner. Two seconds and a shattered plate later, Eva was shouting for me to move.

I backed up against the table, waiting for my aunt to tell me this was a joke. When that didn't happen, I ran up the stairs, taking the steps two at a time. I'd had a theory this day was a fairy tale created in Eva's head. It wasn't, though, because when my throat tightened and the tingling in my body became urgent, the story flipped from fantasy to reality.

As I reached Emily's door, my hand crashed against it, swinging it open with more force than I'd intended. She flinched. My aunt would have killed me if I'd knocked my sister out.

"Tasi! What are you doing?"

"We have to go. Now."

She pulled her earbuds out. Her aqua eyes thinned as they burned into me. "What are you grumbling about? Stop being stupid, and shut the door on your way out." I snatched the phone out of her hand and took off to Eva's room.

"What the heck, Tasi? I was listening to that."

Emily followed. She stood in the doorway, arms crossed, while I rummaged through the closet.

Her arms fell to her side. "You aren't kidding."

"No, now throw on some shoes before Eva comes up here and drags us both away."

I tossed her pink phone back to her and watched as her eyes widened. She bolted out the door.

With backpacks in hand, I ran past Emily's room.

"We have to go, Em—move faster."

Leaping down the stairs in a couple swift movements, I saw Eva standing at the bottom. I swerved so I didn't collide with her. She grabbed one of the packs from me and threw in some snacks and a couple of my special shakes.

"Where is Emily? We have to go."

"I'm right here. Will someone tell me what is going on?" Emily asked. Strapped to her back was a pink duffel bag, bulging at the seams.

"Emily, you have too much stuff." There was a rumble in Eva's voice that was unfamiliar to us.

"What. Why?" Emily asked.

Eva wasted no time. She grabbed Emily's bag off her back and tossed it across the room. "You are only taking what I give you in these backpacks. Also, you cannot take your phones. The last thing you need is to be tracked."

Emily looked at our aunt, opened her mouth, and quickly shut it. She swallowed hard as a visible lump moved down her throat.

"It'll be okay," I said, sliding my hand into hers.

Eva grabbed her keys, ushering us out of the house. "We can talk in the car."

There was a knock at the door, which shook me out of my sleep. One of these days, I would like to wake up refreshed; maybe give the black circles a break.

I rubbed my eyes, trying to focus. Emily sat up, stretched, and let out a silent yawn. I flipped the lamp on next to my bed. The doorknob wriggled as someone—or rather, something—tried to open the door. I was hoping it would find the door locked and move on to another room to find an easier kill. I held my breath. The doorknob twisted again, this time more fiercely. I slid off my bed and slipped on my high-tops. I grabbed Emily's shoes and placed them on her bed.

"Housekeeping." The voice was grimy and melodious all at the same time. He was toying with us.

Emily straightened up. She pulled her knees into her chest as the handle jiggled once again. Nails scraped along the door, and that was our cue.

"Housekeeping." He dropped the pleasantries. There was a grumble in his tone.

Emily was now kicking back her sheets.

"Time to go," I whispered.

Pins and needles traveled along my skin, and my mouth went dry, knowing what lurked at the door. Emily slipped into the bathroom, making her way to the window. I locked the door behind us.

"Little girl, I know you're in there. I've been looking for you, and now I smell your blood. I'm coming to get you." The monster's voice was sweet and taunting. The pins and needles deepened in my skin. He wasn't going to stop until he had us for dinner.

"It's stuck," Emily said.

The palm of my hand pressed against the window's edge. Why hadn't I tried to open this window before? Such a rookie mistake. Emily tried to shake the window loose, gripping the pane. The rattle of the knob stopped. It was replaced by a battering ram.

"Watch out," I said.

Gripping the edge of the sink and pressing my hand against the wall, I leaped, smashing my foot through the glass. The only thing I wanted to do at the moment was run away. If we made it out the window, the approaching sunrise might keep the monster in. If not, we would hide until the sun peeked its glorious head out. Then, by the time nightfall came along, we'd be far, far away.

Emily pulled herself through as the motel room door slammed against the wall. I threw our belongings out and heaved myself through the window, but not quickly enough. The bathroom door swung open, and before I could get out, it grabbed my leg, yanking me back in. My elbow slammed into the side of the window, causing a rippling pain through my arm.

"Tasi!"

Not letting her distract me was essential for my survival. Focusing on my attacker, I used my free leg to kick him right in the stomach. It was like hitting a stone wall, but he stumbled back, and we both landed on the floor. Pain surged through my leg. I ignored it. My strength wasn't the issue here, but my coordination was still off.

He regained his stance faster than I had hoped, and moved toward me again in one swift movement. This time he grabbed my arm, digging his nails deep enough to draw blood. I cried out in surprise as a crazed look filled his features. His eyes shifted from brown to a shimmery black. He was trying to compel me. If I were a human, he'd have me offering my neck to him by now. That was the thing with vampires—they looked human. Their skin was pale, and they had a glamour to them that drew humans to them willingly. This one was tall with sandy-colored short hair and chiseled cheekbones.

He leaned down to lick the blood off his finger and cocked his head toward me. "Yes, you are her—the girl near the nightclub. The girl with the blood that smells so good." He took in a deep breath as if he were getting high. "You taste delicious. Better than anyone I have ever taken pleasure in. Don't worry, little girl, once my fangs drip the venom into you, you will want to give me your blood."

There was a sourness to his voice, and his breath chilled my skin as he moved in closer. My body trembled. My pulse quickened. He looked back at my arm, which he still held, and raised it closer to his lips. Icy needles raced down my spine as I watched his mouth get closer. His tongue lashed out like a serpent and ran across my wound, leaving a tingle running under my skin. Then, licking his lips, he looked at me one last time.

"I'm going to enjoy this."

Feeling his grip loosen as he took in that last bit of blood, I knew I had my chance. The shiver turned to heat, boiling my blood beneath my skin. Using all my strength, I kicked him, catching him off guard. He must really have believed me to be as weak as a human. That moment of disbelief gave me just enough time to lift my pant leg, grab the wooden stake strapped to my body, and stab him in his chest. Again, I had stunned him. With one more push, using all my muscle, I rammed it in farther. His eyes rolled back, and he turned into white ash before hitting the ground, leaving the stench of sulfur in the air. The floating dust particles and smells made me cough.

With the stake still in my hand, I fell against the wall. My breath labored and pain pulsated through me. I remembered Emily and raced to the window.

"I'm okay, Em."

She was sitting against the adjacent building, arms wrapped around her knees, tears streaming down her face. But when she saw I was all right, she jumped to her feet, wiping the wetness from her eyes.

"I'll be right there," I told her. "Just gimme a sec."

I turned back to my assailant, and the reality of the situation hit me. My legs grew weak, and nausea churned in my stomach. A few more seconds and I would have been dead. My aunt had told me I should feed every two days to keep me strong enough to fight. *I guess I now know what happens when I don't listen.*

I found nothing that led me to believe he was deliberately hunting us as I checked through his tattered clothes. It was just a filthy bloodsucker who'd caught me off guard. I wiped the ash off my stake, then concealed the weapon once again.

Thinking through the series of events, I thought I'd been clever in my escape but realized he must not have stopped searching for me. Maybe I should have burned my clothes and the towels that had my dried-up blood on them. I'd been incredibly stupid, and had put Emily's life in danger by leading him back to her.

I headed over to the sink to assess the damage and clean myself up, then ripped the towel and tied it around my wound to keep the blood from dripping. The black long-sleeved shirt I had on hid my new makeshift bandage. Waiting a few seconds more, I checked to see if the bleeding would push through the towel, but it didn't. My body should heal the cut before anyone noticed. With my hands on the edge of the sink, I tightened my hold, staring at my reflection. It was time to stop hiding and start finding answers.

Pulling myself through the window was hard to do, and I decided to go feetfirst this time. Even though my assailant had left me aching and bruised, I landed as gracefully as I knew Emily had.

Emily closed the gap between us, burying her face in my neck. "I thought I had lost you. Who was that?"

"That, Em, is what we're running from. I think now that

you're thirteen, we need to talk about a few things." I avoided eye contact and straightened my ponytail. "First, though, let's get breakfast and go shopping. It's time we head for New York City, like Eva wanted us to. We can chat about all this on the way."

"Okay." Emily smiled back at me. "Can I buy some new shampoo? That motel soap was ruining my hair."

This made me giggle, albeit a shaky one. "Of course—we'll get a small bottle of the one you like."

She clapped her hands and her smile grew. She was so patient. Had someone told me they had a secret regarding my weird life, I would have bitched until they told me. Emily trusted me to do what was right—but at this point, did I even deserve that trust? This wasn't a small lie. This was big. There was an ache in my stomach that wouldn't go away. I could only hope she would understand and this secret wouldn't break our trust once I told her everything.

3

Despite the eventful morning, the day turned out to be pleasant. The warm air wrapped itself around me. Every few minutes, a cool breeze brushed against my face, jolting me and reminding me autumn was upon us. I thought about how much I was going to miss Maine. A pang built within my gut, twisting my insides and filling me with more guilt.

With our backpacks strapped on, we each picked up our one shopping bag and headed off to buy some train tickets. On our shopping trip, I'd picked out a fresh pair of blue jeans and a black zip-up sweatshirt. Emily bought two new sweaters, one pink and the other aqua blue. I preferred dark colors, and she was the queen of pastels, kind of like our personalities. She was always so positive, especially for a thirteen-year-old. Eva always said she was the same as our mother—filled with patience, love, and empathy. I was told I was like our father—strong-willed and with a lot of fight. That was her nice way of telling me I was stubborn.

We started toward the platform, spotting the bench farthest away from other people. Emily gazed out into the crowd. Her forehead wrinkled, and her eyes dulled the harder she fell into her thoughts.

"What's on your mind, mini-me?"

She looked down at her shoes. "Will we ever stop running? Like, have a chance to settle down somewhere I can have friends and a normal life? I hate not knowing where we're going to sleep next, and I'm tired of carrying my life around in this backpack."

Putting my arm around her shoulder relaxed her a bit, and she leaned her head on me. "I know," I told her. "I'll make it right. I'm not sure how yet, but I promise you, we'll figure something out." It hurt me knowing she longed for something I hadn't been able to give her.

"I wish Eva was here."

A tear rolled down her freckled face and plopped onto my hand.

"Me too, Em. I wish none of this was happening to us." I pulled her into me, wrapping my arms around her. Her body trembled as she held back the sobs only I could hear. "Once we are safely on the train, I'll tell you everything I know."

"Thanks, Tasi." She intertwined her fingers with mine while we waited. Knots twisted in my stomach, tightening. I was about to change everything in her life.

Boarding the train was quick and easy. We headed toward the back so we could be alone. Emily slid into the seat first, so she was near the window. Any threats that may come would more than likely come from the aisle, allowing me to keep her behind me while taking care of the problem.

Emily had been told very little about us because she was so much younger. She was never part of the long conversations between Eva and me. She didn't know about my training sessions or that I drank blood. The only information she was privy to was what Eva had told her in the car ride during our quick departure. Basically, the short, short version: our parents had been alive when we thought they were dead, and they'd pretended to be dead because some people wanted to kill us because we were different. My parents thought it was safer for us to live with Eva in Maine than with them in Washington.

When Eva got the phone call that changed everything, it was my mother telling Eva my father was dead. In Washington, he'd had a woodshop, where he'd spent most of his nights making furniture. That night, he had been working on some new ideas. The security cameras failed, and by the time he realized it, those monsters had overrun the property. He called my mother, who was at the main house, and told her to move us and make the necessary preparations, which included him taking his own life. My father—a man who'd survived almost two thousand years— took his own life to protect us. To ensure no one could use him to find and hurt his children. The thought of him putting us first always sucked the air out of my chest. Whoever those monsters were wanted to end our entire family line, and they were getting closer to making that happen.

Now, without Eva, it was my duty to break the news to my little sister. When Eva told me, I was Emily's age. Eva was so strong and easy to talk to that I'd known it'd be okay even as I cried. Now I had to pull it together so I could be Emily's strength. We huddled close so no one around us could hear me speak.

Here goes nothing.

"Em, you remember everything Eva told us in the car when she dropped us off at the bus station in Bangor?"

"Yes. When she told us to meet her at the Lincoln Park fountain the next day but never showed."

Eva never showed because she was dead, just like my parents. There was no other explanation.

"Well, the thing is . . . the thing is . . . well, Mom and Dad were . . ." How could Eva do this so well, while I sounded like a bumbling idiot? "We are different."

"Tasi?"

Emily's face turned pink as she picked at the tips of her nails, the way she did when she was guilty of something or when she knew something she wasn't supposed to.

"Oh, come on. You were going to make me go through the entire story, and somehow you already know."

Her eyes caught mine, and her complexion changed from pink to white within seconds. "Sorry—I overheard you and Eva talking last year. It was more like eavesdropping. I was so pissed that you didn't tell me at first, but then I thought, how does a person tell somebody they're only half-human? So I waited until you were ready to tell me. That's all I really know about us. I swear." The color came back into her face. "And I'm going to be really honest. You suck at delivering news—like, majorly suck."

My body, which had been tense all morning and was still swimming in a dull pain from the earlier attack, finally relaxed. Knowing she had the basic idea of what we were made me feel less stressed. Eva had told me over and over at first, because who would believe someone when they say things like, by the way, you're only half of a human? I slouched back in my seat.

"You're handling this pretty well. I guess I should trust you can manage more than I give you credit for. I just wanted to protect you from all this craziness."

"I get it, Tasi, and that's why you are the best big sister ever, but maybe it's time to treat me more like your equal than your kid sister. We're both having to grow up pretty quickly, and we're in this together, remember?"

She was right. I'd tried to shelter her from this, and she'd patiently waited for the truth, knowing only that she was half-human. She was more mature for her age than I was at thirteen.

"I'll try my hardest to treat you as an equal. I can't guarantee I'll let the big-sister role drop right away, but I promise I'll try."

"That's a start. So, now that you know that I know, do you mind telling me what the heck we are?"

"We're dhampyrs. Our mother was human, and our father, well, he was a vampire. Although, I prefer the term half-breed, since it makes it sound way less formal."

"Dhampyrs? That seems like I should live in a forest with elves and fairies and goblins." This made me laugh, a little louder than expected. She continued, "So, we're half-vampire? I thought they only existed in stories. I mean, really half-vampire? If anyone other than you told me this, I'd think it was a total prank." She wrinkled her nose at me.

"It's a lot of information. It took time for it all to sink in when Eva told me, and you're taking it way better than I did. That thing that attacked us back at the motel was a vampire. I'm not sure if it was hunting us or we just had horrible luck, though I think it was the latter."

"Hunting? But why?" She furrowed her brow.

"I think it is because of what we are—we're considered a threat to the vampire world." I shifted my body toward her, and our knees touched. "Eva told me folklore states dhampyrs were once vampire hunters, and excellent ones. We have all the vampire abilities—powerful senses and quick reflexes—but none of their weaknesses. Well, except one."

She leaned into me, eager for the knowledge, and I knew no matter what I said, she'd have to learn to accept it.

"At thirteen, we go through a change, which is why I wanted to talk to you."

"Tickets," a gruff voice called out, startling us.

I handed over our tickets to the conductor, hoping he hadn't heard our conversation. It was highly doubtful, but I waited to continue until he was far enough away. Once Emily went through the change, we wouldn't have to worry about people overhearing us. Putting the stubs in my jacket pocket, I watched as the conductor strolled down the aisle collecting tickets before turning back to Emily.

"So, is it a change? Like an appearance change? Is that why you look so tired all the time?"

Ouch. That stung a little. I knew I needed to take better care of myself, but hearing it from her was confirmation.

"Appearance is part of the change in who we are. You'll get really sick one day, and to cure it, you'll need . . ." I scratched at my jeans and breathed in a big gulp of air. "Blood, Em. You'll . . . crave it."

Her eyelids flickered. "No way, that's nasty. Wait. Do you crave blood? Do you drink it? Oh my God. That's why you leave at night sometimes, isn't it?" She flinched away from me.

"Em, it's not like that, I swear. I don't go seeking people to bite. I keep a supply of blood that I take from the nearest hospital. I promise I've hurt no one."

Emily shuddered. "I believe you. I just don't want to go through all that."

"I know this won't sound very good, but when I mix it with coffee, it actually tastes okay, and gives me a little more pep."

"You're right. That's extremely disgusting." She nestled back into me until her body calmed itself back down. "When will this happen to me?"

"Sometime this year. You just have to let me know when you feel so sick that you think you'll die. Almost like a nasty flu, but more painful."

"Sounds wonderful."

"It's uncomfortable, but it passes."

This was a lie. When I went through the change, *uncomfortable* was an understatement. Eva had kept Emily out of my room for a few days as my body changed. Most noticeable was my height—I grew four inches overnight. Remembering my bones cracking, breaking, and growing made me nauseous. Other than that, all my senses became really clear. They were better than normal before, but after, it took time to get used to them. When Eva and Emily were talking in the kitchen, if I concentrated, I could hear them from my bedroom, even just a whisper. The smell of flowers from the neighbor's garden would tickle my nose when they weren't even in full bloom yet. It was incredible and strange all at the same time. Saying it was all effortless was a blatant lie.

"Wait, hold on—is that why Eva always made you a special shake every few days? You aren't anemic, are you?"

"No, I'm not anemic."

"And if you don't get this *nourishment*, what happens?" She scrunched her face and stuck her tongue out.

"I'll eventually grow weak and die." This I refused to sugar-coat. If I had died this morning, Emily would've gone through her change not knowing what needed to be done or how to take care of herself. I'd had Eva and the safety of my home to aide me through the change. Emily only had me and, right now, the unknown. My keeping any of this from her continued to put her at risk.

"Okay, I think I need a break. This is a lot to take in, and my brain feels exhausted." She pulled her knees up onto the seat.

"I'll wake you up when we reach Boston. We'll connect to New York once we get there. You should definitely try to get some rest."

Emily buried her head and shut her eyes. I stayed up to keep an eye out for anything strange, just in case the attack at the motel this morning wasn't an isolated incident.

4

When we pulled into Boston's South Station, it was late afternoon. People were hustling through the crowd, pushing their way off the train, so we took our time gathering our belongings before stepping onto the platform. A man with a briefcase came barreling out the train's exit from behind, shoving his way through and slamming into me as he rushed across the crowded platform. My bag slipped from my hands as my shoulder knocked into some stranger.

"Excuse me," the stranger said. His voice caused a knot to form in my stomach. "I believe this belongs to you." Our fingers brushed, making me flinch. My eyes met his, and the world around me stopped. There was no air to breathe. The deep chocolate color of his eyes bore into me, inviting me to sink deeper into him.

I was no longer in a train station. An image of this boy flooded my head. It was like trying to watch a drive-in movie on a foggy night. Were we friends, enemies, lovers? I couldn't make out the scene that danced through my head.

It took a few moments before I came back from wherever I had gone. He ran his hand through his brown, windswept hair, giving it a little tug. His eyebrows furrowed as he watched me watching him. And those full, heart-shaped lips . . . Snapping out of it, I reached for Emily's hand and headed away from the train platform, straight into the daylight, without looking back. I didn't know what trick he'd played in my head, but if our eyes reconnected, I couldn't guarantee that I'd be able to pull myself out of them again.

"What the heck was that about, Tasi?"

"I don't know. His touch was icy cold, but warm at the same time. It felt distantly familiar, and like no one existed at that moment except him." There was no way I would tell *anyone* about what I had seen in my head. That couldn't be real.

"Was he like the thing at the motel?"

"Maybe, but I'm not sure. Something about him was different, though. Either way, we aren't sticking around to find out what it is."

As we increased the distance between the train station and us, I thought about how his hand felt when it touched mine. Thinking of the electric pulse that wrapped around the chill of his hand made my heart stop all over again. The way he'd looked at me, it was like my presence didn't shock him. It seemed more like he was in awe of me. I was obsessing, and I needed to stop, so I shook the thought out of my head and focused back on the task at hand: New York.

It would be two hours before the next train came, but since it was already late afternoon, we decided it was best to stay in Boston for the night and pick up another train in the morning. Neither of us wanted to show up in New York City late at night. It would be the ultimate breeding ground for bloodsuckers, I was sure of it.

We stopped for a bite to eat and asked the waiter if he knew of a place to stay that didn't require a credit card. Luckily, he did, giving us detailed directions.

When we rounded the corner to the place he'd described,

before us stood a timeless red-brick building with a cherry-red door and black awnings. Each step on the cobblestone path brought more excitement as we approached the entrance. The boutique hotel was inviting.

Upon entering the building, the first thing I noticed was the cream-colored walls, dark wood furniture, and warm lighting that made my muscles ease. The cozy fireplace was surrounded by other travelers, jovial and conversing with one another over cocktails. It reminded me of home, something I hadn't experienced in a long time. I certainly hadn't expected to feel it in a big city like Boston. Just as the waiter had said, the girl at the front desk took care of us, and checking in was a breeze. A two-hundred-dollars-extra-a-night breeze, but hey, at least we weren't sleeping on the street. We made our way to the fifth floor.

This was my first time using a key card, and I wasn't any good at it. After five sets of blinking red lights screaming at my inability to open the door, Emily giggling all the while, I finally figured it out. The door clicked open, and serenity overcame me. The walls were trimmed with gray-and-white striped wallpaper. There were white fluffy pillows and a lilac comforter on the bed. The scent of lavender tickled my nose. We dropped our stuff and plopped onto the bed at the same time. This was a room fit for a queen.

"This is how I want the rest of our room experiences to be," Emily said, pulling the pillow into her face. "It smells so clean."

"Don't get used to it."

"Party pooper."

I stuck my tongue out at her the way she always did to me. She pressed her hands to her heart, which made me laugh.

"That's not very adultlike, Tasi."

"Whoever said I was an adult needs their head examined." I flung her backpack over to her. "Let's condense our stuff while we're here."

I ended up throwing a ratty shirt with a few pin-size holes in it into the trash. Emily did the same with some of her clothes. Then, as if it were the most natural thing in the world, I lifted my pants and took off the stake strapped to my right leg. I reached down to my left and pulled one from that leg as well before placing both stakes on the bed. When I went through my change, Eva had given the stakes to me. At first, I'd thought it was a joke, but when training started, I soon understood they would be part of my everyday life.

Emily's eyes went wide as she looked at the wooden weapons. She inched her way over to me, never taking her eyes off the stakes. I studied her face. Biting her bottom lip, she ran her fingers along one edge of the wood. When she reached the tip, a small breath left her lips.

"I never knew you had such an interest in stakes." I gave her a crooked smile. She jumped at the sound of my voice, pulling herself out of the daze she'd fallen into.

"That's because I was pretending I didn't know you had them." She continued to touch the edge of one. "I told you I was patient."

She looked like she had been waiting forever to touch them. There was a hunger in her eyes I'd never seen before.

"Go ahead, pick it up."

"Really?" she asked, eyes sparkling.

"Yeah, you'll have to learn how to use one eventually." There it was again, like a glow radiating through her. She rested it delicately in her hands, almost as if she were offering it to me on a platter. I snatched the stake, surprising her, and put it tightly into her palm, closing her fingers around it. "Tight, Em, hold it tight. Remember, if you have a stake in your hand, then your life depends on it. So that's the way you hold it."

She tightened her grip, not taking her eyes off it, almost as if it held the secrets to the universe.

These stakes were handmade by my father from lignum

vitae, a hardwood found in South America, and were rather attractive to look at. Toward the top of each stake was a four-inch notch where manila rope had been wrapped flush against the wood. This helped with gripping the stake. Unfortunately, it also left room for ash to become embedded in the crevices. The rope had been impossible to clean, and the ash left the rope black around the edges. It was sculpted with intricate designs from the rope leading down to the point. There was a letter branded into the wood at the top of the stake: *V* for Vasile, our family name. Whittled into the side of the stake were also the words, *One who will be reborn, immortal*. It was the meaning of my first name, Antanasia.

"Do you think our father was an evil vampire?"

Flashes of a tall thin man with ebony hair and dark eyes filled my memory. I could still feel his loving touch as he pretended to be my horse, galloping around the house while my mother cooked dinner. He would often take me for long walks in the woods, and carried me on his shoulders whenever I asked.

Emily and I never talked about our parents when we were living in Maine. I had brought them up many times to Eva, and she always changed the topic—probably because she was hiding the fact that they were still alive and was scared she would slip. Bile rose in my throat. I pushed it back down. Now, nothing was holding me back from talking about what I remembered.

"Em, the father I knew wasn't a monster. He was kind and loving." I told her stories about things I remembered, like how he was always there when I fell and scraped my knee, and how he would play Candy Land with me over and over because I asked him to. Or how he would always hold Emily and sing her to sleep.

Tears welled in Emily's eyes. The surrounding skin grew pinkish as she continued to hold back the river from streaming down her face. Her back straightened, and she looked down at the stake she held in her hand.

"I'll be strong, Tasi. I promise." There was such conviction in her voice. She meant every word.

I lifted her chin until our eyes met. "You're already strong. I see it every day. Now we need to get you trained, like Eva did for me."

The tears trying to escape evaporated. "When do we start?"

"As soon as we get settled in New York, I promise. First, we need to recharge my stakes."

Emily cocked her head to the side. She may not be training physically yet, but there were still a few things I could teach her. "Let's take a walk." Strapping the stakes back to my legs came naturally. It was a part of who I was. I pulled my bag over and rustled through it, pulling a second set of stakes out, crisp and new, along with two leather holders.

"For me?" She took in a deep breath and put out her hands, wiggling her fingers.

"Yes. You'll need to get a feel for them. I remember how much the stakes annoyed me the first time I put them on. No better time than the present to figure out where you want them. You have two sheaths, one for each stake, and they can be combined to wear on one leg or split to wear them separately, as I do. And, Em, these stakes were made for you by our father when you were born." Emily's full name was Daciana Emily Vasile. Pointing to the words etched into the side, I continued, "Daciana means 'full of strength.' Father knew you were strong from the day you were born. Now you need to believe it."

Her eyes widened. "Oh my God."

"Yeah, pretty cool, right?"

"Yes, extremely cool." She fastened both of them to her right leg but grimaced as the leather holder slid to the floor. Kneeling, I lifted her pants and showed her how to strap the top part securely, then the bottom. With one more pull against her calf, everything settled into place.

"Do I have to leave them there? It's very uncomfortable." She scrunched her freckled nose.

"No, as long as they're accessible and concealed when you're in public, then wherever you like is fine. This is what works for me."

"I'll try it out." She wiggled her leg, making sure they wouldn't come loose.

At the front desk was the same young woman who had checked us in earlier. Her bright smile, peach-colored lips, and warm hazel eyes made her very approachable. I asked the woman if she knew of any churches nearby, and she gave us directions.

The sky was still blue, but I saw the sun pulling in orange hues in the far distance as it set, which meant soon enough it would be sundown. The streetlights had yet to come on, and since we only had to walk a few blocks, I figured we would be back before darkness blanketed the city.

We headed toward the church. The walkway was narrow and lined with red-brick townhouses. There were black wrought-iron embellishments and entry gates throughout. The path itself was made of gray cobblestone. Trees umbrellaed the passageway, giving it permanent shade. Green moss coated the bricks, making some of them slippery. I felt as if I was in a fairy tale.

"What do I need to know, Tasi?" Emily was taking this a lot more seriously than I had at her age. It made me proud.

"Straight down to business. I like it." I shoved her shoulder. "Okay. Stakes kill vampires. A blessed stake makes cleanup much easier, because the vamp will turn to ash. Otherwise, you are left with a body."

"Oh, wow." She paused. "Wait—does that mean we can scare them off with crosses, like in the movies?"

"No, crosses don't bother them, despite what the stories say. Well, I take that back. Maybe if the cross was wooden and soaked in holy water. Huh, never thought about that scenario."

Emily giggled. "Is that something you're going to try now?"

"Nope. If I have one piece of advice, it's find a weapon you are good at and don't ever deviate from what works. Don't play with your life. Vamps are crazy-hard to kill as is."

"What if I don't like stakes?"

"Once you start training, you may find something else you like. But give the stakes a try first. I think you'll find them to be effective." Emily and I kicked some stones back and forth as we headed down the path. "Now, a vampire can't go into a church or onto any sacred ground. They ignite, just like if they went out in full sun. A cloudy afternoon won't fry them, but it tires and weakens them. They will regain their strength in a few hours. But if you catch a vampire out in the day, they're probably trying to die, or just stupid," I explained.

"I don't get it. Why would a vampire walk outside, then, if it wasn't nightfall?"

"I don't really know, but they do." I gave her a side-glance to check in on her. Her posture was relaxed, so I carried on. "Last item is garlic—I'm not sure where that rumor started, but it won't help you."

"Got it, I think."

"It's a lot to take in, but you'll catch on." I wrapped my arm around her shoulder. "Come on, there's the church."

Before us stood a large Gothic-style church. As we entered, I knelt respectfully in the foyer. In my periphery, I watched as Emily followed my lead. The church was grand and full of grace. The statues filled the room with a holy presence that made me feel protected. I took a few moments to bask in the tranquility. There was no one in the church, so we headed toward the holy water. The marble bowl was large enough to submerge our stakes, which was always a plus. I pulled out my stakes and dipped them into the water while whispering a prayer. After a few minutes, I removed the stakes, which now glimmered.

"Rinse and repeat," I said to Emily.

She took out her stakes and looked at me. "What do you say?"

We weren't religious, but I had been taught to respect all religions. "I ask for the stakes to be blessed and for us to be protected against evil and all it brings to this world."

Her eyes looked me over, and she mimicked what I'd done. She slipped the wet stakes back into place after allowing the water to saturate them, and then we headed back outside. I knew we'd been in the church longer than planned, and stepping outside confirmed it. Dusk had already come and gone. The blackness of night was upon us. Streetlights lit the area around the church with a soft glow. But the route back to the hotel was short, and I was confident we could make it. My eyes darted around the perimeter, and I spotted a young man nearby.

The familiarity was instant as our eyes met. His eyes were deep brown and almond-shaped with beautiful lashes. His dark brown hair was disheveled, yet stylish. He was tall and . . . well, just perfect. He was leaning against a streetlamp, and my heart beat a little faster. He ran his fingers through his hair, and out of nowhere, anger flitted through his eyes. He bared his teeth as he stepped off the curb and began walking toward us. My eyes remained locked on his.

There was a faint voice in the back of my head calling my name, and then a tug at my arm, and another. Finally, I broke free of his gaze when a stinging sensation coursed through my leg and into my back—Emily had kicked me.

"What the hell was that about?" I asked.

She snatched my arm and tried dragging me back into the church. When I looked back to where the guy had been, he was gone. Emily dropped her hand from my arm in clear defeat. I snapped back into protective mode and pushed her behind me as we retreated into the church. Leaning against the wall, I put my hands on my knees and caught my breath. It was all I could do to keep my body from falling over as I shook uncontrollably. My body was betraying me, as if I were fighting a sickness. Why had I lost my mind that way?

"Can you tell me what just happened? That was the same guy from the train station. Do you think he is following us? Why, though?"

It was obvious some of those questions weren't directed to me, but to herself. Not knowing why he had such a hold on me, I straightened up, becoming furious with myself. I'd been weak. This guy made me vulnerable. Now I was positive he was a vampire, but what did he want? In my life, I had met four vampires. My father was the only one who had a grip on his humanity, allowing him to act human. All my other encounters prior to today had been savage creatures out to drink my blood. We were food to them, and I'd been forced to put them down like the foul creatures they were.

This mysterious guy was different. Not quite like my father, but it also didn't seem like he was here to feed on us. But why did my presence make him look so angry?

"Earth to Tasi? Can we go back now before we're stuck here until morning? I don't want to sleep in the church . . . unless you think it's the only way." There was a tremor in Emily's voice.

If we headed back to the hotel, we risked running into him. Could I take him in a fight, or would my feet become cement boots? If I couldn't move, I'd put Emily's life in danger. The right thing to do would be to camp out and sleep in the church until morning. But, to be honest, I wasn't looking to do the right thing now. My gut told me he wouldn't hurt me. Not that my gut had always been a reliable source in the past, but part of me wondered if I *wanted* to run into him again, which sounded stupid in my head. Either way, we had to hurry if we were going back.

Emily was watching me with a tortured look in her eyes. She saw the fight I was having within and was understanding enough to let me figure it out.

"Let's go back, but we'll run the entire way. The faster we get back, the better." I searched the church for the best way out before pointing to the door on the left. "That way."

Emily nodded before we took off. It was a ten-minute walk. Running cut the time down tremendously. Emily wasn't used to running this fast, and I could hear her struggling to keep up. If I hadn't been holding her hand, she might not have made it. We reached the room unscathed, even though I was still tangled up in my thoughts. This vampire was distracting me as no one ever had before. I dropped onto the bed and stared at the ceiling.

"I'm sorry, Em." It was all I could say.

"You did nothing wrong, Tasi. Whatever happened, happened, and now we move on from it. We're both alive."

She placed a hand on my shoulder before heading off to take a shower, allowing me to work through what had happened alone. What had happened? I knew I hadn't had a lot of experience outside of my sheltered life, but no one had ever made me feel so stupefied by their presence. All I knew was the faster we got out of Boston, and away from this mysterious vamp, the better.

5

South Station was bustling with people. The building had high ceilings, lots of shops, and from the aroma swirling through the air, some tasty eateries. Chatter filled the atmosphere, and as we approached the lower platform, horns blared from trains pulling in and out. Announcers over the loudspeaker called out train numbers and destinations. Emily had said little to me all morning, knowing I was still beating myself up over last night. She knew how stubborn I was and that I might snap if provoked. It's not one of my best attributes. But when I was ready to talk, she would know.

I glanced over at my sister. She gave me a small, knowing smile. Her voice echoed in my head. *We're both alive.* I knew I was acting stupid. As long as that was a onetime mistake and I didn't put Emily at risk again, I had to let it go.

Emily shifted her weight. Her lips were tightly pressed together as she wrinkled and unwrinkled her freckled nose. I bumped her with my elbow, then turned to her, extending my arm. "Hi, I'm Tasi, and I'm done being stupid and feeling sorry for myself."

She let out a giggle. "Finally." She ignored my arm and gave me an enormous hug. I leaned my cheek against her forehead. "If I had to sit on a train in silence until we reached New York, I think I would have lost my freaking mind."

"Yeah, me too." The tightness in my stomach lifted.

Our embrace ended as they announced our train. We headed for the back and found some empty seats together. The seats were arranged in fours, which could be an issue, depending on who filled the seats facing us. I hoped no one would sit there, or at least would leave us alone if they did.

While we waited, I watched the hordes of people filing onto the train. Some whispering to each other, dressed in casual attire. Others with their suits on, storing briefcases overhead. The murmurs grew louder as more people boarded the train car. My body was tense, and it became hard to separate the oblivious people from the ones who may be threats.

"If we have time, can we go to the giant toy store in Times Square?" Emily asked. "It has an indoor Ferris wheel!"

"Yes, once we find Sonya. I want to make sure we find a place to stay before we start sightseeing."

"Okay." She clasped her hands together.

As we continued talking, a girl not much older than me stopped in front of us. Her hair was a thick golden blonde. It was pulled back in a half ponytail, and the curls bounced with her slightest of movements. Her lips were narrow and cheekbones high.

Sickness stirred in my gut, and the hairs on the back of my neck sought refuge.

"Are these two seats open? My friend is running late, which is so typical. It's hard to find a good traveling partner these days. So annoying." Her emerald eyes sparkled like gems.

"Sure." Prickles coated my skin as she eyed me.

She sat down across from Emily. "I like the window seat. I hope you don't mind." She directed that to my sister.

"No . . . no, it's fine." Emily gave her a small smile and focused back on me. She saw what I had.

Our seats were in a section too close to other travelers for either of us to do anything. We were safe for the time being. However, my first thought was to lead the girl somewhere private so I could kill her.

She sat still as she looked out the window, her flawless complexion hard as stone. Yup, she was one of them, but did she know who we were? The train jerked forward, reminding me we were in this for the long haul. The trip was about four hours; that was four long hours with a filthy vampire sitting across from us. That's the problem with big cities. These large transportation centers provided enough shelter so vampires could hide out there during the day.

"So, are you guys headed to the city? Business or pleasure?" She studied my eyes, as if waiting for me to stumble or hesitate.

"A little of both." I showed no fear as I locked my eyes on hers. "You?"

"Business, mostly. I hope my friend made it. It'd be such a shame if he had to catch a later train. Plus, our boss would be really unhappy with him if we screwed up our task."

Great. I hoped he missed the train, because if it was a friend of hers, I didn't want to meet him.

Turning to Emily, I noticed her apprehension. She was readying herself for the worst. Part of me wished I hadn't given her those stakes. Our eyes met, and I hoped she deciphered my visual message to relax. Still feeling a little rebellious, I pressed my luck. "So, what kind of business, if you don't mind me asking?"

Her ringlets fell off her shoulders as she leaned closer, showing me her venomous fangs. "Pest extermination." She scowled.

Before I could reach across and grab her by the throat, a familiar scent wafted from nearby. The fragrance was intoxicating and brought back the feeling of electricity pulsating through me from head to toe. *Self-control.* I had to restrain myself, no matter what. Losing it like I had yesterday showed weakness, and I wouldn't be that pathetic again. I slowly regained control and waited as he drew closer. Emily must have felt the war brewing inside me, because she touched my hand to let me know she was there if I needed her.

"Stop being such a jerk, Lizzie." He slid in beside her, shoving her hard into the window.

"What? I was having a little fun. She's the one who was trying to bait me."

The two bickered for a few minutes. Emily leaned into me and whispered, "Should we go?"

In unison, they stopped and focused their full attention on us.

"You two aren't going anywhere," the brown-eyed boy said.

Heat filled my cheeks. Who did he think he was, and what made him believe bullying me was the best way to persuade us to stay? The electrical stream that flowed between us fizzled. I leaned in with narrowed eyes.

"Let's get something straight—I don't know who either of you are, but we know *what* you are. So, if you want to live, then you won't dictate where my sister and I can and cannot go."

He looked at me unimpressed as he leaned forward. The scent of vanilla rolled off him and filled the air around us. The thudding in my chest quickened. "Now *you* get something straight. If you want to live, you stick with us. If you prefer to watch your little sister bleed to death in front of your pretty little eyes, then go your separate way." The air around us turned frosty as he sat back, eyes still locked onto mine. "Oh, and my name is Ethan. Nice to finally meet you."

As he sat there, arms crossed, his once-warm brown eyes now blazed through me like a raging four-alarm fire. He waited for my retort. There was the same wrestling look in his eyes as last night. Refusing to glance away and give him the satisfaction of knowing that last comment about Emily dying had gotten under my skin, I sat there staring at him with hatred brewing in me.

Lizzie said, "Are you two done playing googly eyes at each other? If not, can you let me know when you are, so I can stop throwing up in my mouth?" She made an all-too-perfect gagging noise.

Emily, who had been quiet this whole time, let out a nervous giggle.

My head snapped in her direction as I shot her a disapproving look.

"What? You both are a little ridiculous, so it is kind of funny." Her voice was timid.

"I thought so too." Lizzie winked at Emily.

Ethan pressed his lips together and looked away.

"So, now that we're all acquainted and we've put our differences aside, let's get a game plan together," Lizzie said.

Was she serious? My game plan was to stake her and her boyfriend in the heart the minute I had a chance. Did they think I'd become all buddy-buddy with them? Or was this their way of enticing us into an alley to kill Emily and me? No. I would not be weak this time. "The *plan* goes as follows," I said. "We reach New York, we get off the train, and we—meaning you two and us—go our own ways before *you* end up dead."

Lizzie gave me an irritated look. "You know, the sooner you accept the fact that Ethan and I are here and not going anywhere, the easier this will be on you."

Ethan turned to Lizzie, then to me. His eyes scrutinized me before giving me one last look of exasperation. "I say let them go. They were clear—they don't want our help, and I don't feel like babysitting a bratty kid, anyway."

He talked to Lizzie as if we didn't exist. Dismissing me this way made me angrier, even if he was giving us a way out.

"You know as well as I do that is not an option. These two half-breeds are coming with us." Lizzie turned her focus solely on me. "Even if I have to drag them by their hair."

"You know what, bloodsucker, I'd love to see you try."

"Keep talking, and I'll give you an early preview."

Ethan tried to say something, but it was Emily who spoke up next. "Enough, already. Listening to you all is exhausting. Can't we just talk about why you're here looking for us instead of acting so childish to each other?" She cocked her head toward me. "Is this what Eva dealt with when you and I bickered? Because you sound stupid." Shock filled my face as Emily took a deep breath. "Sorry, Tasi, but this is ridiculous and getting us nowhere."

She was right, but why did she have to be right in front of them? A small smile crossed Ethan's face, and I wanted nothing more than to smack it off him. He probably loved seeing me being scolded by a thirteen-year-old. My ears burned, and my cheeks flushed with anger at the thought. I rethought my strategy. If I was going to devise a foolproof plan to get away from them, I needed to gather as much information as possible. Taking in a deep breath and swallowing my pride, I turned back to Emily and tried my best to compose myself.

"Emily's right. We call a truce, for now." She let out a sigh as I continued, facing the two vampires. "I'll bite. Why are you guys following us?"

"None of your business."

Lizzie smacked Ethan hard on the arm. Ethan exposed his teeth, before getting up and walking away.

"Sorry, he desperately needs something to control his mood swings. So, Tasi, why are you so bitchy?"

Her attention had shifted back to us, but all I could see was Ethan. The farther he walked, the less of a connection I felt to him. He looked furious and bewildered, which left me feeling similar. Emily elbowed me. I flinched.

"Let's start with the fact that every vampire we have met since we had to leave our home has tried to kill us," I said. "What makes you so different?"

"I guess you've met the wrong ones. Plus, I'm sure you didn't give them a chance to talk. You, Tasi, are super feisty. Have you ever thought about anger management?"

Emily spoke before I could revert to my sneering ways. "From what I just learned, we were taught to fear and kill you guys. That all vampires would want to kill us because of what we are."

Lizzie looked kindly at Emily, and for the first time, I didn't hate her as much. "I can see most vampires hating you or even wanting to feed on you. Dhampyr blood is said to be exhilarating and rare. I won't lie; if I were a rogue vampire, there would be no second thoughts. You'd be lunch."

This made Emily shrink back into her seat, but I shook my head. "Then you aren't 'rogue,' or whatever you call it? What does your kind do, ask politely before feeding off people?"

"Funny. We're predators—I won't deny what we are. Rogue vampires drink to kill and take whatever they want without permission. They are miserable, insignificant scavengers. *We* train ourselves to drink to survive, not for sport."

I ran my finger along my lips. "Is that why you seem more human?"

"I think so, but no one truly knows. My best guess is that we never let thirst dictate our lives. Rogue vampires spend their lifetime hunting for blood. We spend our time trying to survive and live as close to normal lives as we can."

The information was dizzying. What had Eva been training me for, if not to kill vampires? No, I'd kill them when we got to New York, or we'd run away. They were deceitful and rotten creatures, rogue or not.

"Fine, we'll cooperate until I feel we are unsafe. Then and only then will we leave."

Ethan sat back down next to Lizzie, eyeing me. I saw there was a look of distrust in his eyes. He probably noticed I was returning the same look. He said nothing, and turned to Lizzie and handed her his phone. She read something on it, then smiled.

"Anyone care for a drink?"

Lizzie pulled out a thermos from her bag. I looked at Emily, who stuck out her tongue as Lizzie poured a thick red liquid into a cup and handed it to Ethan.

"Tasi, do you want some?" Lizzie asked.

The burning sensation came first. It started in my nose, traveling through to my throat, then farther down into my gut. The more I inhaled it, the more I yearned for it. It hadn't been long since I'd had a drink myself, but the sweet metallic scent sitting before me was bringing out a desire I didn't know existed. I couldn't concentrate. Envisioning the red liquid hitting my tongue and sliding down into the pit of my stomach was becoming too much. They all stared, waiting for an answer.

"No. No thanks." It took everything inside of me to pull those words out of my mouth. "I have my own on hand if needed."

The smile on my face was forced, trying and failing to convince everyone I didn't need the fresh, sweet-smelling blood. What I drank every so often was days, if not weeks, old. Why was I craving this blood so much? Did aging blood lose its potency?

"Okay, your loss. Emily?"

"Gross." Sickness filled her features.

"Ah, you haven't changed over yet," Lizzie said.

"No, and I don't want to."

Ethan stared at her as he gulped down the last bit and licked his lips.

Emily's face changed from a slight greenish hue to full-on

green. Pushing through me, she bolted down the aisle, one hand over her mouth and the other over her stomach.

"Idiot." My eyes drilled into Ethan.

As I took off running, I saw Lizzie smack him in the head.

"Jeez, it was only a joke. Why's everyone so sensitive?" Ethan asked.

Reaching the bathroom door, I knocked. "It's me, Em, open up." My head was pressed against the door, my hand still raised and ready to knock again. Several moments later, the door clicked open. Stepping through, I shut it behind me.

The bathroom was tight for the two of us. I rested against the door as she settled into the wall opposite me. She was no longer green, but she still wore a frown on her face, and her eyes looked vacant. Reaching out for her, I pulled her to me.

"Are you okay?"

"Fine, just scared." Her voice was meek. "Between the look in your eyes when the blood came out and Ethan taunting me with it, well, it all freaked me out, that's all. Soon I'll be like that, and I don't want to be."

I had hoped she didn't notice my desire for the blood. "Yeah, sorry about that. I don't even know why I reacted that way. I guess my need for it is growing. I've been drinking small amounts to keep me going."

"It's okay. I mean, it's what we are. It's just all new to me." She pulled away from me, taking in a deep breath. "I'll be okay, Tasi."

"Good, but before we go out there . . ." I lowered my lips to her ear, whispering so low no one could hear me, not even with supersensitive hearing. "We're getting away from them when we get to New York."

She leaned toward my ear to respond. "Are you sure that's a good idea?" Nervousness filled her voice.

"I have no clue what their intentions are, but I don't want to find out. We'll find Sonya, as Eva told us to. Plus, it'll still be daylight when we get there. If we quickly make our way outside, we can get away."

Emily gave me a thumbs-up.

When I opened the door, Lizzie stood in front of me.

"Don't worry, we're coming back."

"Trust me, Tasi, I wasn't worried. I came to see how Emily was doing and apologize for Ethan. I'm not sure what's gotten into him, but ever since we spotted you guys yesterday, he has been, well, a jerk."

"You mean this isn't his normal self?" I asked.

"Nope. Are you feeling better, Emily?"

"Yes, thanks."

We headed back to the seats with Emily's hand resting in mine.

The rest of the ride was quiet. The lull of the train along the tracks was rhythmic and musical. Lizzie and Ethan spoke to themselves mostly. We were going to run, so I didn't bother trying to mingle with the two, especially since Ethan would probably jump down my throat again. Sometimes he would stare at me with such distaste it made me glad I wouldn't be around him much longer. At full rest and with a bit of surprise, two dhampyrs could surely outrun two vampires for the short distance needed to get to the street so the sun could do the rest in keeping them away.

6

"Ten minutes, folks. Penn Station in ten minutes." The muffled words sang through the loud speaker.

"So now where to?" I asked.

"Need-to-know basis," Ethan said.

A fire seared under my skin as I pretended his contempt for me meant nothing. In reality, his disregard caused my heart to twist in pain. I hated that my body was betraying me. I didn't want to feel this strange connection to him. All I wanted was to despise him, to look at him like the evil vampire he was.

To cover my angst, I snapped, "Can we stop at a store along the way? Lizzie, you mentioned getting something for Ethan's mood swings. I feel like someone could use some extra-vampire-strength right about now."

Emily and Lizzie both let out a small chuckle. I saw Ethan glowering from the corner of my eye, but I didn't want to give him the satisfaction of looking his way.

As the train pulled in, I picked up both my backpack and Emily's before standing up. Lizzie also stood, staying close behind. I led the way through the train, then patiently waited for my turn to step out onto the underground platform.

People were pushing their way through the tight crowd. It was my moment. I pulled Emily in front of me, allowing me to turn around and shove Lizzie so hard she fell into Ethan and one other person. My hand found Emily's, and her fingers interlaced with mine.

"Run!"

We took off. Commuters jumped out of the way as we shoved through the massive sea of people. Distantly, I heard Ethan swearing, along with the sound of footsteps almost as quick as ours, trying hard to catch up. I was right—we had matching speed, and catching them off guard allowed us to be a fragment of a second faster.

With no time to waste, I continued through the mob, all oblivious to what was happening. Yelling filled the space around us as we dashed through. We began our ascent up the steps, Emily's hand held tightly in mine. Without warning, a shooting pain ripped through my arm as Emily slipped, bringing us straight to the ground. We were quick to get up, but then pressure on my shoulders forced me back down. Ethan had caught us. Still on the steps, I rolled onto my back. He tried hard to keep me flat against the stairs by pressing his arm against my neck. The rage I saw in his face sent chills through my bones. He was pissed, and Lizzie was not far behind him.

Our eyes briefly met as I gave him an apologetic look and mouthed, "I'm sorry." My apology surprised him, and this time, I didn't hesitate. With all my strength, I kneed him. He fell back, stumbling, but was quick to get back up. Emily caught my hand, and we prepared to start our run again. The problem was that Ethan was close enough to latch on to my ankle. Fortunately for us, there was a blessed stake strapped to it. He let go and swore as Emily and I ran. I glanced back and saw Lizzie looking at Ethan's hand. Ethan, frozen in place, stared at me, brows crumpled together.

Our feet stomped through the station. The door to our freedom was in reach. We jumped into the first cab available, pushing a man in a suit out of the way. He protested, but I couldn't care less.

"Sorry!" Emily yelled to the guy.

"Times Square," I said to the driver as I caught my breath.

With one last look, I saw there was no Lizzie or Ethan in sight. We had done it. Relief overwhelmed me.

"Do you think we did the right thing?" Emily asked.

"I think so. We've been on our own for this long—why should we change now? My job is to get us to Sonya, and I'll do that without the help of vamps."

Deep down, I wasn't sure if this was the right move, but I had to keep Emily thinking I was confident in my decisions. It didn't make any sense, but part of me wanted to be back with Ethan. The electricity that ran through me whenever he was near was still at the front of my mind. I missed how it flowed within me, and I wished I knew how it affected him. Maybe that's why he was angry with me. Maybe what was electrifying to me was hateful to him. Caught up in my thoughts, I neglected to notice the cab had stopped.

We paid the driver and stepped out onto the streets of New York City. The smell caught me off guard. Bitterness and sweetness churned through the crowd of people. The sound was also a lot more overwhelming than the odor, which surprised me. Horns, sirens, conversations, shouting, music—it all came from every direction, slamming into my ears. I wasn't sure what I had expected of New York, but it was surely different from our hometown in Maine. Emily and I continued to gape at the large metal and stone towers standing around us. More impressive was the number of lights and colors that painted everything. The flashing gaudy restaurant signs, bright twinkling advertisements, and giant video screens filled the area. We must have looked like tourists, for sure. People were bumping into us as they scurried around. Once the awe had passed, my mind reeled as I considered where to start.

"We have to get moving and find a place to stay before nightfall."

Emily stared at the massive toy store in front of us. "Can we?"

"Once we figure out what our next steps are, we'll come back. I promise. Let's first get settled in. It's getting late, and I don't know if anyone is going to want to give us a place to stay."

Emily slipped her hand into mine. We headed down one of the side streets, not knowing what we would find. Hotel after hotel turned us away. Either they were full or wouldn't take cash.

After stopping at several places, we took a break to find food. The sun was now hiding behind a thick bed of clouds. We probably wouldn't run into any vampires yet, but there was still the possibility if it continued to darken outside. We found a quiet pizza place away from Times Square and slid into a booth. The restaurant was small, with a brick interior finish. A large man dressed in a white chef's outfit and apron to match fiddled with pizza boxes. There was a restroom and an exit toward the back, which gave me some relief. When the server came over, we ordered a large cheese pizza. I also asked to borrow their phone book. She gave us a puzzled look but accommodated the request.

"I should've known this would not be as easy as I thought," I said as I shoveled a piece of pizza into my mouth. There wasn't one Sonya Bourne in the entire phone book. I slammed it shut. "Back to square one, I guess."

"Can we find her by hiring a private detective?" Emily asked.

That idea wasn't half bad; something to keep in our back pockets if we kept hitting dead ends. Emily looked satisfied, as if she could read my thoughts. But before I could confirm her idea was a good one, I heard something that made my head perk up. From Emily's reaction, I knew she had heard it too.

I hadn't noticed him enter, but a man now sat at the counter with a slice of uneaten pizza in front of him. He wore all black clothing, including his baseball cap. On the side of his neck, there was a small X tattoo. He was on his cell phone, describing us to whoever was on the other line. Homing in with my dhampyr ears, I heard him say things like, "No, they don't know we're following them," and, "Do you want me to restrain them?" One human didn't scare me, but whoever he was talking to might be another story.

"We need to go."

"From the look on your face, I figured as much," Emily said, blowing out a long sigh.

Trying to get the server's attention was more complicated than I'd thought. The restaurant was empty. One would think she would be readily available. We played it as cool as possible because the last thing we wanted to do was give away that we were aware this guy was watching us. I heard the man at the counter pick up his phone again.

"Hurry, they're getting ready to leave. We can't lose 'em again." The man snorted.

"Again?" I muttered. "I guess we didn't lose Ethan and Lizzie like we thought. Damn it."

"Yeah, but you know that guy at the counter is human. So why would he be helping them?"

"To become like them, probably—he helps them and then gets turned into an evil creature of the night. That would be my guess."

"Disturbing," Emily said.

"Worst part is, I don't think I can kill a human. It's one thing to kill an undead creature, but to take a human life seems wrong." The server wasn't paying attention and was taking too long to come back, so I pulled out a fifty-dollar bill and threw it on the table. "All right, we need to go out through the back, just in case they're waiting for us out front. Let's pretend we're going to the bathroom."

Emily nodded, and we started our trek to the back of the restaurant.

"Do you always have to use the bathroom every time we stop?" I said loudly.

Emily played along. "Tiny bladder, what can I say?"

Across from the bathroom was a door marked EXIT. I glanced back and saw the man staring at us as Emily and I rushed through the door. The man yelled into his phone, while the server yelled for other reasons.

We ran as fast as we could, pushing through the back storage area. More screams and some curses continued as we rushed through the rear of the restaurant. There was a long alley in back. I ran to the right after a second of evaluation. The burly guy sitting at the counter was now running after us, still yelling into his phone.

I knocked over some wooden crates as we ran by them, hoping to slow him down. There was a dead end up ahead, with a large chain-link fence on one side.

"Over the fence," I said.

We climbed as fast as we could, preparing to jump over it, but the burly man grabbed Emily.

"Tasi, help!"

Jumping from the top of the fence, I pulled the man off Emily, then took a defensive stance between the man and her. He moved closer. I shoved him back. He faltered but caught himself.

"What do you want, you disgusting excuse for a human being?" The anger boiled inside me as I kept Emily sheltered behind my body.

"I'm not the abomination here." His words dripped with disgust. "You are, and when we kill you, it won't be too soon."

He pushed forward. Without wavering, I kicked him. He flew back and crashed to the ground. Three more humans appeared from around the corner, all wearing matching black clothing. One guy was bald, with piercings and tattoos all over his face. He stood there, cracking his knuckles like someone getting ready for a brawl. The other guy was tall, with sandy-blond hair shaved close to his skin. He had a gun, and was pointing it directly at me. Finally, there was a woman. She looked like the meanest one of all, with her brown hair pulled back tight in a ponytail and what looked to be a Taser in her hand. They all had the same small matching X tattoos.

With Emily still pressed against the wall, I reached down and pulled out the two stakes strapped to my leg. Emily followed suit. I didn't expect her to fight, but it wouldn't hurt to keep those stakes handy for self-defense.

Keeping my eyes on all four targets, I whispered to Emily, "No matter what happens to me, run. Don't let them catch you."

She let out a small gasp, but agreed.

Twirling the stakes in my hands, I focused on the two biggest threats, the gun and the Taser. As I glanced between them, the woman stepped closer. The space between us continued to diminish as she closed the gap. Her jaw tightened, and she stared at me with squinted eyes.

"I guess you want to die first," I said, not taking my eyes off hers. "If you were going to kill us, you wouldn't have a Taser. So what do you want?"

"Well, aren't you observant? Don't worry. We plan on killing you . . . once we drain you of your blood."

Ethan's words rang loud and clear in my memory. *If you prefer to watch your little sister bleed to death in front of your pretty little eyes, then go your separate way.* I'd messed up.

"Over my dead body," I said.

"So be it. If we can only have one of you, we'll take the little one and kill you." She scowled and turned to the guy holding the gun. "Marco, kill her."

There was a loud popping sound, and then a burning sensation rolled across my shoulder, causing me to drop one of my stakes. The bullet had only grazed me, but under my pierced skin, an inferno blazed. It took me a few seconds to regain my composure, and when I did, I could suddenly see Lizzie fighting the guy with all the piercings. Ethan was on Marco, and a new vampire was beating up the burly guy from the pizza place. Their presence changed the story line. I didn't think, I reacted.

The Taser woman was noticeably caught off guard. Her back was to me, so I rushed her. My arm snaked around her neck, yanking her to the ground. The Taser skidded across the alley. She quickly recovered, spinning around to face me. There was a crackling sound as her jaw met my fist. The sharp wooden stake scraped her cheek, causing a river of blood to flow from her face. She staggered back. Sweat dripped from her brow. Her hands shook as she touched the dripping blood. She swung. Fiery pain streamed through my body as her palm pressed into my injured shoulder. Pain didn't matter—the only thing I could think about was Emily's safety.

Blood splattered as I let loose a flurry of punches. Her body rocked as each blow smashed into her. Finally, she keeled over, but I wasn't finished. My fingers intertwined in her hair. I yanked her head down, landing one last jab. She fell back onto the pavement. Her body was still. I kicked her, and she swayed like a rag doll.

Ready to help the others take down the rest of the attackers, I grabbed my stakes again. It was too late—I saw them all standing over the human bodies. Emily ran into my arms, which made me wince as she jostled my injured shoulder. She was sobbing harder than I had ever heard.

I looked at the three vampires standing across from me and waited for them to do something—I don't know what I expected. Were they my friends or enemies? Everything I thought I understood about vampires continued to be challenged, and I was beginning to think I knew nothing after all.

7

"You are the dumbest girl I've ever met!" Ethan yelled. "Why did you take off? I told you they'd come after you."

The temperature rising in my cheeks now trumped the stinging pain pulsing through my shoulder. "You didn't tell me anything! All you kept saying was that it was none of my business. I'm no one's puppet. Either you treat me like an equal and tell me what's going on, or you get the hell away from me!"

"Oh, yeah, now you can say 'get the hell away,' after we save your stupid—" Ethan threw his hands in the air.

His cool, sweet breath tickled my nose. The pounding of my heart thrummed in my ears. It grew quicker and more demanding. Was it because he was pissing me off to the point I wanted to tear his head from his neck, or was it another reason? Finally, Lizzie put her hand on Ethan's shoulder, pulling him back.

"Walk it off, Ethan."

His shoulders sagged, and his eyes left mine as he turned away from me, leaving me standing there, feeling vulnerable and naked. I hadn't noticed until Emily wiped the tears from my face that I was crying. I hugged her tight.

"We didn't know," Emily said.

"And now you do. Maybe we didn't handle the information part very well, but it's not like you would be receptive to anything we said. You pushed us away from the start," Lizzie stated. She made a valid point. She let out a long sigh. "Let's make this easy. We stick together so no one touches you. Just realize that you're lucky humans came after you and not thirsty rogue vampires by the handful. It's New York City, after all," she pointed out.

I bit my lip. But why did *humans* care about two dhampyrs?

Pulling away from Emily was hard. Partly because I continued to feel like I didn't have a clue what was going on, but also because I could've lost her, and it would've been all my fault. I stared at Lizzie and nodded. She shook her head at me but gave a small smile.

"Damn straight." The unfamiliar voice came from behind Lizzie. The boy moved toward me and ripped off one arm of the long-sleeved thermal shirt he was wearing.

"Tasi, Em, meet Cas. Be right back. I need to chat with Ethan," Lizzie said. My eyes followed her for a moment, hoping for a glimpse of Ethan.

Cas was tall and looked younger than me. He had baby-blue eyes and sandy-blond hair. I could picture him hanging ten on a surfboard somewhere.

"What's up, girls?" he asked as he ran his hand through his hair, wearing an infectious smile while baring his fangs. "Unlike Ethan, I'm glad you ran away. It gave me a chance to put my skills to good use. Especially while it's still a little light out—weak or not, it's been confirmed: humans are no match for us vampires."

"Glad we could help with your science experiment." My jaw tightened.

"Let me look at that shoulder." He helped me out of my shirt. "Not too bad. My sleeve should stop the bleeding for now, but you may need a stitch or two to help heal up a little quicker.

Their bullets are typically laced with a chemical that slows the healing process in vampires, or in your case, dhampyrs."

"How do you know that?" I asked.

"I study weaponry, and the humans who know about us have gotten good at finding ways to prolong the hurt of vampires."

He wrapped his sleeve around my wound, tying it tight. His blue eyes, which had once looked inviting, became dark and glassy, and his head jerked to one side in an animalistic way. The last time a vampire looked at me that way, my stake met his heart.

"Your blood—it smells so extraordinary."

I stepped back, stakes ready, as his face grew darker. Did he think I was his dinner?

"Sorry," he said, shaking his head. "I've never smelled dhampyr blood before. Someone once told me how intoxicating it is. They described it as feeling human again. As if the air around me would seduce my senses. Embracing me as the sun tickles my body. Their description doesn't do it justice. Standing here while the scent burns a desire inside me . . . a desire that has been forgotten . . . the only way to describe it is . . . euphoric. It caught me off guard. I didn't mean to freak you out."

His eyes returned to the baby-blue color they were previously. He continued to apologize as he finished the makeshift bandage, then helped me put my arm back through my sleeve. There was a slight struggle going on within him, but he seemed to get it under control. I found his ability to stop the hunger quite intriguing.

"Thanks." I backed away.

"We need to go." Lizzie strolled over to us, hopping over the bloodied bodies. "The last thing we need is to be here when the cops come."

"Emily, is it?" Cas asked. "Let's let them talk. You know, I can see it already—we're going to be best buddies."

He reached for Emily's hand, but she just looked back at me, biting her lip. Looking at Cas closely, I saw that his struggle with thirsting for my blood had disappeared entirely. I had never thought a vampire could regain control like that. She walked away, ignoring him.

"Dissed." He put his hands over his heart like he was heartbroken and followed her down the alley.

Lizzie laughed. "Let's try to get this right this time around."

"I'm so confused. Vampires are bad. Humans are good. That's what my aunt told me. Now I'm not sure what to believe."

"I get it," Lizzie said. "You grew up not knowing all the truths. We can talk along the way, but you'll need to talk to the head of our coven. She can fill you in on the missing details and answer any of your questions."

As we headed out of the alley, I saw Ethan resting against the wall, kicking around stones. He ignored us as we passed. His scent shadowed me, and the desire that had flooded my emotions the first day our eyes met was back. His footsteps fell into a rhythm behind us.

"Hey, did you hear me, Tasi?" Lizzie asked.

"Not really."

Lizzie rolled her eyes, giving me a look that told me I was annoying her. I'd never noticed how beautiful she was. When I had met her on the train, I'd seen her as less than a person—a monster, someone who was there to hurt Emily and me. Now she stood here simply as a girl, someone like me, and even after fighting someone twice her size, she looked so perfectly put together.

"Let's start again," she said.

"Good idea." I looked back at Emily, who was walking with Cas. They were talking now, and her body looked to be a little more relaxed.

"Don't worry," Lizzie said. "She's in great hands with Cas. He'll watch over her while we talk."

"She's my life, you know. Nothing can happen to her."

"And nothing can happen to you guys. You two are a rarity." I froze. Lizzie stopped a few steps ahead before turning back and smiling. "Got your attention now, don't I?"

Ethan said nothing as he passed by us with his hands in his pockets. I pulled my attention back to Lizzie as we continued down the block.

"What do you mean, a rarity? We're just two half-vampire, half-human girls who got dealt a really unlucky hand in life."

"You're way more than that, Tasi. You two are the only dhampyr girls known in existence. We have been looking for you ever since they killed your parents."

"Which time, the first or second? Sorry, that's not your fault. My mouth has a mind of its own sometimes."

"Sometimes?" She looked thoughtful again. "It's okay. Losing your parents can be rough. I don't even remember my parents, or any of my human life, actually."

"You're that old?"

"No, I'm not that old," Lizzie said. "I just don't remember. One day I woke up a vampire, and I couldn't remember anything earlier than that day. It's like all my memories were erased."

"Ouch."

"Don't feel sorry for me. For a long time, I tried to figure out why I couldn't remember. Now I live life to the fullest, like I would if I were still human. I refuse to turn into a full-on brutal vampire killing machine. Plus, I'm hot. Those rogue vampires forget all about their hygiene."

"I'm sorry."

"I told you, I've come to terms—" she began.

"No, I'm sorry for judging you the way I did. It was wrong." Admitting I was wrong was always hard for me to do, but it was necessary. I hoped she could sense my sincerity.

"I get it. I would have probably done the same thing, so no

worries. All that matters is that you guys are safe now." She bumped me with her hip. "C'mon, Sonya will explain the rest."

I stopped. My feet were planted on the sidewalk. Lizzie called ahead to Ethan. Emily caught up to me, eyebrows furrowed.

"What's wrong?" Emily whispered to me.

I was still focused on Lizzie, who raised an eyebrow. "What'd I say?"

Ethan took a protective stance next to her.

"Please tell me Sonya's last name isn't Bourne." My words came out almost accusatory.

"How did you know?" Lizzie asked.

"That's why we came to New York. Our aunt told us to locate Sonya Bourne because she would help us," Emily said. "But how did you know to find us in Boston?"

"Sonya sent us to Maine to check out rumors that two dhampyr girls were hiding out and brawling with rogue vampires. If I knew all I needed to do was say 'Sonya Bourne' and you would've come, this would have been a lot easier." Lizzie shook her head.

"I still wouldn't have come so easily. It's who I am." Thinking about how we could have avoided the events of today made me exhale loudly. "Lead the way, vampire girl."

Ethan's stance relaxed as he listened, but he didn't say a word. When we finished talking, he strode off. My eyes followed him. The fluttering in my stomach faded the farther away he was. I wished I knew how to control that. When he was near, it hurt to breathe.

We reached a terra-cotta brick building after walking quite a few blocks. Its three-story-high presence dominated the street corner it sat on. The main entrance was up a few steps, through a covered archway, allowing plenty of room for vampires to stand in the doorway during the day. I noticed a few cameras hidden in the crevices. Cas punched in a code on the door's security pad.

"Ladies first. Ethan, that means you too." Cas threw me a wink.

Ethan scowled as he walked into the building.

Lizzie punched Cas in the shoulder. "Leave him alone." I watched as Lizzie ran to catch up to Ethan.

"Man, I've never seen him like this," Cas said, shaking his head.

"You know, Lizzie said the same thing, but this is the *only* way I've seen him. So it's obvious he hates me," I said.

"Or maybe he likes you," Emily added teasingly as we walked through the entryway, then through another set of doors leading into a large room.

"Oooh, that's a good guess." Cas put his arm around Emily. This time, she didn't pull away from him. "Yes—finally, you accept us as inseparable pals."

"'Inseparable'? I don't know if I would go that far," she said.

"Fine, baby steps," Cas replied amiably.

I stopped to take in my surroundings. If I thought the outside was magnificent, the inside was breathtaking. The main entrance had brought us into a massive room. The subtle smells of antique books and embers from a fire lingered, making the place feel like a vintage library. Straight ahead was a vast, beautifully finished staircase that led to an open second-floor hallway.

"Where are we?" From the look on Emily's face, she was as captivated as me. I guess I had expected a run-down building for bloodsuckers.

We ventured into the middle of the room, and then I heard someone behind us. A tall slender woman with light brown hair and dark brown eyes walked toward us. Lizzie and Ethan flanked either side of her. Her heart-shaped face and round eyes made her beautiful, but the way she pursed her lips as she stared at me told me she was dangerous as well.

She stopped a few feet from where we stood, eyeing both of us curiously. Cas stepped back from Emily's side, leaving the two of us standing alone in front of her.

"Hello, Antanasia. Hello, Daciana. I'm Sonya. How was your trip?"

My mind was reeling. Lizzie, Cas, and Ethan were vampires, so why *wouldn't* the head of their coven be a vampire? My human aunt and mother had told me to seek Sonya, a vampire. That information would have been good to know while trying to find her on our own. I crossed my arms across my chest.

"It's Tasi, or Tasia, and Emily, not Daciana, and it was . . . eventful."

The corners of her mouth turned up as she looked at me. "Tasia. Yes, I hear you gave my team a lot of practice today." She glanced back at Lizzie and Ethan, who just stood there like statues. Her persona was cold. I sucked in my cheeks, locking my eyes on hers.

"So why are we here? I don't mean to be disrespectful, but it's been a long day, and I'm tired of being the last to know what the hell is going on. Plus, I would like to have my shoulder looked at." The pain was becoming a nuisance.

"Let's go take a seat. Ethan has informed me of your injury, and I have someone prepping the infirmary for you. We can talk in the meantime." She reached her arm out toward a sofa near the fireplace. I walked with Emily and took a seat.

Sonya dismissed the others, and they disappeared into a room off to the left of the stairs. Only Ethan turned back. His face looked concerned, until he realized I was watching him. He then tried to change his guise to distant, but it was too late. His eyes betrayed him.

"So, why are we so important? Please don't give me half-truths either. I want the full truth, whether or not it pisses me off."

"I love how you aren't afraid to speak your mind, Tasia. Just remember, you don't want to get yourself, or Emily, killed with that mouth of yours." Her eyes narrowed.

"I get it, but why do you need us?" I let out a long sigh and shifted my weight from one leg to the other.

"Tasia, we don't need you." Sonya pressed her lips together before she continued. "What I'm about to tell you stays between us. We're keeping you alive because you and your sister are invaluable. You're the only two known dhampyrs, and you carry the blood of an original. Because of this, there's a group of humans looking for you—"

"Why would humans want us? That doesn't make sense."

Her face remained expressionless. It made me wonder if such composure and control came with how old she was. She ignored my question.

"That group believes they can mutate your blood into a disease that will wipe out all vampires. I can't let that happen. I also can't let my kind know your blood may indeed have the means to do this, as I suspect there would be vampires who would want you dead in order to avoid the threat completely."

She circled Emily and me like a ravenous animal checking out its prey.

"I made a promise to your father a long time ago to keep you safe, and I plan to follow through on that promise, no matter the cost."

"Our father? Is it possible he's still alive?" Hope fluttered in my stomach. Emily gripped my hand tighter, and sweat built between our palms.

She looked us in the eyes before answering. "No. Your parents both died in their home, right before your aunt sent you away."

My hand slipped from Emily's as flashes of the parents I

knew flittered through me. The way her grip loosened and slid away from my hand, I could tell she had the same reaction. I don't know why I had hoped the outcome would be different from what Eva had already told us. My eyes locked on the fireplace as I held back tears. This was a moment when I didn't want this head vampire to see me vulnerable. She might mistake it for weakness, and I wasn't ready to trust her yet. Emily rested against me, shaking me out of my thoughts.

"So, why don't you just kill us and be done with it? If you did, there would be nothing for them to get their hands on, and the bloodsuckers would all be safe."

That question made Emily freeze.

"First, because we are not inhumane creatures, like you think. We value life and where we come from." Her eyes bore into mine. "And second, I told you, I promised your father I'd do everything possible to keep you safe." She paused. There was something in her eyes that told me she wasn't telling us everything. "You girls seem tired. Let's talk more after you get some rest."

She ignored my feeble protest and went to the room Ethan had walked into when she dismissed him.

I had nothing left in me. I didn't understand what was going on. Eva had trained me to kill vampires, not humans. There must be something I had missed. I ran through what she told us the last day I saw her alive.

No matter the threat, Tasi, you take them out. They'll come at you from all angles if they find you. A stake to the heart will kill anything or anyone. A knife won't kill a vampire, but bring one with you, just in case. They're great in sticky situations. A gun is too loud—stay away from them altogether. You don't want to draw any unwanted attention. They want your blood; do not let them have it.

Those words—*they want your blood; do not let them have it*—rang in my head over and over. I had assumed that meant the vampires needed it. Had I misinterpreted what Eva was teaching me? How stupid of me. She'd prepared me for all threats—vampires and humans. I wasn't listening.

I sank into the couch, waiting for Sonya to return. The world around me was spinning out of control. One thing was for sure: my aunt and parents wanted me here with Sonya. So here we would stay, at least until I could figure out the missing pieces, or until we were no longer safe.

8

The drumming in my ears magnified. There was so much going on, I hadn't noticed it until we were abandoned. Waiting was a test of my patience; it felt like hours had passed, and my tolerance was diminishing quickly. Not healing fast was new, and honestly, I didn't envy humans at the moment—pain sucked.

What I wanted was to get out of my blood-soaked shirt. It surprised me that a vampire hadn't attacked me yet. I knew they could smell me. Maybe that's why I hadn't seen anyone.

The creak of a hidden door behind the bookcase perked me up. Ethan and Sonya walked out from behind it—Sonya, with her grace and elegance, and Ethan, who was so gorgeous my heart thumped faster as he closed the gap between us. It was too bad he was such a jerk. Emily was passed out and curled up into my side. I shook her slightly as the two approached, waking her.

"Ethan will give you a tour of the facility and also show you to your quarters," Sonya said. "Once you are settled, I would like to evaluate the training you have had thus far. We will also need to start Emily on a training routine. It's not something we take lightly around here."

"Fine."

Emily stood up groggily, putting her weight on me to steady herself. She let go of my hand, and we wiped our palms on our pants. As we walked away, I turned back to see Sonya's dark eyes watching us. She was hiding something. I could feel it.

Ethan left no time for small talk. "The upstairs is where all the different learning and training rooms are—media, study, art, so forth."

"There's a school up there?" Emily asked.

"Yes. We have to learn as much as we can. Times change faster than we do, and we need to keep up with it. You'll probably use it to further your education. If you're staying with us, you'll have to finish school. It's a Sonya rule."

Emily sighed before letting out an unexpected yawn.

He led us through the hidden entry, which doubled as a bookcase. Behind it was a long, dark hallway with many doors on either side. There were antique sconces mounted on the walls every few feet, giving the hall a faint, flickering light.

"Why is this hidden?"

"Safety."

His tone told me he was uninterested in anything that came out of my mouth. Emily gave me a sympathetic smile, picking up on his brief answers, and asked a follow-up question.

"So why safety? Isn't the building safe enough? I mean, you need a code to get in."

"It's safe, but while we sleep, we prefer to stay hidden, in case someone learns how to bypass the key code."

Ethan spoke gently to Emily. It infuriated me. He didn't seem to have an issue talking to her, but with me, daggers shot out of his eyes, repeatedly stabbing me over and over. I shouldn't care at all, but it bothered me.

"It's peaceful around here," Emily said.

"Most of us are still sleeping. Give it another hour or two. Once the evening rolls around, everyone will be up."

"The lack of sleep might explain some attitudes around here," I said.

Ethan stopped. I braced myself for the backlash, but before he could turn to say anything, Emily smacked my arm, making me cringe. She was lucky that was my uninjured arm.

Emily kept the conversation going despite my snide remark. "So do we need to switch our sleep schedule?"

"You should try. It may take a few days, but you'll get used to it," Ethan said, leading us to our room, which was the last one on the left.

Emily grinned like the Cheshire cat upon entering. The cream-colored walls, dark wood trim, and plush chocolate-brown rug made the room comfortable. The lighting was warm and inviting. It was what I thought a ritzy boarding school might look like, except there were no windows.

Rushing in, Emily threw her backpack on the desk farthest from the door. She then jumped onto the bed next to it, scrambling under the covers.

"Can I stay here for the rest of tonight? Please, I need one night," she said.

"I don't know, Em. I mean, it might take a while to get my shoulder patched up, and we just got here. We don't even know—"

"If you're worried about her safety, I promise, she'll be fine here." Ethan placed his hand on the small of my back. The electricity zoomed through me, tickling my fingertips. He flinched, then pulled back. But that small moment between us had sent me the comfort I needed.

"Please, Tasi," Emily begged, fingers interlaced as if she were praying.

"Okay, but only because someone is betting his life that you'll be safe."

"I'll give your sister the rest of the tour. She can show you around tomorrow."

"Thanks, Ethan. Thanks, Tasi." She reached for the pillow, wrapping her arms so tightly around it that if it were alive, she would have taken its last breath.

"No problem, Emily," he said. There was a hint of a smile.

Throwing my stuff on the other desk, I gave Emily a wink and headed out. Ethan and I looked away from each other. My guess was there wouldn't be a lot of conversation happening from this point on.

Ethan must have thought the same thing, because he put his hands in his pockets and headed toward the last door, marked SECURITY. That was probably for the best, because a small part of me worried I would fall into those eyes if I had to look at him for too long.

There was a steep set of spiral stairs leading downward. We walked in silence, hearing only the clinking of our feet against the metal steps. When we reached the bottom, there was another long hallway. This hall was cold and industrial-looking. The walls were white, and the doors were made of metal. Each room had a small window on one side. We stopped at the only set of double doors, to our right.

"This is where the control room is."

We stepped into the room. Two men were sitting in chairs, monitoring about a dozen large screens that covered the wall. Most of the pictures on the screens were of the area outside the building. Some were of the main entrance, and the others were of different angles from the main floor. I saw none of the sleeping quarters or learning rooms Ethan had pointed out earlier.

Both men were good-looking, with short dirty-blond hair and stunning topaz eyes. I thought they might be related.

"Hey, you must be one of the Vasile girls. Heard a lot about you guys," one of them said with a huge grin plastered on his face.

"Hopefully all good things," I said.

"Nothing but good. This here is Leonard, and I'm James."

"You can call me Len."

"I'm Antanasia. Some people call me Tasia or Tasi for short, but whatever is fine."

"Okay, 'Whatever,'" Len joked.

James roared with laughter, which made me giggle.

"Come on, let's keep moving," Ethan said. "These two will keep you talking all day."

They continued to laugh as James said, "He's right—pretty girls don't visit us very often."

Ethan rolled his eyes and hurried me out, but not before my cheeks burned in embarrassment.

"Sorry, they're like Tweedledee and Tweedledum. I just don't know which one is which." Ethan talking directly to me made me smile a little. We continued down the corridor, and he appeared a little more relaxed. "These are where some of our weapons rooms are as well as storage and infirmary rooms," he pointed out.

"Weapons?" I asked, keeping my questions short.

He stopped at the door labeled INFIRMARY and opened it, letting me walk past him into the room. "Sometimes we confiscate weapons from our attackers, plus we keep a supply of our own on hand—never know when one might come in handy." A knowing smile crossed his face.

My heart leaped into my throat. Standing behind me, he leaned in, stopping me in my tracks. His silky lips brushed along my ear, tickling me with his cool breath.

"Don't worry, we won't be taking your weapons away. But I wouldn't let on that you have them either. Some of us might find it threatening. Although, soaking them in holy water—genius."

I caught a trace of his warm brown eyes as he maneuvered around me. It made something happen in my stomach I had never experienced before. I wasn't sure what it was, but it felt as if someone were tickling me on the inside, in a good way. My eyes locked onto him for a few more moments before returning to the room.

I supposed this was what a doctor's office would look like. Since Emily and I were dhampyrs, we'd never gone to the doctor. Along the back wall, there was a counter with a built-in sink. A small mirror decorated the wall, and a plethora of bandages and gauze in containers rested on the shelves. There was an examination table against another wall, raised high enough so someone could stand while checking out their patient.

"Is it shoulder time?"

"Yes, it is." He pointed to the table. "Your wounds need to be cleaned. God knows what germs are crawling around in Cas's shirt."

Being with Ethan in this moment felt natural and right. He was actually being nice to me, and I was trying hard to keep my snide comments to myself instead of self-sabotaging, as I usually did.

I jumped up on the table, but misjudged the height and slightly lost my bearings. Ethan, with quick reflexes, grabbed me by the waist, and I held on to his shoulders as he helped me stabilize.

"Careful there—I don't want to be responsible for taking out a Vasile girl." His smile was genuine.

He let me go once I was safely sitting on the examiner's table.

"Very funny."

I looked around, paying closer attention to the details. The room felt frigid. Everything in it was white and metallic. The tools on the counter glimmered like newly polished silver, even though most of it looked as if it belonged in a horror movie.

Ethan picked out a few supplies before putting them on a tray and walking back over. I tried to keep from staring, even though all I wanted to do was fall into those big brown eyes of his. He gracefully hopped up next to me. Our eyes met one last time, and I looked away.

"Do you want me to get someone else to do this for you?"

My answer came out too fast and too loud. "You can do it. I want you to do it."

His eyes searched mine for the truth. It must have satisfied him, as he turned toward my shoulder. Pulling my arm out of my sleeve would be a task, but I didn't hesitate for fear he might actually find someone else. I winced. He moved closer to help me, and our fingers touched. That desire for him ran through me again. My stomach tightened as I watched him delicately run his hands along my skin, trying his best not to hurt me. He was gentle and purposely kept his eyes off mine.

Delicately reaching under my shirt, he helped me take it off. My heart raced. Underneath, I had on a black tank top that was damp with my blood. Was it hard for him to be near the blood, like it had been for Cas, or was he being distracted by something else?

He moved closer and untied the bandage Cas had made with his sleeve. My eyes followed his every move, his every touch, and caught every stolen glance. I bit my lip, trying to keep my composure. Turning back to the tray, he grabbed some cotton and dipped it into a clear liquid.

"This may sting a little, but the good news is you don't need stitches. It looks like the chemical they used doesn't have as much of an effect on dhampyrs."

"Good to know."

He wiped off all the dried blood that had streamed down my arm. Then, slowly, he moved up to where the bullet had taken a bite out of my shoulder.

Studying his face, I thought about how he'd been so hot and cold with me. "Why are you being nice to me right now? I mean, typically, you're angry at me. Like that night at the church, you looked like you were going to kill me."

He stiffened, then let out a long huff. "I swear, you're the only person I know who can infuriate me within seconds."

"So that's the reason? I piss you off? Then why didn't you kill me that night? That way, you could've rid the world of me."

So much for keeping my mouth under control. The cotton fell from his hand as he eyed me in disbelief.

"Jeez, Tasi, you seriously need to let someone finish talking before you jump down their throat." He picked up another piece of cotton and dabbed it into the liquid. "I scared you back into the church because there was a group of six rogue vampires heading toward you. If you had gone their way, they would have ripped us to pieces—all of us."

Before I could protest, he interrupted me.

"And don't say you could have waited it out in the church. You still don't get it. You two dhampyrs have a smell that is far more exquisite than a normal human's. It would be like having expensive champagne instead of sparkling cider. Get it? Rogue vampires don't give up when they smell something they want. They lack the self-control needed to sit and endure the temptation."

I thought back to the vampire at the motel and how he'd found me, how he'd tried to pass himself off as a housekeeper to gain access to the room. I wondered if he'd risked getting stuck in the sun to find and kill me, all because he was obsessed with the smell of my blood.

"Oh. I'm sorry. I thought—"

"It's fine. You didn't know, but maybe you could find out all the facts next time. You have a habit of thinking the worst right away. Not everyone wants to hurt you." He picked up a piece of gauze and placed it over the wound. Taping it up, he looked at me.

Blood raced to the surface of my skin, and my cheeks

burned, this time from embarrassment, not anger. He didn't understand. How could he? Everyone I trusted had lied to me, and now I was trying to figure out a puzzle with a ton of missing pieces. When I looked up at him, my breath caught. His eyes sparkled as he watched me. He took my hand and placed it in his, palm up. With his other hand, he touched my fingers, outlining them. A tickle ran up my arm.

"You're strong, Tasi. You're a survivor," he said in a low voice, before jumping off the table and carrying the tray back to the counter. After a while, still turned away from me, he said, "Put your shirt on, and I'll show you the rest of the place."

Squeezing my eyes tight, I pulled on my shirt. We continued the tour, heading upstairs, then across to the other side of the main hall. When we reached the kitchen, a dark-haired boy was sitting at the far end of the table. Ethan leaned into my ear. His scent was dizzying. His hand slipped around my waist, and I immediately felt vulnerable. I hoped he couldn't tell how much I liked it.

"That's Austin. He's one of the oldest vampires in this house. Unfortunately, he's also the biggest jerk."

"I heard that," Austin said, standing up and moving closer to us. Before he could say anything else to Ethan, his eye caught mine. "Fabulous, you found the half-breed. Did Sonya give you a cookie, Ethan? How about a pat on the head and a 'good boy'?"

"No, but you could get the hell out of my way before I knock you across the room."

"*Tsk, tsk*, Ethan—we have a guest." He looked me up and down, grimacing. "So what's your story?"

"No story—staying for a while until I can figure out what's going on." My voice was shaky. Something about Austin made me nervous.

"Good luck with that. Somehow, I don't think you'll get very far. If you get bored, sweetheart, you can stop by my room." He leaned into my neck. "You smell wonderful. If you want, we could get together sometime."

Before he could say another word, Ethan grabbed him and shoved him up against the fridge. "Touch either of the Vasile girls, and I will rip your limbs off and use them as firewood."

Ethan looked deadlier than I had ever seen before, but Austin just laughed in his face. "Relax, I won't touch your precious girlfriends. Not unless they want me to." He winked at me.

His words made me cringe. I wasn't sure if Austin was implying I smelled edible, but the thought of any vampire biting me made me sick. Austin pushed past Ethan and smiled at me one last time before leaving the kitchen.

"One day, that guy is going to make the wrong move, and I'm going to be there to rip his head from his neck," he said. "C'mon, I'll take you back to your room."

He led me back through the main hall. It was early evening, and I saw a couple people wandering around now. They stared at Ethan and me as we walked back to the dorm area.

"Here you are," he said.

"Thanks again for bandaging me up, taking me around, and ... stuff."

"No problem." He opened his mouth to say something else, but instead, he let out an exasperated huff and left.

9

I ran through a field, grass whipping my bare legs. There were horses behind me, maybe twenty of them. They were stampeding as fast as they could, eyes fiery red, glaring at me as I looked back. My feet were fast and kept me a small distance ahead of them until I stumbled. Pain surged through my face as it scraped the ground. The galloping sound replicated, nails being hammered into my skull over and over. I looked back one last time. The horses had multiplied, and I was about to be trampled. Not giving in so easily, I tried to get back up and run, but I tripped over my feet. Covering my face and bracing for impact, I yelled, "Stop!"

The field faded, and I was now cocooned in my blanket, flailing about. The more I kicked, the more I became entangled. The horses disappeared, and I was lying in a hopeless mess of bedsheets.

That's when I heard it more clearly, right above me. *Thud! Thump! Fwap!* I rolled over toward Emily's bed, hoping she was sleeping through the loud explosions happening in the room above ours. I rubbed my eyes, trying to focus, until I noticed there was no Emily. I jumped out of bed. The desk and closet looked untouched. Her backpack lay on top of her neatly made bed, but had been riffled through. I grabbed my jeans and a clean tank top and threw them on.

I didn't know what time it was. Waking up before my brain said it was time to get up had made me wobbly, and I made a bleary-eyed pit stop at the bathroom. I turned the faucet on and splashed water on my face. The cold water shocked my body, telling it to wake up, and it did.

Lifting my head, I looked in the mirror. I still looked sickly, with my gray eyes and pallid skin. I ran a brush through my hair, trying to make it presentable. And to think, I'd wondered why people, mainly Ethan, had been cold to me. I was an utter disaster.

I sighed heavily before heading out to find Emily. There was a pang in my heart, not knowing where she was. We always woke up in the same house or room, and never in a place so big and so filled with vampires.

Upon entering the main hall, I noticed a few unknown faces, and some doors were open on the second floor. I saw no one I knew, so I headed to the kitchen, where Lizzie and Ethan were sitting at one end of a table with another girl I didn't know.

I walked up to stand behind Lizzie.

"Anyone seen Emily?" My voice sounded groggy.

"And hello to you too, sunshine," Lizzie said. "She and Cas are in the training room. Up the stairs, last room on the right."

"Above the dorm rooms?" I asked. *Stupid horses.*

"What's the matter? Disturb your beauty sleep? I don't think it's going to help. Sorry, doll," Ethan spat out, getting up to leave.

What happened to the sweet Ethan from last night? Did he suddenly realize how much he hated me again?

"Why's he such a jerk?" I mumbled under my breath.

"Hey, don't talk about him like that. Ethan is amazing." The redheaded pixie-looking girl sitting at the table stared me down with her dark-green eyes. She was trying to bare her teeth at me without looking like she was intentionally doing it, but it would take a lot more than that to intimidate me.

I saw Lizzie sit back.

"Then go be with Mr. Amazing, whoever you are," I said in a squeaky voice, mocking her.

She stood up, palms firmly pressed on the table, and looked at me. "You can't walk into our house and act like a big shot, half-breed. I don't care if your dad was Adrian Vasile." She snorted. She flipped her hair, stuck her nose in the air, and ran after Ethan, who I hadn't noticed was holding the door for her.

"Do you typically clear out a room when you enter it?" Lizzie said. "I wish I had her on camera. Her face was priceless."

"Who was that, anyway?"

"Ethan's on-again, off-again girlfriend, Clover. I think since yesterday, they were on again. Well, at least that's what she says—Ethan usually rolls with whatever."

My fingers gripped the edge of the table tighter as the heat in my face grew warmer. I tried to relax the tension building within me, but I could feel my lips pressing together tighter. The thought of Clover rattling me before I could even have some coffee to wake myself up annoyed me.

"She has a knack for getting under people's skin. Don't let it get to you."

Lizzie's words brought some calm to me. Then my heart crumbled as the word *girlfriend* rang in my head. I must have imagined everything from last night. I needed to learn how to read people. My aunt had taught me everything I knew, but social skills weren't on that list.

"Here, sit and drink some of this. It will take the edge off."

She slid a blue coffee mug over to me.

"What is . . ." That was all I could say before I sensed the sweet scent of iron swirling through my nose. I turned to Lizzie and, in a whisper, asked, "Is this blood?"

"Duh, Sherlock, and it's not a secret—we all do it." Laughter overtook Lizzie. "You're not so clever today. Trust me, drink some." She eyed me curiously. "It'll be good for you."

I hesitantly picked it up, holding it to my lips for several seconds. Slowly, they parted, letting in the thick liquid. It was warm, and before I knew it, I was chugging it down. It slid down my throat and flowed into every inch of my body, all the way to my toes and fingertips. My body was alive again. A familiar feeling filled me, almost as if I'd found something once forgotten.

I turned to Lizzie as I wiped my lips with the back of my hand. "Whoa."

Now she was hysterically laughing. "Oh, Tasi, I have a lot to teach you. You're so lucky to have found me."

She stood up and poured me a little more from the coffeepot on the counter. It was clearly not filled with coffee. Placing the mug back in front of me, she handed me a banana nut muffin before sitting down again.

"Why is it that when I drink my concoction, I don't feel like this?" I asked, taking a bite of my muffin.

"I don't know. How do you drink it?" Lizzie asked.

"I would dilute it with coffee, a lot of coffee, actually, or juice. Sometimes water too. I had to make it last, so I drank only a little at a time every few days." I took another gulp. "I always thought blood on its own was so gross. I can't believe how much I like this."

Lizzie shook her head. "You're half-vampire, or did you forget?"

"Yeah, I guess there is a lot I don't know." I shoved the rest of the muffin in my mouth.

"Come on, let's go find out how Emily is doing with Cas."

I took one last gulp, rinsed the cup out before putting it in the sink, and then ran to catch up with Lizzie. She was now watching me from the bottom of the stairs in the main hall with a grin on her face. Her smile baffled me as I headed over.

Along the way, some people stopped and gawked. Others broke out into whispers. Lizzie's laugh echoed in the hall as more people stared at me. Finally, I spotted Ethan, whose eyes didn't leave mine. Even as Clover pulled at his arm, he just watched me.

Something must be on my face. Oh God, did Lizzie set me up? Are there remnants of blood on my face? My temper flared. I pulled my attention back to Lizzie, who was now heading up the stairs.

"Was this a sick joke?" I asked as I grabbed her arm, piercing her skin.

"Hey, careful—your grip is too tight. Stop."

I loosened my clasp. Lizzie still wore a smile on her face.

My breath quickened, leaving my mouth dry. "Why are people staring at me? What's on my face?"

"Relax, Tasi, and follow me." She clutched my arm and carted me to the bathroom on the second floor. "Now take a peek."

"I know what I look like." I turned toward the mirror, then froze as I stared at a distantly familiar face.

"Man, you're good for a bunch of laughs today." She was standing against the wall, arms crossed against her chest, staring at me. "Meet me in the training area when you're finished." Before she stepped through the doorway, she looked over at me. "You're welcome." Her laughter followed her into the hall.

I touched my face, waiting for the mask to fall off to reveal my permanent dark circles, grayish-colored skin, and dulled features. But there was no mask. My eyes were bright, like they had been a long time ago, and turquoise like the ocean. My features were flawless, better than I remembered, with glowing olive skin and lips full of color. I looked healthy.

I smiled a genuine smile for the first time in a long while.

Then I headed out of the bathroom, right into Clover, who had her hands on her hips, breathing so hard she might start spewing fire.

"Oh, come on. Can't you find someone else to bother?"

Her lip curled back, revealing more of her fangs this time. "I'm going to say this once: Ethan belongs to me. I heard last night you two were real chummy. Well, you better watch yourself. I hear dhampyr blood is a delicacy."

I pushed against her, forcing her a couple steps back. She was a few inches shorter than me. "Let's get two things straight, Cloves."

"It's Clover."

"First, if you have issues with your relationship, then take it up with Ethan, not me. Second, my blood will never get near your lips, but my stake will reach your heart if you keep threatening me. So get the hell out of my face before I rip yours off." The heat burned within me as I spoke through gritted teeth.

Clover flinched, and her eyes went wide, but she didn't back down. "Watch yourself!" She stomped off.

Lizzie leaned out of the room next to the bathroom. "You have a fan."

"Is this what high school is like? If so, I wish my aunt were here so I could thank her for homeschooling me."

Lizzie, still as gorgeous as ever, with her blonde ringlets pulled back in a ponytail, threw her arm around me. "Ignore her. She's jealous. Clover used to hate me because she thought I was out to steal Ethan too." Lizzie smiled. "She might have something to worry about with you, though. You're smoking hot."

"And you're not? Please, Lizzie."

"It's different. You're hot *and* exotic." She laughed again.

"By the way, what did you put in that blood? It was so good, and I look like me again."

"Oh, Tasi, why would you think the old, processed blood you stole from a hospital would sustain you? You're lucky it kept you alive. If I drank that stuff . . . nope, that would never happen. This is fresh human blood sent to us within hours of it leaving their bodies. It's why living in New York is such a dream —lots of willing donors."

I shook my head as I entered the training room to see Cas in a defensive stance and Emily attacking him with boxing gloves. He was holding up his hands, letting her jab them over and over. They danced around a little. Emily landed a few punches before she saw me standing to the side.

"Tasi!" she screamed as she ran over to me. "Sorry I didn't wake you, but I figured you could use the sleep. Cas wasn't doing anything and offered to show me some moves. Did you see my jab? Pretty good, huh?" Finally, she stopped speaking and stared at me for a few seconds. "You look like Tasi again." Her voice was childlike, and she hugged me tightly.

"I know, weird, right?" I replied, running my hands through my hair.

Cas handed Lizzie a hundred bucks, then turned to me. "Man, I thought for sure you would have held out for a week at least."

I looked between the two. "You guys bet on me? Really?" I dropped my head, looking at my feet, and let out a sigh.

"Listen, it was a friendly bet, so don't get all mad and stuff," Lizzie said.

I raised my head with a smirk on my face. The three looked at me. "I'm not mad—just realizing vampires have nothing better to do than bet on stupid things like how long it would be until I tasted pure blood." I arched an eyebrow at Lizzie. "You're buying me a latte next time we pass a Starbucks."

"You drank just blood, like, as in, not mixed with anything?" Emily stuck her tongue out in disgust. "Ew, so gross."

"Get used to it, kiddo. Eventually, it'll be you," Cas said.

"Don't remind me. Let's go. I want to beat you up a few more times." Emily bounced around, making jabbing motions.

"Fine, but go easy on me," he said. "I don't want to mess up my hair."

10

Leaving the training room, I quickly realized that I hadn't felt this good since living at home in Maine. The grin on my face pushed my cheeks up so high it caused a tender feeling on my face. Was it really that long since I had genuinely smiled? I glanced at all the reflective surfaces I passed by.

I approached the media center and noticed the door was slightly open. Inside, I saw Sonya and Austin. I stood quietly against the wall, hoping no one would think my behavior odd, and peered through the crack.

"I'm not sure what you're expecting out of this. Those girls don't even like our kind, which means they should leave." Austin sounded annoyed.

"Last time I checked, you work for me. So you will follow my orders, and regardless of how you feel about the Vasile girls, you need to treat them like they belong here. Ethan told me how you were acting last night toward Tasia, and I will have none of that."

"Figures Ethan would tell on me. That girl brought it on herself," Austin said. "Why do you even care?"

Sonya floated the short distance across the room gracefully and lifted Austin, by the neck, about six inches off the ground.

"You will be one of their guards, Austin, because I said so. You're one of our oldest and strongest, so you'll protect them and ensure they remain unharmed. The humans cannot capture those girls. If they do, it'll infuriate me more than your insubordination." She placed him back on the floor and straightened out his shirt. "Now that you fully understand, you'll behave and keep them protected until further notice. Give them a chance. You might end up liking what you see."

He rubbed his throat as she walked away, but said nothing.

As she got closer, I backed into an adjacent room, making sure no one noticed me. Austin followed shortly after. Watching Sonya's interaction with Austin confirmed what I had initially thought. She was dangerous, and I needed to watch out for her. I slipped out again into the media center.

The room was enormous and lined with two rows of tables. Each table had either tablets or laptops on them. Along the wall were more bookcases, like in the main room, along with a few couches—an excellent place to read a book.

I studied one of the bookcases, noticing something strangely familiar about it. The hidden door to the sleeping quarters had a similar look. Of course, curiosity got the best of me. Running my hands along the side of the bookcase, I noticed a latch. When I pulled it up, the bookcase opened. There was a steep staircase leading upward. By the looks of all the cobwebs smothering the air, no one had been through this door in a long time. I brushed away the threads and crept up the stairs like a ninja in the night.

When I reached the top, I pushed on the door. At first, I didn't think it would budge, but I put my strength behind it and shoved harder. It creaked open. I was outside on a small part of the roof. I was confident this part hadn't been on the security cameras, which intrigued me more. A smile warmed my face as the city lights glistened like diamonds scattered across the busy streets.

As I stood there, I realized that even with Sonya and Austin's weird conversation, I felt safe here—safer than I had in months. I wanted to stay here and watch the sun tiptoe up from behind the buildings. I could only imagine how pretty the structures would look as the sun bounced its rays against the reflective surfaces. Closing my eyes, I took a deep breath, but a familiar voice interrupted me.

"You know, it's off-limits up here."

I spun around. Ethan was standing behind me, his hands crossed against his chest. He looked godlike, as usual. Not that I'd admit it. Too bad his eyes pierced through me as if I were indeed an insignificant mortal.

"Why is that? It seems harmless."

"Yeah, everything, I bet, seems harmless to you—like humans." His eyes continued to drill into me, colder than usual.

I squinted. "Don't you have a girlfriend to attend to? Then you can leave me be, pretend you never saw me, and everyone will be happy."

"I'll go when you come back down. I told you it's off-limits." I could hear the frustration in his voice. "Can't you do what you're supposed to for once?"

The tension brewing between us heightened. Ethan's constant need to belittle me and talk to me like a child frustrated me. If he wanted to hate me, then I'd return the favor. The problem was, I didn't want to hate him, and I didn't want him to hate me. My stomach was doing somersaults, and my breath caught as a gust of wind engulfed me in his signature vanilla scent.

"Fabulous—you found the roof," an approving voice said, breaking me away from Ethan's trance.

Ethan and I turned to see Austin standing in the entryway I'd come through.

"What do you want?" we said in unison. Ethan and I looked at each other, and I found my lips tugging upward into a smile for a second. His face replicated mine, before we scowled at each other again.

"Yeah, so Sonya wants to see Ethan. She said it's kind of important." Austin broke the awkward moment. "I'll see that Tasi gets back downstairs."

Ethan looked at me, then at Austin. There was a struggle going on in his head, but I somehow knew Sonya would always win.

"Go," I said, rolling my eyes. "You may not believe it, but I can take care of myself."

Ethan huffed as he walked away. I wasn't sure how smart that was, but since I'd overheard Sonya earlier, I knew I was pretty safe with the other mean kid who disliked me too.

"I guess we should also go," I said.

"We can stay for a few minutes." Austin brushed off a dusty bench. He took my hand in his and pulled me down next to him. I pulled my hand back into my lap.

"What do you want?" I asked, not breaking my gaze from the lightening blue sky.

"Wow, can't a guy spend a few minutes with a pretty young lady just to say hello and get to know her better?" He brushed his black hair away from his face. I met his gaze, and his emerald eyes bore into me as I scowled at him. "Fine, Tasi, I'm sorry I was a jerk to you earlier. What can I say? Seeing you with Ethan made me a little jealous. He and I aren't friends, so when he leaned into you, well, I figured you two were already . . . *close*."

I stared at him. "That's a bold presumption. You sure it's not because you have a weird ulterior motive?"

"No, I don't have any other motives. I was just a jerk, something I often am. Someone told me today I was judging you a little too quickly, so here I am, trying not to judge."

I studied his face, looking for what might have been a lie. But I found nothing. "Fine, then let's start over."

He smiled and took my hand, kissing the back of it. "Austin, and it's my pleasure to meet you."

His kiss was cool on my hand, but the feeling was nowhere close to what shot through my body when Ethan touched me. What would happen if Ethan kissed my hand like Austin had? Would I get electrocuted by his lips? I pushed the thought out of my mind.

"I'm Tasia or Tasi, and it's nice to meet you too."

"Well, Tasi, what do you say we head back downstairs for now? Before people wonder where you are, and I turn into a pile of dust." He stood up and offered me his hand again.

"Yeah, okay. Do you think I could come back up here? I mean, even if it's off-limits, do you think we could make an exception? I like the peacefulness."

Austin watched me. "Quite possibly—let me see what I can do." His smile was brilliant, and he had a way of not showing off his fangs, which made him look less scary. Actually, it made him look good. I hadn't noticed it so much before, but Austin was gorgeous.

We headed down the stairs, dodging a few more spiderwebs along the way. When we reached the media room, Ethan was there, and he looked pissed. I suddenly realized I still had my hand in Austin's. I pulled it away like a naughty child caught sneaking candy before dinner.

"Sonya never asked for me," Ethan said, pushing Austin.

"Oh, my mistake—I guess I misunderstood."

"You did that on purpose." His jaw was clenched, and he spoke through gritted teeth.

"Does it matter?" I asked. "You were just yelling at me, anyway."

I pushed through the two guys, ignoring them both. I remembered I had planned to meet up with Lizzie and Emily.

As I walked into the kitchen, they waved me over. Emily was eating turkey and mashed potatoes, swimming in an ocean of gravy.

"Have you been in the media room this entire time? What were you looking up?" Lizzie asked, waggling her eyebrows.

"Get a grip. We've never been to New York City, so I was doing research. I guess I lost track of time."

Only part of that was a lie, but I didn't want to bring up any of my weird boy drama. I sat down next to Lizzie and across from Emily and Cas. Just when I thought things here would be free of drama, Austin slid in next to me, Ethan sat next to Lizzie, and Clover sat across from Ethan.

"Aw, Tasia, you have a fan following. Even Clover has joined the party." Lizzie fluttered her eyes and grinned widely at Clover. "Let's see—I understand Ethan and Austin wanting to be near the gorgeous Tasi, but why you, Clover? Oh, wait, I get it—you're babysitting Ethan."

"Bite me, Lizzie," Clover said.

"I'd rather bite a rat," Lizzie said.

Cas and Emily made faces at each other. Emily let out a giggle.

"Lizzie, leave her alone," Ethan said, drinking out of a gray mug.

"Fine," she grumbled, then immediately perked up. "So, Austin, what's your excuse for suddenly sitting with us? I know she's hot, but she's also way out of your league."

I now heard a snicker come from Ethan's end of the table.

"Yes, Lizzie, I don't know what I was thinking. It's too bad Tasi and I are just friends. Good friends." He winked at me and continued to address Lizzie, "I mean, wouldn't you want to sit next to the most exquisite girl in the coven?"

"Enough already. How about we talk about a sightseeing trip and take the focus off me?" I said.

"Yay! Where to?" Emily straightened up.

"I was thinking of a museum."

"You'll never get it cleared by Sonya," Ethan said.

"Oh, dear boy, you underestimate my pull around here," Austin challenged.

"Seriously, will you ask for us?" I asked, my voice almost pleading as I turned toward Austin.

"Under one condition: I come along."

"There goes all the fun," Ethan mused.

The bickering was annoying me, and I turned to Ethan. "Like you're so much fun all the time? You're more miserable than anyone I know."

I kicked back my seat, stood, and walked out of the kitchen —right into Sonya.

"Sorry," I said.

"Is everything all right, Tasia?"

"Well, honestly, no, it isn't. When we spoke, all I understood was that we came here for protection. I didn't realize that meant being locked up like an animal." My voice rose in frustration. "I mean, I want to go out, and I understand it could be dangerous, but I've taken care of Emily and myself all alone until now. So why can't we come and go like everyone else?"

"But you are not like everyone else," she said.

"Yes, I get it. I'm not asking to go out alone. Lizzie, Cas, and even Austin and Ethan were talking about tagging along. How are we not safe? I saw firsthand what those guys could do in a dangerous situation."

She considered for a long moment and then looked at me with a kind face and hard eyes.

"I will let you and your friends go, under a couple conditions. First, you complete your evaluation. I want to know you will be able to defend yourself before you are unleashed into the city."

"Easy enough."

"Second, you must always have Austin or Ethan, maybe both,

by your side. The moment either of them reports you were in too much danger, you and Emily are on lockdown until I say so." She paused for a moment, and her eyes told me I had crossed a line. There was a growl in her voice. "Do you understand?"

I wasn't sure if I liked this part of the deal—always having to be accompanied by Austin or Ethan or, worst-case scenario, both? Then I thought of Emily and how her face had lit up when I mentioned getting out to explore the city.

"Fine, but one more thing." I saw the surprise on Sonya's face, probably because no one ever answered back or challenged her last word. "I want in on any discussions or decision-making that pertains to Emily or me. We're not commodities, and staying here benefits us all. Do we have a deal?"

Her face, which had been growing harder the more I spoke, softened up a little. "Very well, we'll keep each other informed," she said. "You're a strong young woman, Tasia. I like that. But remember, don't cross the wrong people."

She walked by me and into the kitchen. I strolled over to the couches in the main hall and slumped down in front of the fireplace, watching the fire dance around the logs. Challenging Sonya and dealing with teenage drama were exhausting.

Emily came out and ran over to where I was sitting. "Are you okay?" she asked.

"Yes, Em, just tired."

"We all heard you in the kitchen. That was cool, standing up for us like that. I don't think I could have done it." Emily's eyes were filled with pride.

Great, now I would be known as the bitchiest dhampyr. "So everyone heard me?"

"Yeah, Austin looked at us and was smiling like he was also proud. Ethan was annoyed, mumbling obscenities under his breath, but he was nowhere near as annoyed as Clover, since no one asked her to go and she heard that you could only leave with Ethan or Austin."

"Great, more drama. Oh well. At least we can escape and not feel like prisoners for a while. I was getting worried," I said, leaning back into the couch and catching my breath.

"Don't worry, Tasi. No matter what, we have each other," she said, leaning back against me like she did when she was looking for comfort. This time, though, she was excited. Maybe this was feeling like home to her, finally.

"True—we'll always take care of each other first."

11

The training room was empty. I really wanted to get out of the house, so I'd scheduled my evaluation for the following day. When I woke up, I got ready and headed straight there. I pulled a yoga mat out from the shelf, rolled it out, and stretched. I wasn't sure what to expect and hoped it wouldn't take too long.

There was a glow coming from the room across the hall, and it piqued my curiosity. I had time before Sonya showed up, so I headed over to what I thought was the art room to see who else might be up here. It was Austin, and he was painting. There was a cloud of sadness enveloping him. His eyes, which were normally a beautiful crystal green, looked muted and dark. He stopped when our eyes met.

"Don't stop because of me." I shouldn't have interrupted him; there was clearly a lot going on in his head. I turned to walk away.

"Tasi, you don't have to go."

I stopped. "Sorry if I interrupted you. You seem so deep in your work, and I feel like I walked in on you naked or something. Not that I'm saying I want to see you naked." I sounded stupid. "I'm just saying you were so engaged in the painting, and I interrupted like I had a right to."

The corners of his mouth turned up, and the sadness was now gone. "So, you're saying you want to see me naked?"

"That's not what I'm saying, even though I just said it. I'm just sorry I broke your concentration, that's all."

I watched as Austin's eyes were drawn back to his painting. I wondered if he was any good and what kind of paintings he created. Were they stick figures because he was no good at painting but enjoyed the idea of it, or funny-looking abstract shapes that were subjective to the artist? This intrigued me.

"Do you paint a lot?"

His eyes moved away from the painting and back to me. "Not anymore—I only paint when I need to think." He smiled again. "Do you want to see what I'm painting?"

"Sure."

I walked over to stand beside him. My eyes bulged and my mouth fell open.

"Do you like it?"

"Austin, this is exquisite." The painting showed a canal with buildings on both sides, a beautiful bridge with arches, and mountains topped with snow in the background. The detail was so realistic I thought I was looking at a photograph. "Where is this?"

"It's Annecy, France. I spent some time there, after living in Italy. It brings me a sense of peace." I watched as his brush gently touched the canvas.

"Have your paintings ever been displayed anywhere?"

"No, my paintings are private." His voice had a finality to it, and I didn't think I should press him. Plus, I barely knew him.

"It's beautiful. I guess I should get back to my evaluation. I don't want to leave Sonya waiting for me," I said with a small smile.

"No, you don't. See you over there."

I stopped and looked back at him. "Why will I see you over there?"

He grinned wickedly. "I told Sonya that I'm the oldest vampire outside of her in this house, so you should spar with me."

My stomach flopped. "Great."

"Don't worry. I won't hurt you too much. I like that face." He winked.

I shook my head and headed back to the training room. I wasn't aware there was going to be a sparring session. When Sonya said "evaluation," I'd pictured me and her in the gym, the way Eva and I would train. Just the two of us, maybe a third when we had combat training. Would there be others besides Austin also coming to my evaluation? Would Ethan be there? Would I have to spar with him also? Questions raced through my mind. The thought made my stomach turn somersaults. My hands began to tremble thinking about Ethan.

I focused back on stretching and trying to clear my head. At least I wouldn't be blindsided by Austin's appearance later. I still couldn't help wondering who else would be joining. Would there be several levels of sparring? Would Sonya even interact with me, as Eva had done, or was she just going to watch?

I was continuing my warm-up routine when my favorite familiar face walked into the room—Emily. She grabbed a mat and began stretching alongside me.

"How do you feel?" she asked.

"Okay, I guess. I was better until I found out I'd be sparring with Austin."

"Really?"

"Yeah, I'm a little nervous because I've never sparred with a vampire, at least not one I didn't intend to kill. Sparring with people at the gym with Eva was hard, since I had to consciously hold back because they were human. Imagine a girl like me taking out a guy who was a foot taller and had a hundred pounds more muscle. People might have wondered."

Emily giggled. "I never thought of that. It's funny, I always thought you went to the gym with Eva to keep her company on the treadmill."

This made me laugh, until I thought about sparring with Austin again. "Now I have to fight someone who may be stronger than me. Not only that . . . what if I bleed? Will I become Austin's next meal?"

This made Emily flinch. "Maybe we should tell Sonya you're concerned about that."

"No. I don't want her involved. I'll just pull out a stake and use it, because *no one* is going to drink my blood."

"Wait—you have your stakes on you for this?"

"Why not? If I'm fighting out in the real world, I'll have them on me, so I should train with them on as well."

"Huh, that makes sense. I'm so glad I have you to learn from. Without you, this would be so much harder. Either way, I know you're going to do great today." She leaned in and hugged me tight.

"Girls," Sonya's voice boomed.

"Sonya," I said in return.

"Tasia, make sure you're ready. We will begin in ten minutes."

"Good luck," Emily said, before getting up and sitting on a bench across the room.

Lizzie, Ethan, and Clover came in and also sat on the bench. Ugh. I had an audience. Cas arrived and started stretching, which made me think he was part of my evaluation too.

I rolled up my mat and put it away as Sonya spoke.

"Tasia, your evaluation today will be on the following: cardio fitness level, offensive and defensive movements, and sparring with one or multiple partners. Any questions?"

My hands were sweating. I wanted to ask if we could postpone this to another day, so I could mentally prepare to do this with others watching, but I didn't think that would bode well for me. I looked over to the side of the room where Emily sat and noticed more faces now. Vampires I'd never interacted with sat there waiting for me, the freak show, to start throwing punches. I wanted to be snarky in my response, bitchy and callous, as if this didn't faze me, but I couldn't do it.

"No questions."

"Great. Let's get started."

The cardio was easy. I had to jump on the motorless treadmill and run five miles as fast as I could. This was something I did at the gym often as a warm-up. But there, I wouldn't run faster than an eight-minute mile. Here I could let loose a little.

Five miles went by pretty quick. I was able to complete a four-minute mile without stressing my lungs. I decided to come back here and test myself on my own to see what I could really do when no one was looking. Sonya scratched something on her clipboard as she chatted with Cas. Her face showed no emotion, making me wonder if I went too slow.

"Tasia, Cas will now take you through some basic movements I would expect you to be well versed in," Sonya said.

I wiped my hands on my pants. Cas stepped up, looking mature and confident. He moved a punching bag to the middle of the room. I stared at it, trying to convince myself that no one in the room was watching.

Cas called out a move, and I performed the act. We repeated this for several rounds. The last move was a combination of kicks, which I easily completed, with the final move being a back kick. I hit the bag harder than planned, and it split open. *Shit.* I didn't want to do that. There were a few hoots and cheers from the bench area. I knew if I looked over, it would be Emily and Lizzie, but I didn't want to acknowledge them and break my concentration.

Sonya scratched something onto her clipboard again and said, "Cas, Austin, clean that up so we can move to the sparring."

As Austin passed me, he gave me a sweet smile.

"I need a quick break," I said, walking out of the room.

"Five minutes, Tasia," Sonya's voice trailed behind me.

The bathroom was a few steps from the training area. I stopped in and washed my hands. *You can do this, Tasi. This is like training with Eva.*

"You okay?" Emily asked.

I looked up. "Yeah, just nervous. There are a lot of people watching. I guess I wasn't prepared for an audience."

"Deep breaths, Tasi. Even if you can't take out your opponents, you'll learn something about yourself."

I continued to stare at myself in the mirror before looking at Emily. "You're always the voice of reason."

She smiled and grabbed my hand. "Come on. You need to show everyone what a dhampyr can do."

We headed back to the room, where they had finished cleaning up my sandy mess.

"Ready?" Sonya asked.

"Yes." With my shoulders back and chin up, I walked to the center of the room.

"Great. First, you will spar with Cas. Three rounds—best of three takes the match. Whoever is on the floor for more than three seconds loses the round."

Cas and I faced each other. "Good luck," he said.

"Same," I replied. Emily's little talk helped, but until this moment I didn't realize how dependent I had become on my stakes. Fighting a trained vamp without them made me feel completely naked. I looked over at Emily once more. Her smile lit up the room. This made my heart beat slower and my palms less sweaty.

Austin stood to the side, refereeing. "Begin."

Cas charged. Blows rained down. I blocked his first punch

and ducked on his second, but his third punch was a direct hit—my body slammed onto the floor, reverberating in pain. I gulped to catch my breath. My feet were fast, though. I dodged his incoming attacks. He reached for me. I jerked away, landing a kick to his face. Blood ran down his chin. With one last strike, Cas smashed onto the floor, blood spurting on impact. He attempted to stand but fell back again, a dazed look in his eyes.

"Nice one," he said, touching his lip.

"Tasi, one," Austin said.

I helped Cas up. "Hope you didn't expect me to go easy on you," I said. I took a few deep breaths and wiped my hands on my pants.

Cas smiled. "Game on, dhampyr girl."

The smell of sweat now lingered in the room. Cas didn't hesitate. The blow rippled through my chest, but my footing held. I returned the favor. He stumbled back, his eyes wide in surprise. I pounced. Cas was taller than me, but not stronger. My nails dug into his throat. His blood flowed coolly, tickling my fingers as I tossed him to the floor. There was a wheezing sound as my knee pressed into his neck. He writhed beneath me, unable to squirm his way out.

"Tasi takes the match," Austin said.

I helped Cas up.

"All the advantages of a vampire and none of the disadvantages—didn't think it would be true, but damn, girl, you are quick and strong," Cas said.

There were cheers from my small fan club. I looked for Emily, but caught Ethan's eyes instead. He had a small smile on his face. Clover stomped off, leaving the room and making me smile wider.

"Well done, Tasia," Sonya said, breaking my concentration.

"Am I done?"

"Not quite. You will go one round with Austin."

"What? Only one round?" Austin said, approaching.

"Yes, one round. Tasia has been testing for almost two hours. You have an unfair advantage, being rested."

"We can do this another day when she is more . . . rested, if that is what she needs. I get it—she is part human, after all." Austin was taunting me. Even if I thought he was being playful, I wouldn't back down. Any fear I'd had previously was long gone.

"Three rounds—I'm ready."

"Don't worry, Sonya, this will be quick," Austin said.

I rolled my eyes as I got into position. He looked at me with his dazzling smile.

Cas stepped in. "Begin."

Austin darted around me. He was faster than Cas, which probably meant he was stronger as well. We grappled. I was going to have to work hard to beat Austin. I narrowly escaped his grasp. He backhanded me. A fiery pain ripped through my body. I stumbled to the floor, blinding spots forming in my eyes from the blow, and in the next moment, he had my hands pinned above my head, with his body on top of me, rendering me immobile.

"I can get used to this position." He smiled, leaning in far enough so I could smell his sweet breath. Again, I rolled my eyes as he let go. I shoved him off as he claimed his one point.

I quickly stretched, hoping no one saw me faltering. I was right; he was strong. I had barely been able to move underneath his body.

This time I didn't delay. My fist zipped by his face. Austin dodged it, smiling, of course. He lurched forward, landing a blow that caused me to crumple to the floor. A violent storm surged through me as I gasped for air. I hopped up and hammered my fist into his face. Pain jolted up my arm and into my chest after each hit. He was stunned. I went to finish him with a kick, but in one swift movement, he flicked me to the ground. There were stars, along with a deafening screech in my ears. I got to my feet before Cas called the match. Austin continued to smile, but this time with a head shake.

"You don't give up."

"Nope, it's not in my nature," I said, dodging his blows.

A flurry of thrusts came at me. The air swirled around us as we danced. Blood dripped onto his shirt as I struck his face, which didn't seem to faze him. I evaded his retaliation and, in a frenzy, threw him to the ground, crushing his body. He wasn't able to move this time.

"Not bad, Tasi. Few people impress me, and that was good."

"I've got more. Get ready."

He walked up to me, leaving little space between us. "As much as you're turning me on right now, you're going down. By the way, you smell good—delightfully good."

I watched him as he readied his stance. I, on the other hand, tried to regain my composure. The comment of me smelling good bugged me. Did I smell like pretty flowers or lunch?

"Are you ready, Tasi?" Cas asked.

"Ready." I shook it off and prepared my aching body.

My ears heard the word "Begin," but my brain took too long to catch up. Before I had a chance to move, I was staring at the ceiling, trying to suck the air back into my lungs. At first, I thought my soul had separated from my body. But no, it was only Austin getting the drop on me. I bounced to my feet, but he was a step ahead. He hurled his fist at my face. Blood dripped down my throat as my teeth cut into the soft flesh of my cheek. Desperate to gain the upper hand, I rushed him, landing blow after bone-crushing blow. My fists morphed into dark hues of purple and blue, and my knuckles scraped and burned with each collision. He grabbed me and tossed me to the floor. I avoided his reach as I shot to my feet. Crimson liquid splattered across me when my foot met his jaw. The room rumbled as he landed. I straddled his stomach. His face matched the color of my fists, and blood continued to drip onto the floor.

He had a devious smile plastered on his face. "Tasi, I didn't know you liked to be on top. Maybe you could wiggle yourself a little lower."

My face grew hot, and I loosened my hold. He rolled me onto my stomach, pressing his body against me. He leaned into me, his cool breath brushing my ear.

"Sorry, beautiful, I'm not that easy. We should have dinner first."

Austin waited for the last count to stand up, then reached his hand out to me.

I grabbed it, pulling myself up. "Smart way to distract me."

"I wasn't sure it would work; you had me." He grinned, wiping the blood from his mouth with a towel Cas had given him. The dark purple colors covering his face and my hand began to heal.

Sonya reached us, and I noticed the crowd had dissipated.

"Tasia, you did extremely well today. I can now see why you and Emily have been able to fend for yourselves. You're rough around the edges, but your aunt did an excellent job training you. Your results will be in my office. I'll make you a copy so you can continue to train and master your skills."

She left the room. I was left with Austin, Cas, Lizzie, and Emily, who slipped her hand into mine at some point. I looked around for Ethan, but he was nowhere in sight.

"Dude, you almost got beat by a young dhampyr. Hang your head in shame, old man," Cas poked fun at Austin.

"Never. It's satisfaction enough to see Tasi fall for my charm." Austin winked at me. "Plus, you're one to talk. You didn't even make it to round three."

I playfully shoved Austin. "This isn't over, old man."

12

It had been over a week since my evaluation, and I couldn't get used to the schedule. Emily had adjusted to her schedule so quickly. She was settled in classes and training. Not me—a nighttime schedule wasn't in the cards for me yet. I stopped staring at the clock beside my bed and got up.

Sonya had pulled some strings to get us into the American Museum of Natural History after hours. I'd assumed that was her way of keeping some control over the situation. Yesterday, I'd learned this so-called safe house was listed as a boarding school for gifted kids. They were gifted, all right—gifted with an eternal curse.

After showering, I changed into a pair of dark blue jeans, a maroon tank, my black zip-up, and my high-tops. Lizzie had given me some extra clothes she had because we were the same size. I strapped on my stakes and headed out to the kitchen to find a drink and relax a little. When I opened the kitchen door, I walked in on Ethan looking through a newspaper.

His back was to me, so I spun around to head back out.

"If you want to be alone, I can leave." He turned his head just enough so I could see his profile. His eyelids hung low, and there were dark shadows under his eyes.

I held the door for another few seconds before letting it go and walking over to the shelves with all the mugs. I reached for the same blue one Lizzie had given me before and looked for the coffeepot. It was sitting on the table in front of Ethan. I bit my lip, and as if he knew what I was thinking, he reached out for my mug.

My heart raced as I handed it over to him before sitting. As he filled it, he never once looked up at me. He then slid it across the table. The warmth of the mug soothed my chilly hands.

"You know, I don't bite," he said, finally looking up at me.

"Maybe not, but you know how to be a jerk to me. Maybe I should say, you know how to be a jerk to me when everyone is around and sometimes nice when it's just us."

"Only sometimes? I thought I was pretty nice all the times we've been alone."

I let out a long sigh. I knew Ethan could see the frustration filling my features, and thankfully, he must have decided not to say anything else to avoid triggering an explosion. As I gathered my thoughts and tried to keep myself calm, I took a sip from my cup, then set my eyes on his. That's when I decided I didn't want to play nice. He gave me no reason to be even somewhat cordial, so I would push his buttons for once.

"So, are you going to tell me why you play Jekyll and Hyde around me, or do I need to guess?"

He looked at me as he shook his head. "Why do you care how I treat you? Aren't you Austin's girl now?" His words dripped with venom.

"Listen, I'm no one's 'girl.' It's not my fault he treats me better than some other people," I said, lifting the cup to my lips.

His face turned the color of my drink. *I think that did it.*

"And you're gullible enough to believe his act. It's Austin. He likes three things in this world: to manipulate people, to piss me off, and his specialty is girls he can use. If that's what you're looking for, then you got it, babe," he said, looking at the newspaper.

"Don't call me babe. Austin and me hanging out is none of your business, so stop acting like you're jealous." I stared at him. "Plus, don't you have a girlfriend? I think you should worry about her and not me. Then she can stop threatening me in the hall."

This news shocked him for a second. My guess was he didn't know about Clover's confrontation with me a few weeks back. The surprise didn't last long, though, and he jumped right back into it.

"Right, I'm jealous. More like you're lucky that tiny dhampyr brain of yours hasn't gotten you or your sister killed yet. You're nothing but a stupid little girl pretending to be all-knowing, and eventually, you're going to end up dead. I just hope I'm there to see it." He sat back in his chair, shook the paper out, and pulled it up over his face.

I stared at the back of the paper for several minutes, finishing my drink. My heart slowly shattered into my stomach, making me feel nauseated. I didn't deserve that, but I refused to cry, to be weak.

Before I could make my legs strong enough to hold me up, he lowered the paper.

"Don't," I said sternly.

"I'm sorry. I didn't mean it. I'm just frustrated with you, as always."

"Yes, and as always, you hurt me. Forget it. You're right—I'm a stupid little dhampyr girl."

"Wait, Tasi—"

"I said don't."

I stood up and headed into the main hall, ignoring anything he might have said next. The sun was setting, and it was almost time for the vamps to start their day. I lay on the couch, waiting for the others.

Staring at the ceiling, I thought about Ethan. It was the last thing I wanted to think about, but what he'd said bugged me. He could be so cruel sometimes, and it was always directed at me. What had I done to him, to make him hate me so much?

"Why the long face, Killer?" Austin stared at me with his glittery-green eyes, arms crossed on the back of the couch. He tilted his head slightly.

"Killer?"

"Yeah. Death Wish was the other pet name I thought up weeks ago, but after a long internal debate I decided on Killer. It has a nicer ring to it." He moved in closer, bringing his voice to a whisper. "Anyone ballsy enough to take on Sonya the way you have and almost kick my ass in a sparring match, well, that person is pretty badass, if I say so myself."

"Whatever."

"Seriously, Tasi, over these past few weeks, you have changed my mind. I truly thought you were going to be a stuck-up girl who thought she was all that when you first got here. I'm grateful to admit I was wrong."

I couldn't control the smile on my face. "Glad I could change *someone's* mind."

He swiftly moved around the couch and lifted my feet so he could sit down. I sat up, pulling my legs into my chest.

"You mean Ethan." He rolled his eyes, brushing his black hair out of them. "He's moody. Ignore him. Plus, if he can't see how fantastic you are, then he isn't worth it."

I rested my head on my knees, giving Austin a small sideways smile. "I'll try."

There was no way I could ignore Ethan. Even though he riled me often, there was something that kept pulling me to him. I wished there weren't, because I didn't want to feel anything for him. I wanted to forget I ever met him.

The rest of the gang was headed over to where Austin and I were sitting.

"Well, well, look who's getting all cozy in front of the fireplace." Lizzie smiled.

"It's not like that," I said, shaking my head.

"Yeah, she hasn't completely succumbed to my charm and brilliance." Austin stood up and straightened his clothes, then looked at me and winked. "Yet."

"Brilliance? A dog is smarter than you, Austin," Lizzie said with an arched eyebrow.

"Yes, and I would say the same about you, but everyone knows it already." He ruffled Lizzie's hair as he passed by her. "Be right back. Going to steal the keys to the Navi."

Lizzie grimaced as she violently fixed her hair. "Horrible comeback, and I hate when he does that." She turned her focus to me. "So, when will you guys have your first date?"

"Who's dating now?" Ethan asked, walking into the conversation.

"The two lovebirds, Tasi and Austin," Cas contributed, which made Emily giggle as they both walked up.

"Can't a girl be friends with a guy? Man, I'm happy I never had to go to an actual high school."

"Yes, Tasi, a girl can be friends with a guy, just not a guy like Austin," Lizzie said with a smile.

"Yeah, I'm going to have to agree with Lizzie on this one. Austin is a girl magnet, you'll see. Wherever we go, women swoon over him," Cas added.

"Enough, please," Ethan said. "I don't want to listen to this all day."

"Yes, why would we want to listen to this all day when we can listen to Ethan and his multiple personalities?" I didn't look at Ethan, but was secretly glad he'd voiced his opinion, not that I would give him the satisfaction of knowing that. I really didn't want to hear about Austin and me all day either.

Austin was walking back toward us, swinging the keys around his finger. Admittedly, he was beautiful, with his messy black hair and crystal-green eyes. His chiseled facial features made him look sophisticated. Then there was his personality. I could see why girls fell all over him. But there was no way I'd be that girl. Yes, I enjoyed talking to him, and staring at him was a pleasant pastime, but I wouldn't be his conquest.

"You might want to stop staring. After five seconds, it becomes noticeable," Lizzie snickered.

My eyes shot daggers at her, which made her laugh, but my face flushed as I realized the others had seen me watching Austin. When I looked at Ethan, he just stood there, lips pressed together.

Lizzie looped her arm through mine and led me toward the doors. "Come on, let's go have some fun."

"Austin, Starbucks, first stop—it's on Lizzie." I watched as her smile dropped to a frown, and I was the one laughing.

13

We reached the museum—that was now closed—as the sun set. It was perfect timing, since I was finishing up my vanilla soy latte, courtesy of Lizzie. I savored the taste now.

We headed inside and met with Annie, the curator who had worked out the details with Sonya. She was tall and thin, with blonde hair and amber eyes; definitely a vampire, and a beautiful one. She led us in and locked up behind us. Who knew being locked inside a building would make me feel so free?

"When you're all set to leave, please call this number. I will be in my office working," Annie said, looking at Austin. She handed him the card, giving him an inviting smile. A tinge of bitterness raced through me. Was she one of his past conquests? Even if she was, I didn't understand why jealously had crept up on me. *He's barely my friend.*

Austin must have noticed my inner struggle, as he winked at me, giving me one of his dazzling smirks. Feeling my cheeks flush, I turned back to Emily, took her hand, and headed toward the ocean room. We were well protected, locked inside the museum like this, so none of us felt the need to stick close to one another. I glanced back to Cas and Ethan. They were joking around. I thought I saw a genuine smile on Ethan's face. Lizzie and Austin were bickering over what tasted better, a tiger or a giraffe. Not a particular conversation I wanted to interrupt.

I focused back on Emily, since we had a little time alone as we walked.

"How're you doing with our new living arrangements? And I mean really doing—don't lie."

Emily paused. "At first, being in a new place with vampires scared me. I still sleep with my stakes. I know that sounds crazy, since everyone seems so nice," she said. Her cheeks grew pink.

I touched her on the shoulder. "No, Em, it's not crazy. It's brilliant." I lifted my pant leg in the front. "See, I still wear them too. You never know, right?"

"Right," she said, standing up straighter. She lifted her own pant leg, and the corners of her mouth tugged upward.

"How about everything else? Cas seems nice."

"Everything else is okay. Cas is amazing, and so is Lizzie. Ethan, I don't know yet—he seems moody." This made me laugh. "Austin, well, according to everyone else, he's a jerk, but he's nice to us, so I guess he's okay."

"Yeah, I agree with you on all of those."

We strolled along, fingers intertwined, the way we used to when it was just us. "There is one thing . . ." Something was on her mind. "Tasi, Sonya scares me. I'm not sure why, but she does. I mean, she says she has good intentions. Eva and our parents trusted her, but I don't know . . . something about how she's always hovering over us bugs me."

"Yeah, I'm still trying to figure her out. Just do as Sonya says, unless she asks you to do something ridiculous—then you need to find me first. I won't let anyone hurt you." I squeezed her hand a little more tightly.

"I know. It's like I always said—you're the best big sister anyone could ever have."

"I second that," Cas said, throwing his arms around us and breaking us apart. "What's up, Small Fry?"

This made Emily chuckle. "Nothing. Talking about sister stuff, you know, the usual. Em, did you brush your teeth today? Did you eat breakfast? Stuff like that."

Em was lying through her teeth. Impressed by her ability to keep our business secret, I gave her an approving grin.

"Wait—I have to use the bathroom," Emily said.

Cas waited with me while Ethan waited farther back. Lizzie and Austin were still arguing over animal delicacies—so gross.

"Thanks for being so kind to Emily. She's only had me and our aunt Eva her whole life, so it's nice that she's making friends." I stared at my feet for a moment before looking back at him. "How old are you, again?"

He laughed. "I'm sixteen."

"For how long?"

This made Cas laugh harder. "Don't worry, I'm treating your sister like she's my sister. I'm not looking for a girlfriend."

"I wasn't implying."

"Yes, you were, and it's fine. Did you know I had a sister before I was turned? She was Emily's age, so I get why you're so protective," he said. He might have been younger than me, but at this moment, I couldn't help feeling young around him, knowing he had lived through so much more than me.

"I'm sorry. Being with Emily must be hard for you, then. You know, hanging around someone who reminds you of your sister."

"I think she's helping me more than I'm helping her. The vampire who killed my little sister is the one who brought me over to the dark side. I couldn't protect her." His eyes glazed over, filled with hurt.

"Wow, I'm sorry. I don't know what I'd do without Emily. She's my family, and all I can think about is protecting her." I gave him a friendly hug. "Seriously, though, thank you again. I'm happy you two found each other."

"Me too. Em's special."

As we pulled apart, Emily came skipping out of the bathroom. "Now I'm ready to see animals and dinosaurs and whatever else we can find." She rubbed her hands, giving us a devious smile.

"All righty then, let's hop to it," Cas said, holding out his hand.

"You guys go; I'll catch up. I need a bathroom break too." They shrugged, then took off, laughing.

When I finished, I turned the faucet on in the sink right before nearly having a mild heart attack. Standing there, looking more magnificent than ever, was my biggest fan.

"Ladies' room? Classy, Ethan." I continued lathering up my hands, ignoring him as much as I could.

"You didn't really think I would leave you alone?" Ethan said from where he was leaning against the wall. His black shirt showed off every one of his muscles.

"No, I guess not, but I had hoped. Then again, the dumb dhampyr girl might forget to wash up—so tragic," I said, holding up my hands. I turned them around for him, showing them front and back. "See, I didn't forget—sparkling clean."

His fingers slid around my arm. The buzz flowed into me, but for once I didn't care. "Don't touch me." I jerked my arm away.

"Listen, I said I was sorry." There was an aggravated tone in his voice, which softened. He must have realized it wasn't helping his cause. He tried to touch my arm again, and I pulled back before he could reach me.

"Yup, and the next time you're mean to me, you'll feel the need to say sorry again. And I'm damn well not waiting for it. Because if you say something like that to me ever again, I will knock the fangs out of your mouth."

He didn't even look shocked as I laid into him. Instead, he stood there, the corner of his lips turning up. "Are you finished? You have to forgive me sometime."

I poked him in the chest. "I don't have to do anything, got it? Plus, give me one good reason why I should forgive you."

He didn't hesitate. He pulled me close to him, wrapping one arm around my waist. His dark eyes stared at me. "Because you have no choice." I wondered if that day at the train station he'd experienced what I had. I thought about asking him and then decided now wasn't the time. He ran his fingers along the side of my face, brushing my hair behind my ear. My heart raced. As angry as I was, I wanted him to kiss me. At least, until I remembered how stupid he thought I was.

"No." I pushed him so hard his back imprinted into the bathroom wall. What did he mean I had no choice? If I didn't want to forgive him, I wasn't going to.

"There you are," Austin said, jogging up to me as I exited. "I thought you might have escaped into the night."

"Nope, bathroom break." I let out a laugh, which was a little too forced. Then I remembered Ethan was listening, and I had an idea. "Why, were you going to rescue me if I ran away?"

"Hmmm. Chasing after a pretty young lady in the dark," he said, spinning me around as if we were in the middle of a dance. "Most definitely. You know, as long as I get a reward at the end." He leaned into me. "Like you."

"Hey, down boy."

He laughed.

"Ready to visit the ginormous whale? Your sister is ogling it." He put out his arm, waiting for me to grab hold.

"I bet she is." I pulled my hands out of my pocket, looping one arm through his. "Lead the way, monsieur."

"Ah, mademoiselle. *Vous parlez français?*" he said in perfect French as we walked.

I sighed. "Um, *monsieur* is the extent of my French."

"Something else I can teach you." His smile melted my heart just enough to take away a little of the regret I had for treating Ethan the way I did.

When we were halfway down the hall, I looked back to see Ethan walking far behind us. His eyes looked through me as if I didn't exist.

When we caught up to the others, Emily was so excited I forgot everything else that was going on.

The rest of our time in the museum was a blast. Cas and Em goofed off. Lizzie and Ethan stayed together. They were both equally annoyed with Austin, for different reasons, but that left me to keep Austin company.

"So, are you impressed?" Austin leaned in. "I mean with where we are, not with me."

His lips, so close to my ear, made my skin tremble. "Yeah, the museum is better than anything I could have imagined. And, well, you aren't such a shabby tour guide either."

He stopped. "Wait, did you pay me a compliment? Let me savor this moment."

"Shut up." I pushed him playfully. "You know what I mean."

"Yes, I do. You like me, admit it."

Before either of us said another word, Ethan strolled over. "Are you guys all set, or is there something else you want to see?"

"Buzzkill," said Austin.

"I think we're all set." I turned to Cas and Emily. "You guys all set?"

"Yes, all done," Emily yelled back.

"I guess that's it, then. Let's call Annie and head out," Ethan said.

"Your wish is my command." Austin bowed to Ethan and then turned to me. "Be right back. Sorry I'm not leaving you to more pleasant company."

I said nothing and just watched Lizzie, Emily, and Cas, who

were playing tag. They were having so much fun I couldn't help but laugh.

"Emily seems to have taken to Cas. I overheard him telling you about his sister. It's heartbreaking," Ethan said.

"Yeah," I said, not looking at him.

"You can't stay mad at me forever, I promise you," he whispered into my ear.

"I think I'll try to for now." I saw Austin coming back. "We all set to go?"

"Why yes, we are." He gave me one of his dazzling, crooked smiles. "What do you say, race you to the exit?"

"You're on," I said, getting ready to bolt. "On *go*. One. Two. Go."

I took off running, jumping over rails and down four steps at a time. The pounding on the floor behind me kept getting louder, but he wasn't as fast as me. The cheers from Lizzie, Cas, and Emily gave me the push I needed to win.

We reached the door almost at the same time, and we broke out in laughter.

14

Standing at the top of the steps, I turned one last time to get a look at the vast building, with its large columns and giant archway. We'd spent three hours exploring its insides, and it was remarkable. I wasn't sure how everyone else felt, but I didn't want to head back yet.

I bounced down the steps until I reached the others. "So, where to next?" I said, disregarding the fact that we were told to come straight back after the museum.

"I don't care. I'm up for anything," Lizzie said.

"Me too," Cas and Emily said, before bursting into laughter.

"I don't know. We should probably get back. Not sure I'm ready to push Sonya with your newfound freedom," Austin countered.

"That's something I'd expect out of Ethan, not you, Austin," I said.

Ethan shook his head. "Let me know what you guys decide." He then walked over to the bottom step and stood there as if he was scouting the perimeter.

"This is our first bit of normalcy in such a long time. Can't you cut us a break? Please, Austin?" I was giving him my infamous pout, which used to work wonders on Eva.

A sigh left his lips. He placed one finger under my chin. "Only if you promise never to make that sad little girl face again."

"Fine. I know just where to go."

We all jumped into the Navigator and headed toward Times Square. I whispered the location only to Austin, who was driving.

"I'm going to drop you guys off. You should be safe enough without me. Promise me, Tasi, you'll head back right after." Austin looked at me. His face was serious. "Call me if you need me. I'll be back in a flash."

"Wait, you aren't coming with us?" My voice sounded a little more upset than I'd expected.

"Don't worry. Remember, I'm just one call away. I have a little surprise to show you. I'll have it ready for when you get back. Plus, I can tell Sonya what's up—I'm sure Annie has already called to tell her we left the museum, and it may be easier to calm Sonya down in person. You know she isn't going to be happy about your additional excursion."

I rolled my eyes, then asked, "What's the surprise for?"

"Let's just say you bring out a side of me I didn't quite know existed." His eyes wouldn't meet mine as he focused on the road. There was a sense of vulnerability coming from him that I didn't think he showed often.

Lizzie made gagging noises from the back seat. When I shot her an evil look, she stopped and started laughing instead.

We reached Times Square, and everyone filed out. Austin grabbed my hand, brought it to his mouth, and gave me a small, delicate kiss. "Stay safe, Killer."

I could feel the heat in my face rise.

When I got out of the car, Emily was jumping up and down. Somehow, her excitement overshadowed Ethan's grave face.

He'd acted chummy with the others all night, but hadn't even glanced at me for hours. I saw a tinge of something behind those eyes; hurt, jealousy, or anger, maybe? Whatever his issue, I pushed it away.

"Please, please tell me we're going to the toy store!" Emily screeched.

"Easy enough—we're going to the toy store!" I repeated.

"Yay!" she said, bouncing around like a kangaroo.

"Awesome idea, Tasi, and don't worry, I'll keep an eye out for her," Cas said, grabbing Emily's hand and taking off into the store.

"Me too." Lizzie smiled and ran to catch up.

This left me with Ethan. Why couldn't he have driven the Navigator back? Then Austin would have had no choice but to have stayed here. At least then, I would know what the mood would be like. With Ethan, I never knew what I would get.

"I know you don't want me here. I get it. Let's just make the best of this for your sister." He placed his hand on the small of my back. His touch sent shivers throughout my body. I'm pretty sure he noticed it, too, because he quickly took his hand away.

"Right, let's make the best of it," I agreed.

I thought the whale at the museum had made Emily's day, but no, it was the Ferris wheel in the middle of the toy store that did it. The inside of the store was massive, and it made me realize that the outside did no justice to the size of the place. There were five enormous floors, and it looked like a rainbow had thrown up on all of them. The place was packed for being so late at night. Wall to wall people, and even young children, strolled through the store. I guess this was to be expected in the City That Never Sleeps.

"Wow, can we go on the Ferris wheel?" Emily asked.

"Sure, right before you guys are ready to leave," I said.

The three took off toward the video games, leaving Ethan and me trailing behind. We stayed silent most of the time, watching as they played with all the toys. We mixed in well with the other tourists.

As we walked, someone shoved hard into my shoulder, making me trip into Ethan.

"Sorry," I said.

"No big deal. I guess this is what it's like to be a parent of three teenagers." He shook his head. I could tell he was trying to break the thick layer of ice that had formed between us.

I gave in. The fighting was exhausting. "There's a thought."

"Yeah, a scary thought." I saw him relax his composure, so I decided to say something, hoping we could reconcile both our destructive behaviors.

"Look, I'm sorry for pushing you in the bathroom at the museum. I'm not saying you didn't deserve it, but I shouldn't have done that."

There was a look of astonishment on his face as he studied me. "No, I'm sorry for what I said today. This one is all my fault."

"Yeah, you were pretty mean . . ." I trailed off. "But let's forget it. We've both had moments of immaturity."

He nodded.

After a while, we stopped following the trio and stood near the escalators, leaning against the rail overlooking the different floors of the store. Emily found Ethan and me as soon as they finished.

"Ferris wheel time," she sang, clasping her hands.

"Yeah, go ahead. Ethan and I will wait up here for you guys. Unless you want to join them?" I asked Ethan. "I don't mind waiting alone."

"No, thanks. You guys have fun and meet us back here when you're done," Ethan said.

"Yes, Dad." Lizzie laughed. "Oh, and Mom, thanks for the trip to the toy store. It was super fun."

The three laughed as they headed toward the escalator.

"Is this the part where we ground them or take away their toys?" I said.

"Both options sound like the right thing to do."

We watched as they rode the Ferris wheel, smiling and laughing as kids should. Then, out of the corner of my eye, I watched as Ethan's composure changed from relaxed to on guard. He slipped behind me with such quickness I barely saw him move. He put his lips to my ear, which caused a tickle throughout my body.

"Tasi, smile like I told you something funny, remain relaxed, and blend in."

I did as he asked without question.

"Two men are standing across from us, leaning on the rail. Slowly glance in their direction, but don't catch their attention," he said. "Keep smiling. They have the same tattoos as the guys in the alley, the ones who attacked you and Emily."

With him still behind me, he slid his hand around my stomach, pulling me toward him. I wasn't sure if the immediate panic that filled me stemmed from Emily not being by my side or the fact that every time he touched any part of my body, I wished I'd melt into him. The longer I stood there wrapped in his embrace, the more my body became attuned to his. He was making it hard to concentrate on his words, but then I saw Emily again. She was laughing and joking, not knowing what was happening. My heart pounded hard against my chest; she was too far away.

"Did you hear me? I'm going to slide in front of you and tell you what we'll do next. If you're with me, nod."

I nodded. Ethan kept his hand wrapped around me as he glided around my waist until he was in front of me. He pushed a lock of my hair away from my eyes so he could gaze into them. Our eyes broke from each other's, and Ethan was back to scouting out the area behind me, looking for more threats.

"Okay, are Em, Lizzie, and Cas still on the Ferris wheel?" he asked.

"Yes. Sitting at the top."

"Good—hopefully, we'll have a few minutes. Stay this way and let me know if they leave the ride. There have to be more of them around here. Lizzie can take out two of them without an issue. Unless . . ." He looked around more urgently. "Unless they called in backup and are waiting outside."

"Did you also notice they're only paying attention to the Ferris wheel? I don't think they know we're here."

"That's good. We'll have the upper hand, then," he said. My body shivered as he pressed into me. I wished that would stop happening. "I'm sorry if I'm making you uncomfortable. Tell me when they reach the bottom."

"I'm fine. They'll be let off next." I looked back over to where the men were standing. "The two men were joined by a third. They're still standing there trying not to draw attention to themselves."

"They want to have the element of surprise on their side. Little do they know what's about to happen." His lips curled into a small smile. "Now, this is important—the second Em, Cas, and Lizzie get off the ride and look up at us, you need to get their attention so those guys focus their attention on us."

Ethan was still looking deep into my eyes. There was a strange longing there, and as much as I wanted to drown myself in them, I knew I needed to focus on the current task. So I watched as the ride stopped and the door to the car swung open. Out of the corner of my eyes, I could see the men watching my sister and our friends. Emily's eyes were the first to meet mine. So I waved furiously, but before I could say anything, Ethan pulled me in and kissed me.

I didn't push him away. Instead, I leaned into him, kissing him back. The jolt of energy that usually raced through my skin whenever he was around now radiated inside my head. His lips were so soft and captivating. I couldn't imagine breaking apart from him. Instead, I brushed my tongue along his fangs as he pulled me deeper into him. The venom dripped onto my tongue, causing a bit of sweet numbness. He wrapped his arms around me tightly. Slowly, I was losing myself in this kiss—my first kiss.

Finally, I faintly heard Emily, Cas, and Lizzie cheering and clapping. I opened my eyes to see Ethan staring at me. Snapping back into reality, I looked over at the three men, who had puzzled looks on their faces. One of them grabbed his cell phone and screamed into it. As I'd thought, they hadn't known we were here. Whatever this was, it was working.

Ethan leaned over the railing. "Run!"

Lizzie immediately grabbed Emily's hand, and Cas flanked Emily's other side as they ran up the escalators toward us. The three men started running, but Ethan grabbed my hand and dragged me toward the others. When we met up, we saw four more of them waiting at the front of the store, which brought the total to seven. I grabbed Emily's hand as soon as they reached us.

"We can take the ones outside pretty quickly," I said. "We don't have much of a choice, unless we find another way out."

"No time to search for another way out," said Ethan. "We should gain some distance from the three behind us by running through this crowd."

We pushed through the mob of people. Our smaller frames and wicked reflexes made it easier to make it through without taking out any humans. I turned to see the other three men struggling to make it through the mass of tourists.

Ethan ran out ahead of us and attacked one of them, causing two men's heads to collide. I watched as they fell, knocked unconscious.

"Go, I'll catch up," he said, punching the next guy straight in the nose.

I didn't hesitate. I knew Lizzie wouldn't leave Ethan if she thought he was in trouble, so I did as he asked.

The four of us took off across the street, gracefully weaving through the cars. As we hit the other side, I turned back to see Ethan running and four guys on the ground. I smiled.

We ran as fast as we could, dodging pedestrians as they got in our way. Once we thought it was clear, we slowed down.

Ethan finally caught up. "Is everyone okay?"

"Yeah, I think so," I replied.

"Let's keep moving so we can get back before they figure out where we are," Ethan said.

We started back toward the school. Emily stayed close to me. I knew it was where she felt safest. Plus, I could sense she was still a little distressed.

My mind immediately went back to that kiss. If you ask me, there were plenty of other ways we could have gotten Emily, Cas, and Lizzie's attention. He could have yelled over the railing and told them to run. There would have still been an element of surprise. But maybe there was more to the kiss than a mere distraction? I played the situation repeatedly in my head and couldn't quite make sense of Ethan's actions. I almost thought it was riskier that he did what he did. If Ethan felt what I had, I don't think he would have been able to break away. But he could, so maybe it was all in my head, and Ethan honestly thought that was the best tactic.

"I have to know. Was that kiss real?" Lizzie asked.

"No. Sorry to burst your bubble, Lizzie. I thought it was the best way to get you guys to give us a loud enough reaction to pull the attention away from you. It worked. They weren't sure what to think when they realized there were more of us," Ethan said.

He was behind me now. Whatever his reasoning, I could imagine what his face looked like—disgust, hate, annoyance.

"Come on, Ethan, you want me to believe that? There was something between you two; I could feel it from where I stood," she said, continuing to probe. "And don't tell me I'm wrong."

"I don't know what to tell you, Lizzie. Just don't fill your head with imaginary ideas. We barely like each other, if you hadn't noticed." His voice was commanding. "Can we not bring this up again? The last thing I need is her new boyfriend getting on my ass about this."

"He's not my new boyfriend." I stared straight ahead, ignoring his snicker. "And, agreed—it was nothing, just a distraction to get your attention and make sure those goons knew we were there too. It's called the element of surprise, Lizzie."

"Fine, whatever you want to believe. I know what I saw."

I stopped walking, making Emily stop.

"Seriously, enough, guys—it ends here. Pretend it never happened." I looked at each of them, waiting. When I reached Ethan, the warm, fuzzy feeling I typically felt near him was frost-ridden once again. "Don't worry. It wasn't memorable. Already forgotten," I said. Ignoring them all, I headed toward the school without another word.

As we entered, Sonya stood in the foyer with Austin by her side. Her face said it all.

15

"You're late." Sonya's icy tone cut through the air. "Were there any altercations, Ethan?"

"Of course not—we're here, aren't we?" My voice was harsher than I intended it to be.

Sonya's eyes met mine. Her features darkened as she took me in. A flashback to a conversation two vampires were having in the kitchen the other night flitted through my head. Rumor had it Sonya once ripped the head of another vampire clean off in front of the entire coven for talking out of turn. *Let's see if we can add dhampyr to her list of the headless.*

Her face softened. "When I address you, you may speak. Until then, learn when and where to open your mouth, young one."

Her eyes hardened, and whatever she saw in me a minute ago was now gone. No matter; I knew she wouldn't back down in front of everyone, but neither would I, and in that moment she faltered, she'd confirmed that my head was safe. Which meant my mouth could have a field day, and the repercussions wouldn't kill me.

"I'm sorry," I said. "I must have missed your memo."

She glared at me for several more seconds, as if she were waiting for me to realize I was out of line, or maybe even wondering if I would apologize. Funny.

I was aware it wasn't Sonya's fault Ethan had again made me feel insignificant. I just wanted to be left alone to wallow in my misery, and Sonya's inquisition wasn't allowing me that. So, doing what I do best, I took it out on the person annoying me most in that moment.

Impatience grew in her face as her eyes slowly drifted from me to Ethan.

"As I asked before, were there any altercations?"

Here we go, the end of our freedom. Sonya had warned that we'd be on lockdown if anything happened, and somehow I knew she meant it.

Ethan pulled his hands out of his pockets and straightened up. "No. We spent some time in Times Square, then headed back here, making sure no one followed us." I stared at him as if he were a stranger.

Keeping her eyes on Ethan, she turned to the others.

"Lizzie, Cas, is this how you recall it?"

"Yup, nothing to tell. Well, other than riding the Ferris wheel. I don't know how I have lived here so long without riding that thing," Lizzie said.

She lied flawlessly. I was pleasantly surprised that she would lie for us—that they all would.

"Yeah, and don't forget the video game part of the store. I totally killed it in there," Cas said.

I heard Emily giggle from behind me.

Why hadn't Ethan told Sonya what happened? Lizzie and Cas, I could understand. They were more our friends than Ethan. Plus, from what I had seen so far, Ethan was genuinely loyal to Sonya. I didn't doubt that if we were with Austin, he would have ratted on us as soon as we walked in. Then it dawned on me: Ethan probably thought he would have to relive what had happened and how we got away. That would mean admitting to a kiss he'd made very clear he had no interest in remembering.

"Are we done here? My feet hurt, and Emily should get something to eat," I said as politely as I could. "Please."

"Yes, finish up your day and get some rest. Emily, you missed most of your classes today, which is fine, but I would like it if you and Cas could get in some training before bed."

"Yes, ma'am," Emily said.

Sonya's smile brightened. "It's nice to see one of the Vasile sisters has manners. Maybe you could teach Tasia one day."

Emily hung her head, as if she had gotten me into trouble.

"No, I don't need manners. I prefer to be a bitch."

"And you do it so well." Sonya turned and headed off to her office. "Ethan, stop by my office before you turn in."

"Will do." He then walked away from us like the good little soldier he was.

When Sonya was out of sight, Austin looked at me. "Killer, you're one brave girl, I tell you." He smiled and threw his arm around my shoulder. "Can't say it enough—I'm so glad I misjudged you."

Emily rushed over, wrapping her arms around me. "I'm so sorry I got you in trouble."

"Please, Em, don't change who you are for anyone. It's not your fault all the sweetness missed me and poured into you. Get something to eat, then finish up your training. I'll catch up with you before bedtime."

Cas and Emily headed for the kitchen. Lizzie walked after them, but stopped in front of me.

"Austin's right; you're a badass. No one speaks to Sonya like that and keeps their head. I'm so happy I saw that firsthand. If you weren't a Vasile girl, I'd tell you to sleep with one eye open." She punched me playfully in the shoulder, yelling to Cas and Emily to wait up. This left me with Austin.

"Told you, Killer."

"Whatever," I said, rolling my eyes.

"So, are you ready for your surprise? It might calm you down a bit."

Sonya had annoyed me to no end, but I was still recovering from that kiss. I couldn't get it out of my head, and all I wanted to do was go to bed and pull the covers over my head until tomorrow. Yet, when I looked at Austin's face, there was excitement dancing in his sultry green eyes. It took me a minute to pull myself together before I agreed.

He took me by the hand and led me toward the second floor, making sure no one was watching as we disappeared into the media room. Once there, he opened the secret bookcase that led to the small rooftop area.

"So, I know it's off-limits up here, but I snuck up and cleaned it up for you. I figured maybe it could be your little sanctuary when you need to get away from the craziness."

He pushed open the door leading outside, and the enchanting glow enveloped me. The outside space was adorned with tiny white lights. There was an old trellis tangled with vines and pale pink roses sloped against one of the exterior brick walls, and an old wooden bench painted dark red along the farthest wall. It was simple but beautiful.

"So, what do you think?" His hand reached out for mine, intertwining our fingers. Normally, I would have stopped him after the day I had, but all the heartache washed away for the moment.

"It's amazing, Austin." I took a few steps forward, looking around the magical rooftop. "Did you do this all for me?"

"Yes, though I'm hoping maybe I'll get invited up here occasionally," he said.

I whirled around; Austin was so close. I looked up, gazing into his sumptuous eyes. "Of course, whenever you want—it'll be our space."

He pressed his hands against my back and pulled me in closer. His mouth was so close, if I inhaled, my lips would graze his. "I know we're only friends, Tasi, but if you one day want something more..."

Before he could even finish that sentence, I kissed him. His lips were soft and tasted like ripe, sweet plums. It wasn't a long, passionate kiss like the one with Ethan earlier, but it was nice. Of course, nice wasn't what I wanted our first kiss to be. It should be butterflies in my stomach, toe-curling, and electrifying. More importantly, I shouldn't be thinking of Ethan when I was kissing Austin.

I pulled back before it could get any more awkward and touched my lips with my fingers. "I'm not sure what I want right now. Emily has to be my number-one priority. Plus, who knows how long I will be here?"

In reality, as wonderful as Austin was in this moment, I knew who I wanted to be sharing moments like this with. He simply didn't want me.

"Understandable. I'll be here if you ever need someone to talk to, okay?" He pulled me back into his arms, giving me a hug and kissing my forehead. "And if you ever decide you want more, well, you know where I am." He gave me one of his sexy smiles, which made me wonder how many girls he'd offered himself to in this manner. I remembered how Annie, the curator, had looked at him.

"Thanks, Austin. I mean it, though. This is our place."

"Okay. We should probably get back before people start looking for us." He pulled away, touching my cheek with the back of his hand. "Beautiful and smart—you're a rare find, Killer."

When we left the media room, the great hall was filled with vampires. Ethan was the one my eyes found immediately. The more time we spent together—good, bad, indifferent—the more I could feel a tether forming. Because of it, we could always find each other in a crowded room. The feeling of hurt quickly resumed as I thought about the disgust in Ethan's voice when Lizzie had asked if the kiss was real. Ethan disliked me, and it drove me mad.

"I'm going to go grab a drink from the kitchen. Are you hungry?" Austin asked.

Taking my eyes off Ethan, I turned back to Austin. "Um, no, I think I may check on Emily, then go to bed. I have one question, though. Do you know who takes care of all the books around here? I was looking for some nighttime reading."

The corner of his lip turned up. "You read too? I don't think I can take all these surprises you keep throwing out."

"Ha ha, funny."

He gave me a devious smile, and before I could object, he kissed me lightly on the cheek, whispering into my ear, "You want to see the girl who sits behind the desk in the back corner behind the stairs. See you tomorrow, then, Killer."

"Are you ever going to get tired of calling me that?"

"Hmm, maybe one day, but for now, it's Killer." He gave me a gallant bow and headed off to the kitchen.

I shook my head as he descended the stairs. My eyes landed back on Ethan, who was also watching me from the corner of the hall. His face was filled with disappointment. Big surprise. I refused to let him get to me, so I walked over to the training room, where I found Lizzie and Emily sparring.

Cas was sitting on the side of the mat, watching the two and critiquing their techniques.

"Leg higher, Emily. When you make contact, try to hit her higher," Cas said. Emily listened, hitting Lizzie hard enough in the side to make her wince. "Great job, Em."

My smile must have radiated around me. Emily was not only adjusting well, but she had also made some excellent friends. Content that she was in good hands, I headed down the stairs to look for the mystery book lady. She sat there silently behind the dimly lit desk, reading. Her long blonde hair was pulled back in a tight ponytail, and her sharp features made her look like a high-fashion model. I went over to introduce myself.

"I know who you are. I'm Jelena." Her smile was sweet and her accent thick—Russian, or maybe Polish, if I had to guess. "I've been waiting patiently to meet you, Miss Vasile. Now, what can I help you with?"

"I was wondering if you had any books on dhampyrs."

"How much do you know about your kind?"

"Well, I don't know much. I do know we have the same makeup as vampires, without all the nasty side effects like not being able to withstand exposure to daylight and holy water." We walked along the bookshelves as we chatted. I also knew my blood was a hot commodity that might be able to wipe out all bloodsuckers, but I thought keeping that to myself would be best.

She reached for a book off the top shelf. It looked old, and the binding was worn. "There are a few things in here about your kind. I'm not sure whether it's information you already know, but it may be good for you to read up on."

"Wow, thanks. Anything I can learn will be helpful. Sometimes I wonder what is going to happen to me in fifty years," I said as I skimmed my fingers over the dusty binding. It was so old, the name was no longer legible. "My aunt told me what she knew about what would happen before and after my transformation. She also told me that the information had been passed down through word of mouth, because there wasn't a lot documented that we had access to."

"It's a good question. I believe there is another book. I will look for it as well. Maybe it will help clear up some of the unknown." She perked up for a moment. "I have an idea—both of you Vasile girls need to learn more about yourselves, and I think I can help."

"How do you mean?"

"Why don't we have a class? It will be an hour long, a few days a week, mostly question and answer. If we come across questions I don't have answers to, I'll research them for you, and we can go over them in the next class."

"That's not a horrible idea."

"Excellent. I'll let you know what time. First, I have to clear it through Sonya, but I don't see why it would be a problem."

16

I didn't know when my body would give in to this new not-so-human schedule, but I woke up before I should. There were no windows in our room to let in the sounds of the city, so the culprit of my restless sleep was the mess of thoughts swirling in my head.

While reading the book on dhampyrs that Jelena gave me before bed, I'd learned about how no one accepted most vampire-human relationships. The only way a vampire could hold a relationship with a human was if the vampire was lord to the human. Otherwise, it was looked down on. I knew my parents were different. From what I remembered, my father treated my mother as an equal.

Children were another issue. Only a vampire male could impregnate a human female. The mortality rate of a dhampyr in the first year after birth intrigued me most. It was ninety-seven percent. I wasn't sure how many vampires contributed to this census, but it made me feel different. Ninety-seven percent of dhampyrs like Emily and me died, and our parents had managed to have two dhampyr children.

The book explained the birthing process and how most

dhampyrs killed their mothers during pregnancy. This was because the baby absorbed all the mother's nutrients while inside the womb, leaving her dead. If the mother survived, the baby was typically stillborn. My mother had survived and cared for us, even if for only a short amount of time. I felt a new appreciation for the time we'd spent together and the love she showed me.

Reaching for the bedside lamp, I clicked it on, hoping Emily wouldn't wake. I sat up, rubbing my eyes and adjusting my pillow. I took the book off the night table and started reading again.

During the thirteenth year, dhampyr bodies transform. They will grow inches taller, become faster, and their strength will become equal to an adult vampire's within days. They also take on more vampire traits, lessening the need for human food as their thirst grows. The process can take from a few days to an entire week, finishing the change with human blood. If the dhampyr child does not receive the blood, their body will immediately grow weak until they die. This change is not pleasant and will cause much pain. If the dhampyr's body is not strong enough, they will die, even if all precautions are taken. This change is known as the body transition.

I looked up, taking in a deep breath. Even though this wasn't all news to me, parts were. *If the dhampyr's body is not strong enough, they will die, even if all precautions are taken*, rang in my head. The thought of there being a chance that I could do everything possible to prepare Emily, but she could still die sent a pang through my chest.

Not wanting to give up yet, I returned to the book.

During the sixteenth to eighteenth year—

My head shot up in disbelief. There were more changes, ones I knew nothing about? I focused back on the book.

During the sixteenth to eighteenth year, the mind transforms and compulsion becomes attainable to the dhampyr. To compel is to influence another's mind to act in one's favor. While a vampire cannot use compulsion on another vampire or dhampyr, only humans, the dhampyr who learns compulsion can use it on both vampires and humans.

Furthermore, a vampire is woken with the ability to compel. Dhampyrs are not. As dhampyr bodies mature, this ability can be acquired only by the strongest, and it must be learned. There is record of only two dhampyrs who have gained this ability.

Compulsion in a dhampyr needs to be monitored closely. It differs from a vampire's compulsion, as the dhampyr's mind is still part human, and there are no records indicating how using compulsion may affect the dhampyr's future mental state. This change is known as the mind transition.

My mind was spinning with all this information. Before I could stop and think about compulsion, the next paragraph caught my attention.

The final change happens at twenty, when the soul transforms and the body no longer ages. Thirst will also be more significant. Daily intake of blood will be a must, and human food will no longer be desired. It is said that a dhampyr's soul tethers to their body, allowing the dhampyr's physical form to stop aging and become immortal. What remains unknown is what is required to successfully endure the change. There are no documented living dhampyrs at the time of this writing who have survived the final change. This change is known as the soul transition.

As tempted as I was to throw the book across the room, I placed it back on the nightstand. Sleeping was not an option now. I crawled out of bed and tiptoed out of the room.

When I reached the main hall, it was empty. That's when I made my decision. Stupid or not, I was going for a walk. I needed to get out and see the world as a human again—not as a dhampyr, and not on a vampire schedule. Perhaps this would relax me before I had to come back and pretend I wasn't rattled by what I had read. Who wants to hear they are likely going to die from a book? Was I being overdramatic? No. Until I found information that countered what was written in the book, in my mind, I was going to die two years from now. There had to be a different outcome. I just needed to find it.

I started my way across the room, listening to my feet echo through the hall with every step. All I thought about was what would happen if I got caught. I'd probably get reprimanded by Sonya, or worse, Ethan, telling me how stupid I was again. I shook the thought out of my head. I didn't care right now. I needed to breathe.

Reaching the front entrance, I opened the door and slipped out.

The sun warmed my skin as soon as I stepped into the city. Even though Halloween was around the corner, there wasn't a chill in the air, just a warm breeze. It was definitely warmer than it should be at this time of year. I hadn't seen the sun so bright or the sky so cloudless in weeks. I stretched my arms, involuntarily letting out a yawn as I headed out the old wrought-iron gate that marked my freedom.

It was New York City, and I wanted a coffee. There was undoubtedly a coffee shop within a few blocks any direction I went.

I headed down the street, taking in the sights and sounds around me. Across the street was a park. Kids played on the swings while adults sat on park benches, reading a book or chatting with each other. Skaters dodged pedestrians as they sped through the crowds.

My smile turned to a frown as I thought about how I'd never get to be that carefree. Instead, I had to worry about preparing for Emily's change. I couldn't lose her. Trying to imagine being stuck in this damned life and living years with her death on my shoulders, I knew it would eventually kill me. Actually, the third soul change would probably kill me, but I needed to put that aside right now and concentrate on Emily. I tried to remember when it had happened to me. As dhampyrs, we didn't get sick.

During the body change, I had just lain in bed, aching from head to toe. Remembering the pain of the bone breaks made my throat tighten.

I jumped when I noticed someone falling into step with me.

"Oh my God, you scared me. Wait—what are you doing? How can you be out here?"

"I can't. I need to get back inside."

Austin had every inch of his body covered, almost as if he were wearing full-blown body armor. Vampires couldn't come outside in this weather—the direct sun would burn him to ash.

"Listen, someone alerted me when you left the building. You know it's dangerous for you to be out alone, right?" Austin's reprimanding voice rippled through me. "What are you doing out here?"

I stopped under the shade of a tree. Austin pulled his hood off, and his skin glistened as sweat ran off him. I couldn't believe he would risk his life to find me.

"Yeah, I know. I went in search of a coffee shop and got distracted. So how much trouble am I in?" I asked.

"If we go back now, none. No one knows you're gone, other than Len."

"The security guy?"

"Yes, he woke me up when he saw you leave. He didn't want you to get in trouble. You're lucky James didn't see. He is strictly by the books. If Sonya doesn't know, then she won't ask questions, and I won't have to tell her."

"All right, I guess I can do without coffee. Plus, there are a few things I want to jot down to talk to Jelena about."

I could see him faltering because of the sun. He yanked his hood back up over his face, and we started walking back. I thought about coffee. If that book was accurate and I didn't die, which at this point seemed the unlikely path, then I would be on a strictly all-blood diet in a couple years. Even though I was used to drinking blood as if it were a regular part of my life, I wasn't sure I wanted to give up food, especially French fries.

"I'm guessing she found you a book to read?"

"More or less."

"And said book has information you were hoping for?"

"Maybe."

"Aren't you a bundle of mystery today?"

I forced a laugh. "I'm just tired."

We stepped back into the building after Austin punched in the security code. That's when I knew, if Austin hadn't come for me, I would have been caught red-handed. I didn't have the code. Before making our way into the main hall, I hugged him. He pulled me in, brushing his lips to my forehead.

"Thanks for not yelling at me for leaving. I was expecting a huge lecture. You risked your life for me out in the sun. That was selfless of you."

"First, the clothes gave me enough protection. It was uncomfortable, but they worked. Second, I need to keep you safe. If anything were to happen to you, I don't know what I would do." A smile crept over his face. "So don't worry, it'll be our little secret. But next time you decide to be adventurous, wake me up. We can be adventurous together."

I couldn't help the smile forming on my face.

As we walked into the main hall, I saw that no one was awake yet, so I decided to try for a couple more hours of sleep. I kissed Austin softly on the lips, as if it were the most natural thing in the world, then headed back to my room.

17

I woke up later than I had hoped. As I was getting ready, I noticed something off in my room. Where was the book Jelena had given me? I riffled through my desk and found nothing. Maybe I'd get lucky and Emily had it. I finished getting ready so I could find my sister and ask her about it.

By the time I reached the main hall, excitement was swirling through the air. Two vamp girls passed me, talking about what they were going to wear and do with their hair. I headed over to where Emily and Lizzie sat to find out the news.

"What's going on?" A yawn squeaked out.

"And here she is, folks, Sleeping Beauty." Lizzie snickered. "I have never in all my existence seen someone sleep like you."

"What? When did you see me asleep?"

"Sorry, Tasi, I was so excited," said Emily. "I asked Lizzie to help me wake you up because I couldn't do it, but it didn't help, so we left you passed out."

"I suggested dousing you with water or getting Cas to come in and jump on your bed, but Em stopped me. I thought that would have been a lot of fun."

"You mean fun for you," I grumbled. Lizzie's smile widened. "So, who's going to tell me what's going on?"

"Oh yeah," Emily bounced on the balls of her feet. "Sonya announced that we would have a party to celebrate the Day of the Dead."

"Like, as in All Souls' Day?" I asked.

"Yeah, and it will be a full-blown costume event," Emily concluded. "Isn't that exciting? I always wanted to go to a school dance."

"So awesome. Sheltered freaks attend a costume party. How remarkable. You and your sister should go as vampires." The voice was sharp. "You know, because you aren't, but you try to act like you are anyway."

My head turned to see Clover standing behind me with her hands on her hips.

"Just ignore her, please," Emily pleaded.

I shot her a look, which made her sigh. Lizzie, on the other hand, wiggled into her seat with a smirk. I stood up to face Clover. "And you're planning on going as a dog, I suppose? You know, a female one. You're already an ugly bitch, so you won't need an actual costume."

Clover inched closer to me, but I shoved her back. She stumbled. Once she regained her footing, she readied herself to lunge forward. Ethan grabbed her by the arm, pulling her away from me right as Austin showed up and put his arm around my waist.

"Let her go, Ethan. You know damn well my girl will beat yours." He held me in such a way that I saw fire burn in Ethan's eyes, and Austin didn't stop there. "Maybe she'll stake her, and you'll need to find a new girl—one not so clingy this time."

Clover broke free of Ethan. A crackling noise echoed through the room, followed by a crunching sound and a yelp. She had swung so hard at Austin that when her fist met his face, the bones in her hand shattered. Ethan wrestled her back again.

"This is your fault!" Clover yelled at Ethan, pulling away and stomping off. "Stay here with your stupid friends."

Ethan glanced back between Austin and me, then shook his head. "You two really are made for each other." He followed Clover.

My gut twisted in knots. I plopped into my seat. "Why can't she just leave me be?"

"The same reason you can't let what she says roll off you and ignore it," Emily said, giving me the same exasperated look Ethan had. "You really shouldn't be so hard on her."

Great, now my sister was taking Clover's side. "Not cool, Em. You are supposed to be on my side."

She opened her mouth, but was interrupted.

"I say she deserved it," Austin said, pulling out the seat next to me. He was rubbing his jaw. "I have to say, she has quite the punch, for such a neophyte." My eyebrows crinkled. Emily had a similar look on her face. Austin's smile grew. "Neophyte vampire; she's a fledgling, new to the vampire game by only about ten years. She should know hitting a vampire my age is only going to result in bad things for her."

"Is she really hurt?" I asked.

"Nah—vampire, remember? She'll heal up pretty quickly," Lizzie said, leaning in closer. "Her ego, on the other hand, well, I think that will take longer to heal."

"Good, maybe she will back off me." I was getting pretty tired of the Clover-and-Tasi drama.

"Or plot her revenge," Lizzie and Austin said simultaneously.

Cas came over to the table but didn't sit down. He looked all business. "Ready, Em? We have to get in an hour of training before your new class begins."

"New class?" Emily asked.

"Is it with Jelena?" I asked.

"Yes, it is. How did you know?"

"I spoke to her already. I'm taking that class as well."

"Cool," Emily said. "Meet me after training practice. We can go together."

"Okay, Em, sounds like a plan. One more thing. Did you see a book on my nightstand before you left the room? It was really old."

"No, I didn't." She turned to Lizzie. "Did you see it?"

"You think I would notice if a book was sitting there or not? No, I was having too much fun trying to wake up Sleeping Beauty."

I rolled my eyes. "Never mind—I will take another look. I probably moved it and didn't notice." Emily left, and I diverted the conversation before further questions arose. "Do you guys have parties often?"

"No, that's what makes this one so exciting. They were banned for years," Lizzie said.

"Really?"

"There is a good reason behind it," Austin said. "One year, a vampire disappeared, and no one knows if it was intentional or not, but they found his clothes in the alley days later. Most of us figured he passed out and the sunlight caught him. Unfortunately, there was no way to say what really happened."

"That's a miserable way to go."

"Agreed. So parties of all kinds were prohibited, but I overheard Sonya talking, and she feels a night of distractions would do us all good," he said.

"And she's right," added Lizzie. "It sometimes feels like someone died around here. If we want a night out with other vamps, we have to go to another coven. Glad we can have some fun on our own turf again."

I thought it strange that Sonya, who was so secretive and wouldn't let us leave the coven without a small army, thought it wise to have a party with two dhampyrs in the house. To me, it seemed like the perfect opportunity to keep us distracted.

"Tasi, you look like your head's going to explode. Is it

because you're sitting next to Austin? That would cause me pain as well," Lizzie said.

Austin let a low growl leave his throat.

"Funny," I said, switching subjects to distract them from my trance. "So, what are you guys going to the dance as?"

Lizzie perked up. "I'm going as a zombie prom queen."

"Nothing far from the truth, then," Austin teased.

She narrowed her eyes at Austin, then looked at me and said, "I'll catch you later. I don't like the company anymore." Standing up, she flipped her hair and strode off toward the kitchen.

"Boy, you sure know how to piss a girl off." I laughed. "That makes two so far today."

"Yeah, well, as long as it's not a certain girl, then what do I care." He nudged my shoulder. "I'm going to talk to Sonya. I have an idea that you'll love, but I need to run something by her first."

"You and your surprises."

"If you don't like surprises, I won't—"

"No, no, let's meet up later, and you can tell me all about your super idea," I said, shooing him toward Sonya's office.

He stood up, taking my hand and kissing the back of it. "Before bed in your—I mean *our*—secret location." He winked before heading off.

Heat radiated from my cheeks. Thinking back to our first kiss, I remembered how nice and sweet it was. There was something about Austin that made me wonder if nice and sweet were okay. Maybe it was better for two people in a relationship to start as friends and build on it from there. He was gorgeous. Plus, he had shown me on more than one occasion that he cared for me. He'd also broken the rules to help me, and never once belittled me.

Then there was that kiss with Ethan. It was still vivid in my mind. The desire that particular kiss had held was mind-blowing. The way his hands had captivated my body, and the electric feeling that pulsed through my veins as I fell deeper into him . . . I couldn't forget any of it. My tongue tingled as I thought about how it had skimmed his fangs.

Ethan had left a lasting impression from the time his brilliant eyes burned deep into my soul. In that moment, my heart had filled with a warmth I'd never felt before, and I wished I could forget it all. He didn't care about me. The way he was always mean with his words, the way he looked at me in disgust. It was clear that, to him, I was insignificant and childish.

Thinking about wanting Ethan and hurting Austin twisted my insides. The decision was obvious, based on how each treated me, and I was becoming a horrible person for wanting them both. My throat tightened.

"Tasia." A voice broke me out of my trance.

"Hi, Jelena. I heard about our class. I'm guessing you cleared it through Sonya?"

She sat down next to me, seemingly hesitant. "Yes, but I need to tell you something. Can I trust you to keep this between us?"

"Of course."

"You can tell no one—not even your sister." She glanced around, looking to see who might be watching, and pulled out a book.

"*History of Vampires*? I thought we would be going over the history of dhampyrs."

Jelena opened the book and pointed to a chapter titled "Ways to Kill a Vampire." I wasn't sure if I should shock her and tell her I was positive I already knew how to do that.

She tilted her head toward me, still pointing to the book, and whispered, "Pretend we are discussing this book."

"Okay. Pretending we are discussing this book."

"Tasia, this is serious." She gripped the book. "When I spoke to Sonya, she said I could teach the class to you and Emily under one condition: she wants to see all of my lesson plans.

When I questioned her as to why, she told me if I couldn't comply, she would deny my request."

"I don't understand why that's a problem. Sonya's always in everyone's business."

"Because she specifically asked me not to share anything regarding dhampyr transitions. That's when I became concerned. Tasia, she asked me to lie to you and tell you I couldn't find any information."

"I don't understand. Why would she do that?"

"I don't know, but then she threatened me and told me people have died for less, so listening to her would be in my best interest. Be careful what you tell her, Tasia." Jelena reached out for my hand.

"Give me a reason why I should trust you, then. I mean, I don't want to sound ungrateful, but how do I know you don't have your own agenda?"

Jelena looked hurt by my accusation, but she didn't understand my trust issues. Lots of people had lied to me over the years, and I wasn't in the mood for it anymore. On good days, I tried to follow my gut, but I'd learned it wasn't always a reliable source, so asking the pointed question seemed to be the way to go.

"Do you know anything about what happens when a person gets turned into a vampire?"

"Yes, they become a bloodsucking vampire."

"Let me rephrase my question. Do you know what becomes of our humanity when we're turned?" she asked.

"It gets turned off, doesn't it?"

"No, Tasia, it doesn't. All vampires have their humanity. Whatever we were in a past life is amplified. So, if you were a murderer in your past life, you would be deadly to anyone who crossed your path in this new vampire life. Most rogue vampires were cruel, dishonest people in their human life. They were also careless, which is why most end up dead pretty quickly," she said.

This was thought-provoking information. I wondered what kind of person Ethan was in his human life.

"Okay, so why are you telling me this? Were you a saint?" I asked.

"No, Tasi, I wasn't a saint." Jelena's jaw tightened for a moment before loosening again. "I was a devout person," she said. "So, as a vampire, I vowed to continue to live as an honest one. I'd accepted my fate as God's chosen path for me, so I would embrace it, hoping for redemption when my time as a vampire finally comes to an end."

"So what does this mean? You won't lie to me?"

"Correct. Whether you choose to believe me or not is up to you. I have nothing to gain from lying. But in telling you the truth, I have my salvation. Here is what I would ask of you, and you can choose whether to trust me. Please, be careful what we speak about during class. Sonya will be watching. We can figure out how to meet up outside of class to discuss topics that Sonya has forbidden me to talk about." She stood up when she heard Sonya's door open from across the room. "Don't tell anyone about the book I gave you either. Hide it." She then said, loud enough for Sonya to hear, "We'll meet in the media room once Emily's training is finished. This is the book we will start with. I look forward to speaking with you, Tasia."

I didn't have the chance to say to Jelena that I had already lost the book she gave me, and I was still debating who needed to know about the last two transitions. I knew I needed to tell someone, especially about the last one. Trying to find out what was needed to survive the third soul transition was going to be difficult alone. I needed help, but whose? Sonya came over and picked up the book lying in front of me. "*History of Vampires.* Interesting reading material."

Jelena gave Sonya a curt nod. "Yes, I asked Tasia to read through it. She is well versed with her human side. She needs to know the other half of where she came from, as it is just as important."

"Yeah, I guess all I know about you guys is that you're bloodsucking murderers I used to kill," I said. "Of course, the more I'm here, the more I think I might have been wrong, but I still know nothing other than you like to drink blood."

My eyes met Sonya's, but as expected, she didn't falter. I really wanted to trust Sonya. My parents and Eva had sent me here for a reason. I just wish they had warned me she was a vampire, and explained why she was so eager to help two strange dhampyr girls. What were her true motivations?

"Right, Tasia. And you don't like blood at all," Sonya said, narrowing her eyes at me. "Jelena, you're dismissed, and Tasia, I would like to see you in my office, if you wouldn't mind."

"Sure, I have nothing better going on, other than learning about murderous vamps." I put my hand out, waiting for Sonya to hand me the book.

Placing it down on the table, she started back to her office.

18

Sonya's office was grander than I had imagined. There was an intricately carved wooden desk, a chair, a wall of bookshelves, and a series of computers. There was a sense of power and elegance in the room. Above the fireplace was a peculiar painting of a woman's silhouette standing over a mountain of dead bodies. It was creepy, and I wondered if it was Sonya depicted in the portrait.

"So this is home for you," I said, running my fingers across the back of the couch. "Comfy."

"Have a seat, Tasia." Sonya's voice was resolute.

"I think I'd like to stand."

"Very well." She leaned against the desk. "I advised you that I would keep you up to date if we had any progress identifying the individuals behind your assault."

She had my attention. All the qualms I had about Sonya evaporated. No matter whether I liked her or she liked me—this was serious.

"Do you know who is after us?"

"Yes. I had a suspicion when you first got here, as this group had been watched by one of our sister covens for some time now, and they confirmed it with me today. The group is called the Deity, or by some, Deity X," she said.

I recalled the humans in the alley and at the toy store. They'd all had a small X tattooed on their necks.

"It is a group of humans dedicated to cleansing the Earth of supernatural beings. The Deity regard the vampire species as their biggest risk, and they believe they could eradicate us if they had the blood of a dhampyr. What they don't realize is that it's not just any dhampyr blood. I believe they need one with the purest blood of an original vampire."

"Why? What makes our blood so different?"

"Tasia, do you know how your father came to be?"

"Why would you think I'd know anything about my father? He died when I was six, and my aunt didn't know much about his past either. She was my mother's sister and didn't even know he was a vampire until after we were born."

Sonya was fidgeting, something I had never seen her do. "I'm going to tell you about your father's origins."

"You know? And you've been keeping this from me. Why?"

"Tasia, now is not the time—unless you prefer not to hear what I have to say."

"Fine." I crossed my arms.

"Yes, I've been around a long time, Tasia, and I remember the story of the Vasiles. There are different versions told throughout history, but what I'm going to tell you is what I know to be closest to the truth."

"I need to sit down." I gripped the edge of the couch and slid into the seat. Sonya strolled over and sat down next to me on the couch.

"At the beginning of the second century, the Roman Empire conquered Dacia, which was where your father was born. Your grandfather, Cristian Vasile, was a widower. He fell in love with a Roman girl, Valentina, after the war. Unfortunately, her family disapproved of their relationship. They did not like that he was

Dacian, had four children older than their daughter, and had been labeled by some as an evil, selfish man."

"Was he? Evil and selfish?"

"No, he was known among the Dacians as a man who took care of his family and his people. He happened to fall in love with the wrong girl, and that was his downfall."

I pulled my knees into my chest and rested my chin on them. "Okay. Go on."

"Valentina's mother was known to be well versed in plants, herbs, and poisons."

"Like a witch?"

"Yes. She secretly created a deadly concoction, pouring it into pitchers of wine. The servants were to deliver a pitcher of poisoned wine to the chamber of each member of the Vasile family the night before her daughter's wedding. What she didn't know was that her daughter was with Cristian, and they shared the wine between them. The Vasile family—and Valentina—died. Two days later, Cristian and two of his children, Adrian and Andreea, came back as what we now call vampires." Sonya shifted. "Do you want me to stop, Tasia?"

This information was overwhelming, but if it could answer my questions as to why the Deity were hunting us, I needed to hear it. "No, keep going."

"There was something in the genetic makeup of the original vampires that allowed three of them to come back. I suspect the Deity are not going to find these same properties in just any dhampyr's blood. Just because all vampires have a line to the Vasiles through venom and blood exchange doesn't mean they have the same genetic makeup. Only a direct offspring of a Vasile vampire will share that connection."

"So basically, the Deity think my family's genetics lives in all vampires, when in actuality it's only the originals and their direct descendants?" I stewed about this, trying to absorb the mounds of information I'd received.

"Sort of. We have studied vampire anatomy, and there are no living properties in any vampire's blood, including your father's —but you, Tasia, are alive. Your heart beats and you have warm blood running through your veins. You are alive. Whatever lived in the Vasiles before they turned into the undead, lives in you and Emily now."

"And the Deity don't know this?"

"The Deity know a version of how vampires came into existence, but they don't know you two are actually the key." She paused, her body tense, and she began to shift uneasily. "I know they don't realize this because they have been trying to breed vampires and humans in hopes of creating dhampyrs in order to farm blood. It is my understanding they have been unsuccessful in trying thus far."

These people were sick. Using humans and vampires as a science experiment in hopes of producing an innocent dhampyr. I pictured someone like my baby sister, small and harmless, being poked, prodded, and what? Killed when they were used up. If they were calling me an abomination, then there was no way they would let a dhampyr live. My stomach tightened.

"I realize this must be upsetting for you, and I know we often disagree, Tasia, but please don't share this knowledge with the others. The last thing we need is vigilante vampires running around seeking to become heroes."

If I heard, "Please keep this to yourself," one more time, I thought I might scream. Why was all this weight being dropped on my shoulders?

"Is this all? I'm not feeling too well, and I have class soon."

"For now—I will keep you up to date as information comes in." Sonya stirred in her seat. "I have another request that I would like you to consider. If you're willing, I'd like a sample of your blood to run some tests. A sample small enough to see if we can understand why your blood is so different. There is very little written about dhampyrs, so your blood may give us a better understanding of your genetic makeup. If you would like, Jelena can head up the studies with me. I don't want to clue anyone else in to the fact that you have shared your blood."

"Can I think about it?"

"Yes, and if it will make you more comfortable, you can talk it over with Jelena. She has conducted blood studies on vampires with me in the past."

Sonya seemed to trust Jelena, but Jelena had told me not to trust Sonya. I didn't know what to think anymore or who to trust.

I started to leave, but turned back. "Sonya?"

"Yes, Tasia?"

"You said there were three originals, and my father is dead. Do you know what happened to my grandfather and aunt?"

"It was said that Cristian went mad and took his own life on the ten-year anniversary of Valentina's death." She paused. "There is no record of Andreea after the seventeenth century. She was presumed dead."

The small flicker of hope that I still had family out there dwindled. "Thanks."

I searched out Emily. She would be finishing up training by this time. When I reached the top step, she was waiting for me on a nearby bench. She looked more like a kid than usual. Part of me wondered if I should shield Emily from all this and leave her in the dark, but she showed her maturity more and more every day. Sometimes she even seemed older than me. Her smile broadened as she saw me, and I decided I would keep what Sonya had said to myself for now. Emily didn't need to carry this weight on her shoulders. She was happy here, and I wasn't ready to take that away.

"Hey," Emily said, hopping up.

"Hi, Em, how was training?"

"Good—I'm learning so much from Cas."

We reached the media room, where Jelena was waiting for us, and I noticed Ethan sitting off to the side, reading a book. He rolled his eyes and let out an irritated sigh when I walked into the room. I found the farthest seat from him and slid into it. Emily sat next to me.

My hand shot up in the air. "Jelena? I have a question."

"Yes?" Jelena raised a brow.

"Why is he here?" I asked, pointing at Ethan.

I saw Emily put her head on the desk in frustration. Ethan looked up at me, eyes squinted.

"Sonya has instructed Ethan to assist us, similar to a teacher's aide."

"Great." I slumped in my chair.

"Trust me, princess, I don't want to be here either."

"Oh my God. You two are going to drive me insane. Kiss and make up already," Emily blurted out. "I'd like to learn something."

That left me both speechless and annoyed. Sinking back in my chair, I focused my attention on Jelena.

"Thank you, Emily. Now, let's get started on the misconceptions of vampires and their vampiric ways."

During the class, Sonya made a surprise appearance. She looked satisfied and nodded to Ethan, who turned his attention to me immediately after she left. After that, I focused back on the lecture, counting down the minutes.

When class was over, Emily wanted to get something to eat. Before I could go with her, Jelena asked me to stay behind for a moment while she gave me some books. Ethan looked us over suspiciously, but left the room with Emily.

"Here, take these books with you. We can chat later about any dhampyr questions you may have." She pushed me along, but I stopped her.

"Wait—Sonya asked me if she could take a blood sample. She wants to study dhampyrs a little further. She said that you could do all the testing if it would make me feel more comfortable," I said, scrambling for words. "What do you think I should do?"

"Do it. I hate to say it, but she's right. I'll take enough so we can run a few tests. Don't let anyone else take any blood unless I am present. Now go."

"Okay, I'll tell Sonya I talked to you," I said, heading toward the door. Again, I wanted to tell her about the missing book. It was bothering me that it still hadn't turned up. Multiple times I had checked under my bed, in my closet, and on my desk. I even checked Emily's side of the room, hoping it had somehow made its way over there.

I wished I knew why someone would take the book, other than wanting to keep the information from me. Maybe there was something on how to survive the third soul transition, and they took it because they wanted me dead.

I intended to drop off my books before hanging out with the others, but ended up stretching out on my bed and falling asleep. A few hours later, Emily woke me up.

"Where have you been? Lizzie, Cas, Austin, and I were watching a movie. Austin was super nice to me. He made me popcorn. Lizzie ended up throwing most of it at his head." She giggled.

"Yeah, sorry about that. I guess I was more tired than I thought." My stomach made a weird gurgling sound, which made Emily let out a wholehearted laugh. "I should grab something to eat and meet up with Austin."

"He asked me to mention that he was waiting for you. He wouldn't say where but that you would know." She shrugged before leaving the room.

19

Seeing Austin meant I should probably pull myself together, which entailed running a brush through my hair and tugging it back into a ponytail like I often did. I also put on some lip balm. That was as fancy as I could manage. I stared in the mirror and quickly realized it wasn't the look I wanted. So I pulled my hair out of the ponytail and changed my shirt. I had obtained a few more clothes since arriving, so I might as well use them.

One last check and I was ready. I headed to the main hall, and the place was like a ghost town. My stomach rumbled again. I ignored it and hoped it wouldn't embarrass me in front of Austin. But why did I suddenly care? We were just friends meeting up to hang out. Friends who kissed each other on occasion. Then I remembered he had a surprise for me.

As I scaled the stairs in the main hall, my heart started beating faster, and my breathing became unsteady, so I paused for a moment at the top of the steps. I was anxious, and it was strange; Austin never made me feel like this. Finally, I moved again slowly in an attempt to control my heart rate.

I entered the media room and pulled back the secret bookcase door. Light snuck in from the outside, and the breeze hit my face before I reached the top step. It smelled crisp, with different facets of the city lingering within the scent.

Austin was standing and peering into the distance, a perfect silhouette in front of the moon.

"Hey."

When he turned toward me, I let out a gasp. The twinkling from the miniature white lights filled his features. He looked more handsome than ever, and I couldn't ignore the way his gray sweater hugged his body. His mysterious green eyes regarded me as I continued to stare at him like an eager teenager. He was flawless.

"Are you going to be okay?" he asked as his lips tugged upward.

I shook it off. "I'm fine. Still a little tired, though. So what's up? I heard you wanted to see me."

He held my hand and drew me closer to him. My heart, which had slowed back down, started beating wildly again.

"I always want to see you. So I figured we should get some alone time to go over our arrangements for the party."

"So that's the surprise?" Disappointment dripped from my lips, and I cringed. *Not how I wanted that to come out.*

He laughed. "No, that's not the surprise, but we'll get to that in a minute." He ushered me over to where the bench was. I spotted a red makeshift tablecloth, two wineglasses, and a bottle of wine. "I thought we could start here."

"If you expect to get me drunk, you have another think coming." Here was the moment everyone had told me Austin was notorious for. Girls threw themselves at him so he could entice them to bed. "I'm not easy, Austin."

"Oh, Tasi, relax. I figured it would be a friendly gesture while we spoke. If you don't want any, it just means more for me." That smug expression that regularly crossed his face was back.

That's when my stomach betrayed me by growling, loud and fierce. The only thing I could do was give in, so I sat down.

"Sorry, I missed most of my meals today."

He reached under the bench and picked up something—two slices of cheese pizza.

"That's why I brought these with me."

The smile on my face returned as he passed me the tinfoil carrying the warm slices of pizza. I stuffed my face, using my manners as best I could, which wasn't saying much.

"What? I'm starving."

"Quite all right. Here's something to wash it down with." He gave me a glass that he'd filled with wine. I stared at him. "Trust me and try it. If you don't like it, I'll drink it."

"Fine." I balled up the tinfoil and reached for the wine.

"You realize you could chew your food? Scarfing down two enormous slices of pizza without savoring the flavor seems so disrespectful, and not very ladylike." He laughed.

"I never claimed I was a lady. If you prefer one of those, look elsewhere."

"No way. You, miss, are perfect. You're beautiful, amusing, and, well, a badass. Plus, did I mention how sexy you are, because my, my, you are so incredibly sexy," he said as he shifted toward me. He was serious.

"Oh." My cheeks grew warm once again. With my hands wrapped tight around my glass, I took a sip of wine. The liquid warmed my mouth, biting my taste buds with the flavor of copper, a taste I remembered well.

"Ah, I think she likes it."

"Is it blood?"

"Yes, I laced the wine with blood—a large quantity of blood."

"It's delicious," I said, taking another small sip. "Let's talk about this dance thing. So, what're you going as?"

"That, my dear, is a secret." He strolled over and leaned forward against the brick wall, looking over the edge.

"Now you're keeping secrets from me? Not certain I can endorse this behavior." I took another sip.

"You'll forgive me once I tell you my real surprise. I've asked Sonya for approval to go shopping this weekend. The dance is fast approaching, and we need costumes."

"Seriously? We get another day out?"

As I stood up, I couldn't tell if my feet were dancing in circles or my head was spinning. After a few seconds, my balance finally came back.

"Yes, I'm serious, and you shouldn't have anything else to drink." His hands grabbed on to my waist, steadying me. "Maybe that stuff is stronger for dhampyrs."

"I don't know, but I feel terrific." I didn't think I was drunk; it was only some momentary wooziness as the floor spun beneath my feet. The light captured in his eyes was now drawing me in. "You have such wonderful eyes."

"Yeah, no more alcohol for you." His finger followed my jawline, delighting my skin along the way. "If you were some other girl, I would take advantage of this moment."

The cloudiness impairing my thoughts cleared up. My jaw clenched, and my palms became sweaty at the idea of not being good enough.

"Why is that? Am I not pretty enough for you? Not pretty enough to sleep with, just fun to piss off Ethan with?"

"Tasi, you must be kidding me right now. You're gorgeous, and if it were up to me, we would be back in my room doing all sorts of naughty things." He pulled me in tighter. "You are by far the most alluring girl I have ever met. Any guy would love to be with you. And I don't mean just to sleep with you."

"Not every guy—I know of one who despises me."

His hold loosened around me. "So that's it. You have a thing for Ethan."

"No. Wait. Who? What?" I said as I struggled to figure out the correct words to back myself out of the corner my mouth had gotten me into. I had created a mess once again.

He smiled and shook his head. "I suppose it's a good thing we're just friends, right?"

Why was I tormenting myself? In front of me stood a fantastic guy who wished nothing more than to make me happy, and I was still thinking about Ethan and that stupid kiss we had, while Ethan had made it evident on several occasions that he didn't even like to be around me. Plus, with my impending doom in two years' time, maybe I should spend my efforts on the guy who actually liked me.

He watched my internal battle closely, then finally let go.

"No, Austin, wait." I stepped in closer to him. "Listen, I don't know if I'm ready for a relationship. There's a bunch of stuff going on with me right now, things that I'm not ready to talk about."

"It's okay, Tasi. I told you before, if all we can be is friends, then I'll take it. I like spending time with you." He brought his finger under my chin and lifted it so my eyes found his. "You don't owe me any explanations."

I reached up, sliding both my hands around the back of his neck. "Maybe if we tried, it would work."

"I don't know, Tasi. You said it yourself—you aren't in the proper mindset. It's almost as if you are forcing yourself to say these things so you don't hurt me."

"Honestly, Austin, I've never had a boyfriend. So I don't know if I'll ever be in the right mindset. And you're right, I don't want to hurt you if I'm not ready for all this. You deserve better."

He studied me further. "I have an idea. How about the night of the dance, we go on our first date?"

"What do you mean, exactly?"

He wrapped his arms around me again. The giddiness that had me whirling had now passed. The only emotion that lingered was the tremble I felt when he touched me.

"I mean let me pick you up at your room, escort you to and

from the party, and let me dance with you." Before I realized what was happening, Austin twirled me around. "You should let me get your drinks and hold your purse." His breath was luscious as he leaned in close. "And when the night is over, if you let me, I will sweep you up in my arms and—"

Before he could finish that sentence, my mouth moved to his. The kiss was delicious, interwoven with the metallic aroma of the wine. There was an urgency in the way our tongues danced. He pressed his palms against my back. Our bodies melted together the closer we stepped in to each other. My hands reached deep into his hair, driving his lips closer to mine. I didn't want him to stop, but he did.

Pulling back ever so slightly, he was smirking at me. "You understand I'm going to need a cold shower after this, right?" The brush of his fingers across my lips sent quivers through my body. He leaned in for one more kiss, moving his lips from my mouth to my jawline and down my neck. I stiffened. "Relax, lovely, I wouldn't bite you. I only wanted to tell you once more how breathtaking and ridiculously sexy you are." He grazed my ear with his tongue before pulling back.

"Sorry—still getting used to the whole vampire thing," I said as my face flushed.

"It's fine, Tasi, I won't do anything to you without your permission, okay?" he said, his tone gentle. "We better get to bed. Sun's coming up, and I don't want to be here when it does. Plus, that cold shower is calling."

"I should probably get to sleep anyway, before I try to join your cold shower." His eyes brightened. "Just kidding. I have class tomorrow."

We cleaned up the mess, stealing kisses from each other along the way.

"So, what's the deal with that class, anyway?"

"Jelena is teaching us about vampires and dhampyrs. It was her idea, and I guess Sonya thought it would be good for us to learn the truth, so we would stop killing you guys off." I considered myself close with Austin, but I couldn't tell him about everything going on. Not yet—there was no way to know if he would run back and tell Sonya everything.

"Interesting."

As we headed back through the main hall, I saw Sonya coming out of her office. "Hold on a sec." I broke off our hand-holding and ran over to talk to her.

Startled, she gave me a haughty look. "Shouldn't you be in bed, Tasia? Alone, I might add." She pursed her lips, watching Austin, who was waiting for me.

The blood rushed to my cheeks. "I'm going to bed alone, trust me. What we talked about earlier—the answer is yes. I spoke to Jelena, and she said she would help."

Sonya's face lightened up. "Excellent. We will make arrangements within the next few days. Once we are ready, Jelena will take you after one of your classes."

I nodded just as Ethan walked out of Sonya's office, narrowing his eyes as he looked at me. I wondered what he disapproved of now, the conversation I'd just had with Sonya or the fact that I was with Austin. Maybe it was a little of both.

20

The last few classes with Jelena had been boring. Emily still looked attentive, but I couldn't tell if it was an act or not. The limitations Sonya had placed on the class left Jelena talking about vampire and dhampyr information Emily and I already knew. What I really wanted to talk about in this class was the fact that I might be dead in the near future. Jelena, Emily, and I should be researching the material I learned from that book. Instead, today we were wasting time on the ethics of vampire and human relationships.

If Ethan weren't there eavesdropping on us, maybe we could have talked a little more freely. Teacher's assistant was such an awful lie. He was more like a spy, and as soon as class was over, he would be off reporting everything to Sonya. What was worse than his snitching was that the harder I tried to pretend he didn't exist, the more my eyes betrayed me. Sometimes I'd catch him doing the same thing. There was an uncomfortable feeling when one of us would notice the other. He would writhe in his chair or turn the page a little more forcefully as he quietly read his book.

Today, Jelena was going to take my blood while Emily met

Cas and Lizzie for sparring practice. Thankfully, none of us could stay bruised long, because they weren't holding back during their fighting classes. From what I'd seen, Emily held her ground well, and the better she got, the more I saw Lizzie and Cas facedown on the mat. I was almost excited for Emily to go through her transition and put on a few more inches. I bet after that, she'd be able to take both of them simultaneously.

Class ended, and Jelena and I were now alone. Ethan had rushed out of class quicker than usual.

"Sorry I haven't been able to meet with you," she said. "Ethan has been watching me a lot lately, which is odd, because he paid no mind to me before you came along. I don't think he's fond of me."

"I'm not surprised. He doesn't like me much either."

On the way to the infirmary, Jelena caught me up on conversations she'd had with Sonya. Nothing new—only more talk of Sonya's threats about not discussing certain information.

The infirmary was cold. The tiny hairs on my arms twitched, then stood on end as the chill crept over me. I jumped up on the table and rolled up my sleeve. We kept the talking to a minimum as she prepared the needle and other items needed to take my blood. I tried not to rattle off questions. Like, how many times had she done this before, and what did she expect to find? Then, just as I had built up the courage to ask a question, Ethan was there.

"Ugh! What now?"

"Nice to see you too," Ethan replied, before shifting his attention to Jelena. "Sonya wants to see you in her office."

"Can it wait?"

"Apparently not. You know how Sonya gets when she wants something."

Jelena sighed and clutched my hand. "Five minutes, I promise."

I decided I didn't want to talk to him. The last time he was genuinely nice to me was at the toy store. Since then, he'd been rude, snarky, and a big jerk. I chose not to deal with it today. So I sat there, my skin freshly swabbed with alcohol, pretending to be alone.

"So, you and Austin?" he said. "I hear you guys are going to the dance together."

I ignored him, glancing over at the needle, which looked like it had grown a few inches since Jelena left.

"That's fine. You don't have to talk to me. I'll just talk to you. Do you want to hear about all of Austin's past conquests? There are many, so this may take a while, but let's start with Lani. She's a spitfire. Maybe he will introduce you to her, and all the others, at the dance."

That did it. I snapped, "Austin and I are none of your business."

"In all seriousness, be careful who you decide to befriend, Tasi. You don't want to get hurt."

"I have been choosing my friends carefully. Didn't you notice I stopped talking to you?"

This made him smile—not the reaction I was going for. "Yeah, I guess. What about Jelena? Do you trust her?"

"Why are you probing, Ethan?"

I could feel the frustration growing inside me. I was on the verge of punching him. The chilly temperature in the room didn't seem to matter anymore because my body temperature was rising pretty fast.

He moved forward at a slow pace. I hadn't noticed how close we were until he reached out and pushed pieces of my hair behind my ear. And again, his touch took my breath away. In a moment of weakness, I sank into his warm, chocolate eyes, which filled me with a desire for more of him.

Finally, he broke the gaze and stepped even closer. The sweet scent of his breath tickled my senses.

"You know, the best place to talk to someone privately is in your room. You don't really think I'm buying that your classes with Jelena are to cover topics about the basics of vampirism and dhampyrism, do you? So if you want to talk to Jelena privately about anything, take her to your room."

"What?"

"You heard me. Privacy is where you sleep. Now slap me in the face, as if I told you something to piss you off, and make it convincing. I don't want anyone thinking we're friends." His lips brushed my ear one last time.

He leaned back on his heels, looking me in the eyes with a smirk. Before he stepped back, I slapped him. He graciously touched his lip, which my fingernail had conveniently sliced open, and strolled over to the opposite side of the room. There was a smile on his face as he licked away the blood that slowly began pooling.

"What is wrong with you?" Part of me wanted to know why he'd told me that, and the other part just wanted to know what was with the multiple personalities.

"What can I say? You looked so hot sitting there, I thought maybe you wanted to give me a quick kiss before Jelena came back. Trust me, it'd be worth it." He winked at me. At that second, he reminded me of the Ethan from the toy store. He was helping me, but why?

"Don't you have a girlfriend?" I played along, and in the process decided I should get a few things off my chest while I had the chance.

"Actually, no, I don't. Clover likes to think I'm still hers, but we haven't dated for over six months. She was too tiring. Always wanting to break up, then get back together. She liked the thought of a boyfriend, not an actual boyfriend. I don't bother correcting her or anyone else, though, so everyone thinks we're a thing."

"Way to lead a girl on, jerk."

"You should talk. Austin's leading you on, and you don't think he's a jerk," Ethan said. "I'll try not to say I told you so."

Jelena finally walked in. "What's going on in here? Are you fighting again?" She pulled Ethan's chin to her so she could examine his lip. Then, glaring back at me, she said, "Did you do this?"

"Yes, and I'll do it again if he doesn't stop hitting on me."

"Okay, enough, you two. Let's get this over with."

Ethan hopped up on the table across the room from mine.

"Why are you still here?" I glared at him.

Before he could answer, Jelena replied, "Because he has to report back to Sonya when we're finished."

Ethan's grin widened as I scowled in his direction.

"Fine, let's get this done."

When Jelena completed the task, she had two vials half filled with my blood. She placed both vials into a tiny fridge with a keypad on it. As Ethan left the room, our eyes found each other one last time.

That last glance was all I needed. Ethan was helping us for some reason. Jumping off the table, I pretended to get dizzy.

"Whoa, the room is spinning. I should have eaten something before class today."

I stumbled a bit, reached back to the table, and held myself up as if I was going to pass out. *Man, I could be an actress with this performance.*

Jelena ran over to help keep me upright. "Yes, maybe a little food is in order. Let's get you to the kitchen."

"No, I need to lie down. Can you walk me to my room, please?"

"If that is what you want."

On the way back to the dorms, I used Jelena as support. She helped me inside, and I pulled her down beside me on the bed with more force than I intended.

"There are no cameras in here. Can we talk now?"

"You aren't dizzy or ready to pass out?"

"No. Ethan reminded me we could talk in here privately. I don't know why," I said.

"That seems strange, yet helpful." Her fingers went to her lips and she lost herself in her thoughts for a moment.

"Agreed. I thought it was weird as well."

"Let's not waste any time. Do you still have the book I gave you?" she asked.

"No, I woke up the other day, and it was gone from my nightstand. I asked Emily and Lizzie, who were also in my room the day it went missing, and they hadn't seen it either. I didn't want to make a big deal about it, so I dropped it," I said.

"That's the best thing you could have done," she said, a tinge of disappointment lacing her words. "What questions do you have for me? I'll see what answers I have or can find."

"There are two things I need you to look up. At my age, a dhampyr goes through a second, mind transition. I have no idea if I went through it or not yet. It allows a dhampyr to learn compulsion if they are strong enough, and I was wondering if we could find out more about it and what I need to do to tap into it."

"Interesting. I wouldn't suggest trying anything until I can research it first. Don't keep your hopes up. The chances of me finding anything detailed related to dhampyrs and compulsion are likely to be slim. What else?"

"This is the most important thing—there is a final, soul transition, a third change, and the way it reads is that it's just as dangerous as the first transition, if not more. According to the book, there are no known dhampyrs who have made it through this last transition. Which means in less than two years, I'll be dead. If no one else has survived, then how can I assume I would? Could you please try to find out if this is still true and whether there is any information on what is needed to survive the transition?"

I tried to keep my voice even because I didn't want her to know how scared this made me. This life I had been given wasn't a fair one, but I still wanted to live it.

"Yes, Tasia, I'll do what I can to find the answers." She slipped her hand into mine, giving it a gentle squeeze. My heart steadied itself.

There was an urgent knock. We looked at each other, and I scrambled under the covers as Jelena hustled to answer it.

"Sonya, what a surprise."

"Is Tasia all right?" Sonya asked.

"Yes, she's fine. How did you know she wasn't feeling well? We left the infirmary and came straight here," Jelena said.

"Ethan told me she was looking pale when he gave me his update, so I figured she would have either gone to the kitchen to eat something or come here to lie down." There was a strange tone in her voice. I thought it might be concern, but decided against trusting that—Sonya was an outstanding actress.

"Of course, I forgot Ethan was there. Well, she is feeling better, if you must know. I was going to grab her some food and bring it back here. I didn't want her friends questioning her."

As I lay there watching the two vampires interact, I could feel the tension brewing between them.

"No need for that, Jelena. You're dismissed." Sonya stepped out and rolled in a metal cart loaded with orange juice, a blue mug full of what must be blood, and some banana nut muffins.

Jelena shrugged behind Sonya's back and disappeared down the hall, clearly trying hard not to draw unwanted attention to the situation.

"Thank you," I said, sitting up in bed and reaching for the orange juice. I kept my movements slow, making my story more plausible.

"Look at that—she has manners," Sonya said, sarcasm lacing her words.

"Don't get used to it," I scoffed. "Is my blood safe in that fridge in the infirmary? I don't want to be blamed for unintentionally killing off any bloodsuckers."

"Ah, there is the snippy Vasile girl I know. I thought you were truly sick for a moment there." Her voice became stern. "Don't worry, only Jelena and I know what the code is, and the only other people who know it's there are Ethan and you. So if it goes missing, I know which heads I am coming for."

"Well, that's where you're wrong. You forget, the security guys know too."

"Actually, no, they don't. I control the cameras from my office. Someone conveniently turned the infirmary feed off this afternoon."

"As always, you make everything feel so reassuring." The cynicism rolled off my tongue. "So then, why are you here?"

"Just making sure you were okay, like I said. I know you don't have any trust in me, Tasia, and that is fine for now. But there will be a time when you'll need me, I guarantee it." There was conviction in her modest speech, and it made me gag on the inside.

"Sure, whatever you say." I took a sip of the juice as she unloaded the muffins and mug onto my night table. "Oh, hey, before you leave, could you get me the book sitting over on my desk? It'd be a real help."

She scowled at me and strode over to the desk.

"Thanks. I usually leave books on my nightstand, but for some odd reason, they seem to disappear from there. You wouldn't know anything about that, though," I said, staring at her as she turned back and put the book on my bed.

Her eyes slithered their way back to mine, and there was an underlying warning as she looked at me. "Rest up, Tasia. Your friends will be looking for you shortly."

21

Today was going to be awesome. My friends and I were going on an adventure: costume shopping. Emily was so excited when she first learned we were going a few days ago that she'd searched for Austin to give him an enormous hug. He had hugged her back, picking her up off the ground and squeezing her tightly. The interaction between them melted my heart a little.

We headed down to the main hall, where Austin and Cas stood near the ginormous fireplace.

"Just the four of us and Lizzie?" I asked.

"Yes. Are you disappointed, Killer?" Austin reached around and pulled me into him. "I know I'm not Ethan, but you'll have to make do." He kissed the side of my forehead, making my cheeks warm.

"You're so melodramatic," I said, poking him in the side.

"Okay, enough from you two lovebirds. Can we go?" Lizzie asked.

Nothing could dim my mood right now. Letting go of Austin, I ran over to Lizzie. "What's the matter? Do you miss my attention?" I wrapped her in a big hug and planted a kiss on her cheek.

She froze. Everyone laughed as she wiped her cheek vigorously. "Don't kiss me with that mouth. Wash it first. Who knows where it's been." She looked at me, then pointed to Austin, before sticking her finger down her throat and making a retching noise.

Austin strode up to Lizzie and put his arm around her. "Don't be jealous. If I liked blondes, you would be first on my list of girls to chase after."

"Don't flatter yourself, Austin. I wouldn't touch you if you were the only vampire alive. I'm not that crazy," she scoffed. "No offense, Tasi."

"None taken, Lizzie."

Just before we left the property, Ethan ran outside and called Austin over. We stood off to the side discussing costumes, but I paid more attention to Ethan and Austin's mannerisms than to Lizzie raving about her fantastic costume idea. Austin looked frustrated.

"Fine, but you come with me so you can prove it," Austin said, before turning his attention to us. "Be right back, guys. Sonya needs to talk to me real quick."

The two boys headed back into the building, leaving us alone. Neither of them looked happy, which meant Sonya must have something up her sleeve. After a few minutes, Ethan came out holding keys in his hand, and Austin looked irritated.

"Cas, come here for a minute," Austin called.

"Really? Come on, already—we're wasting time. All this waiting is getting on my nerves," Lizzie groaned.

"Relax, Lizzie," Ethan said. "We have a scheduling conflict. I'll get the Navi. It'll save some time."

I watched in confusion as Cas and Austin spoke. "Leave your cell on in case I need to ask you something," Cas finished.

"All right," Austin said. He waved me over next.

"What's going on?"

"Sonya needs help and wants me to do it. She told me yesterday Ethan could, but today she changed her mind. Go figure," he said. "Don't worry, Ethan is taking my place. Remember, you can't leave unless you have one of us with you. So enjoy the day away, okay?"

"But maybe if we leave later . . ." I said, hopeful I had found a solution.

"Then the store will be closed. It's okay, Tasi. Have fun. I'll have to wait until the dance to see your outfit. I'll make it up to you, I promise." He ran his fingers along my chin, lifting it toward him and giving me a small kiss that lingered a few seconds too long. "Cas is picking up my costume, so I don't need to worry about that either."

I gave Austin one last hug before I left. When I turned back to the others, Cas, Lizzie, and Emily stood there staring at me.

"What?"

"Um, I wasn't sure if you noticed, but Austin kissed you. Like, really kissed you," Emily said. "Oh my God. Are you two a couple?"

"No, I told him I didn't want a boyfriend. It's too distracting."

"Yes, because a hot guy who isn't your boyfriend kissing you goodbye isn't distracting at all. I can definitely see the logic in that." Lizzie snickered. "Your reasoning, as always, is good for a few laughs."

"Whatever."

Ethan pulled up to the front. No one mentioned the kiss after that. My guess was that no one wanted to ignite the fight that always started when we were together.

I sat in the back with Lizzie and Emily. Lizzie was insisting on sticking with her original costume. The thought of Lizzie, gorgeous Lizzie, running around in zombie makeup made me laugh. Emily wanted to be a black cat. I had no clue about my own costume.

"I was thinking maybe a fairy or pirate," I said. "But I don't know."

Ethan, who'd been quiet until now, said, "I was thinking more like a witch."

No one said a word in anticipation of what would come next. "Funny, Ethan. I like it, though." My voice was even. "You know, if you need help picking out a costume, I have an idea for you. It rhymes with Venus."

Lizzie busted out laughing, along with Cas and, to my surprise, even Ethan. Emily turned to me with a confused look on her face.

"I don't get it," she said. This made us laugh harder. I watched as Lizzie leaned in to Emily. Emily's eyes almost fell out of her head. "Antanasia," she scolded.

I gave Emily a kind smile. "You sounded like Mom right then."

Her face lit up at the thought. "Really?"

"Yes, it was like being scolded for drawing on the walls again."

We reached the store, which broke the silence that had formed in the car. I gave Emily one last knowing smile as we filed out of the vehicle. We were all in good spirits. Even the tension between Ethan and me had dissipated.

It drove me crazy that I couldn't figure him out. I never really knew what he was thinking about when I was around. Thinking back to the infirmary, I wondered if he was the one who had tipped Sonya off. Even more so—did he tell me to talk to Jelena in my room so that Sonya would get there in time to catch us chatting about dhampyr transitions? Or was it all coincidence? I tried to push the thoughts out of my head. There was nothing more to think about, other than finding a costume for the dance. However he treated me, I would roll with it.

We entered the store. Flapping bats and shaking ghosts lit up the aisles, howling as we walked by, waking them from their rest. The place was pretty big, two whole floors filled with Halloween stuff. How many costume choices could one possibly need? We wandered around looking for the best outfits. Ethan and I were slower than the others, secretly glancing at each other and even smiling when caught. When we turned the corner, it didn't surprise us to see Cas and Lizzie having a sword fight in the aisle. Emily stuck close to Cas as usual, so I didn't worry too much. Ethan and I watched them playing as regular teenagers did. I shook my head.

"Ready to take on the parental role again?" Ethan said.

"If we must. This time I can do without the crazy humans, though."

"Agreed."

We walked for a bit, laughing at some costumes and jumping at others.

"Can I ask you something without you telling me to mind my business?" I asked.

"Depends what it is." Ethan gave me a half-smile.

I stopped for a moment, giving a little more distance between us and the others. Ethan followed my lead.

"Well, when you helped me out in the infirmary. You know, before you told me to slap you—which, by the way, was so much fun for me."

I saw the corner of his lips twitch upward. "Figured you'd like that."

"Then why did you tell Sonya I wasn't feeling well? You knew she would go straight to my room. I only had about five minutes with Jelena before Sonya showed up with food, saying you told her I looked sick," I said.

"Are you two coming?" Lizzie yelled to us.

"We'll catch up. Just don't leave the store," Ethan said. Lizzie turned away, but not before rolling her eyes and making sure we noticed. "Tasi, I didn't tell Sonya anything about you. I told her the samples were ready. I had no idea you didn't feel well. Think about it—I left the infirmary before you were even off the table."

He was right. Why hadn't I put that together before? I was so quick to blame him because he was Ethan. How could he have known I'd try to get Jelena back to my room right away?

"You know, Sonya has cameras in her office," he said.

"I know, she told me, but she said she turned the infirmary camera off, so the security room wouldn't see me give blood."

"The video feed that goes through the security room goes through her computer first," Ethan said. "She never turns it off in her office, even if she shuts it off in the security room. So my guess is that she was watching you."

I stayed quiet for a moment. "That makes sense. Sonya probably blamed you for telling her because normally, I wouldn't be asking you to validate her story."

"Tasi, never forget she watches your every move."

"Yeah, so? I already knew that."

"Do you? Are you sure you know how much she is watching? Did you know there's a camera installed on the roof where you and Austin have made your love nest?"

Hurt and anger dripped from his voice as he said that last part. Then I remembered the night I was with Austin and how icy cold Ethan was when he walked out of Sonya's office. He must have seen everything. I tried to swallow without getting choked up. I started walking again, keeping quiet about what he might have seen. A lump formed in my chest.

"Why do you want to help me, Ethan? We barely talk, and when we do, we're usually bickering back and forth."

My voice was gentle as I spoke. Normally, I would have jumped down his throat for irritating me, but that never got me anywhere with Ethan. This emotional roller coaster we always rode needed to stop. All I wanted was a genuine answer.

Ethan sighed. "Let's finish shopping, drop the kiddies off, and then we can talk, if you're up for it."

"Sure."

"When we get back, say you left your wallet at the store. I'll volunteer to bring you back and get it. We won't be too long."

22

When we arrived back at the house, I did as Ethan asked, and it sort of worked.

"I should come with you guys," Cas said.

"No, tell Sonya we will be no more than thirty minutes, and Tasi will be safe."

"It seems way too risky, man. Plus, Sonya is going to kill you two when you get back."

"And you want to die alongside us? Please, Cas, stay with Emily and make sure she's protected. I'll be back soon." I placed my hand on his.

"Dude, hurry back."

Ethan drove to a small coffeehouse that wasn't too busy. Upon entering, a sudden warmth fell over me. The smell of freshly brewed coffee tickled my nose. Ethan headed over to the young girl behind the counter. She looked at him, almost lost in his presence, but he barely noticed her. What in the world was he going to tell me? I caught his eyes once, then pretended I wasn't staring, trying my best to be patient.

The ambiance was relaxing. The walls were brick, and the floors were dark wood. There was a multitude of couches, and bookshelves filled with books and board games. Under different circumstances, this would be a quaint hangout.

We found a table in the back corner, which the antique chandelier only dimly lit. My hands wrapped tightly around my hot coffee. Ethan pulled out a small flask and poured its contents into my drink. No one noticed.

"Why, Ethan, you rebel, you."

I gave him an approving smile as he put the flask back into his coat. Again, there was a moment of silence as our eyes met. This time intentionally. I took in his features in the dim lighting, which hid the true glow that usually radiated off of him. His eyes were dark, almost black. The hair that was usually so neatly combed had taken on a mind of its own.

"So." I broke out of the mystical trance.

"So." He furrowed his brow.

"So, you were going to explain to me why you are helping me? I mean, I know you don't like me—"

"It has nothing to do with me liking you. I mean, I do like you, but . . ." He took one more deep breath. "It's a long story—one I rarely talk about. I'll try to get through it all, because we don't have a lot of time.

"I was turned at the same time as my father. We were working out in the barn. My younger brother, Isaac, was feeding the animals, and my mother had just left for the market to sell vegetables. When she got home, we would all have breakfast together. She was an amazing woman." He drifted off for a bit, clearly lost in memories.

"She sounds wonderful." I slid my hand across the table. The hum from his touch reverberated into me.

"Anyway, it was early morning. The sun was still hidden away when we heard Isaac cry out. My father and I ran toward the sound of squealing pigs and a screaming boy. A rogue vampire stood over his lifeless body, draining him until he looked like a pile of bones covered in skin. I attacked the vampire, who picked me up by my throat and sank his teeth into my neck. The venom changed my body, scorching me on the inside, making me contort into impossible shapes. Then, when he fed me back his blood, I screamed repeatedly from the burning in my veins until I passed out."

"I'm so sorry."

He shifted in his chair before continuing, "My mother dragged my father and me into the house. She tended to our wounds, not knowing what had happened. When I woke, I was in my bed. My brother was in his with a sheet over him, hiding what that monster did to him. My father came into the room first. He tried to talk to me, tried to keep me sane. But all I could think about was the monstrous creature that took my brother from me, and took my happy family and tore it apart. The beast that made me into the miscreation he was."

I squeezed his hand, which was jittery. I could see this tearing him up inside, and my heart hurt for him.

"Do you need to stop?"

I wanted him to keep going. I wanted to know all about him, to understand him, but his need outweighed my selfish desire to hear what he'd held inside him for years, maybe even centuries.

"No, we need to keep going."

"If you need to stop, it's okay." He reached out and touched my face, rubbing my cheek with his thumb.

"When my father couldn't get me to calm down, my mother stepped into the room. She embraced me, crying, her face streaked with layers of different shades of red. She had been crying all day, stopping and starting again every time she realized one son was dead and the other and her husband were monsters. As she let go of the embrace, I hesitated for a second before lunging in to bite her. My father must have picked up on it, because he plucked me from where I was. He was stronger than me. He also had the power of my mother's love on his side. He would never hurt her—not as a human, and not as a vampire. So before I could do anything else, he tossed me out. He told me never to come back unless I could control myself. So I had no other choice but to go."

"Where did you go? That must have been incredibly hard, watching your family fall apart like that."

"Wherever I could. I sought out other vampires and stayed with them. It was incredibly hard, but I did what my father said."

"You went back."

"I went back after eight years. I still wasn't sure if they would accept me. When I knocked on the door, I braced for the worst. My mother answered, and she immediately threw her arms around me. She asked me in, and then told me that my father had gone out one night and never came home." Ethan stopped for a moment.

"Maybe he left and is alive somewhere?"

"No, he wouldn't leave my mother and sister. My father was too noble for that, and I'm sure he loved them."

He stared at me as if he was waiting for something. What was it he was waiting for? Sympathy that he missed his family and never got to say goodbye to his father?

Then it hit me like a boulder. I gasped for air before I could get the words out. "Oh my God. You had a dhampyr sister. Didn't you?"

"Yes. I helped my mother raise her as best I could. She was six, and I immediately fell in love with her. I tried my hardest to find information anywhere I could. No one knew a half-vampire, half-human could even exist. When Alice turned thirteen and got sick, we thought she had some disease."

"She didn't make it through her first transition."

"First?" Ethan asked.

"Oh. I said that out loud. Please, finish telling me what happened, and then I will tell you all about it."

Ethan watched me suspiciously before continuing, "Well,

when she died, it tore us to pieces. My mother ended up dying as well. I don't think her frail body could take any more tragedy. That's when I left. I'd heard of safe houses where vampires gathered, so I headed to New York City, thinking it was my best chance for a new life. That's where I met Lizzie, and I've been here ever since."

"Is this why you are helping me, because if someone was there to help your sister . . ." I thought about how different life could have been for Ethan.

"You and Emily are alone, like we were. Leaving things to chance could kill you both. As mad as you sometimes make me, I don't want you or your sister to die because someone withheld vital information from you. If that means I have to turn my back on Sonya, Jelena, or even Lizzie, I will."

He was putting Emily's and my lives before everything, and it made my heart blaze. "Are you sure this is the right thing for you? I mean, Sonya isn't very forgiving."

"I can take care of myself." He was chewing on the inside of his mouth. "What first concerned me was that when Sonya found out you two were out on your own, she began acting very strange. She was being secretive on the phone, setting up additional cameras throughout the building, and her open-door policy for Austin and me was revoked. Three vampires actually left the coven after that, and I think that's why the rest have avoided getting to know you guys. Sonya's behavior didn't go unnoticed."

"Let me get this straight. That's why you're mean to me when other people are around? You don't want anyone knowing you're helping us."

"I decided as soon as Sonya told me I was going to find you that if I were to be of any help to you both, I had to play the asshole, and it had to be believable to everyone. I need to be close to Sonya to figure out her secrets and what she's not telling you. Because, Tasi, there is definitely something she's not telling you."

"I figured as much. She is so hard to read, and sometimes she acts really weird around me." I picked at my fingernails.

"And if she finds out I took your side over hers, I'm afraid she won't allow me near you anymore. She may even send me away, or worse, add me to her headless vampire collection. Think about it—why did she pull Austin from this trip and ask me to take his place? It's possible this is her way of not letting you get too close to him."

He had a point. I was wondering why Austin and Ethan were switched out last minute. Sonya had always treated them equally, yet suddenly, Austin was asked to do something else during a trip *he* had planned.

His hand reached for my cheek once again, which immediately triggered fluttering in my stomach. "Jelena is another one. I know little about her, so I've been watching her."

"She noticed. When I was talking to her the other day, she mentioned it to me."

"Good to know. I don't trust Austin either, and you should be careful. I swear, if the situation were different..."

"The kiss in the store. It wasn't fake, was it? You felt what I did."

"Yes, I've always known there was something between us, since—"

"Since you saw me on the train platform that first day in Boston," I finished.

"Yes, which makes pretending to hate you a lot harder."

The thumping in my chest had moved to the rest of my body. It was aching for him so much my body quaked. All the denial in the world didn't help the feelings I had right now. I wanted him more than he could know, but he'd already said we couldn't be together. Not if he wanted to keep me and Emily safe. I was clenching my jaw so tight there was pain rippling through my head.

It also triggered my mouth to speak before my brain could kick in. I know that, because what I said next would have been better kept in my head. "You know, Austin is not as bad as you make him out to be. I know you guys have your petty rivalry, but he is like you are now—sweet."

This made his face harden. "Please don't compare me to him, ever."

"Sorry," I said, and my heart dropped into my stomach. I didn't want to hurt Ethan, but I couldn't deny how close Austin and I were. I watched the fire ignite in his eyes.

He looked up at the ceiling. "We better get back before they come looking for us."

"Did you want to know what I meant by *first transition* before we leave?" I asked. "You know, before you have to go back to hating me."

"Yeah, I guess."

My stomach turned over, leaving a sour taste in my mouth. The connection we'd had a few minutes ago seemed severed. I wasn't sure what I had hoped he would say, just not that.

"I found out there is a second transition that has to do with the mind. I'm not sure, but I may have already gone through it. If I did, I can learn compulsion—and not only learn it, but use it on humans *and* vampires."

"Really?" he said, sitting up straighter. "That could be something valuable for you. How do you learn it?"

"That's the problem—I'm not sure how it all works, and I don't know how to try it out without asking random vampires to do things for me. I'm thinking that'll give me away, or make Sonya suspicious."

"Okay, so what do you need?" There was life in his eyes.

"A willing subject to practice on." I laughed at how ridiculous that sounded.

"Done. If I can get away with no one knowing, I'll sneak into your room around bedtime so we can practice."

"But, Emily . . ." I thought about what he was saying and how crazy it sounded. "I don't know if that's a good idea."

"This is something we should include Emily in. Remember what happened to my sister. You shouldn't be hiding anything from her. What if something happens to you? What happens to her then? Think about it," he said, getting up. "Come on. We need to go."

"One more minute, and you might want to sit for the next part." I hadn't been sure if I was going to tell anyone other than Jelena about my impending demise, but after Ethan opened up to me the way he did, I trusted him.

"There's more?" He ran his hand through his hair, giving it the usual tug.

"Yes. So, there is a third and final change, which is called a soul transition. It happens when I turn twenty, and it doesn't seem like the outcome will be good for me."

"What do you mean?"

"Jelena gave me this dhampyr book, which someone stole out of my room before I finished reading it, but that doesn't matter right now. In that book it talked about learning compulsion and one final change at twenty, which would be a death sentence for me. The book said there were no records of dhampyrs surviving it, basically because no one knew how to treat it. Again, I don't know where the book went, so I'm not sure if it was elaborated on."

I met his eyes as he spoke. "So, what you're saying is, I'm going to lose another person I care about because no one has any information on how to fix this."

I reached out my fingers, touching his. "I care about you too."

That look he had when he was telling me the story of his sister had returned. "We have to go, but this conversation is definitely not over," he said, standing again and reaching for my hand. He pulled me up and right into his arms, then studied my face before leaning in and kissing me.

His lips were so soft. They brushed against mine, slowly at first. His hand made it to the back of my neck, where his fingers tangled in my hair. I couldn't stop myself. There was an urgency for me to kiss him faster and harder. I was consumed by his presence. I don't know how long I let him kiss me, but finally, I pulled back.

"We shouldn't, Ethan. I want to, but I can't." I couldn't look at him now. If he looked into my eyes, they would betray me. They would tell him how much I longed to be with him.

"But it's okay for you and Austin? I'll only say it once more—you can do so much better. He's manipulating you." He turned away from me and headed toward the car.

"Like you? Is that any better? You say you're pretending to hate me; then why not ignore me, instead of treating me like garbage? What a catch," I said, keeping up with his fast pace as we made it to the car.

Ethan just sighed. "Let's just forget it."

"Great, we can agree on something."

Ethan didn't get it. If he'd told me this was why he was so hot and cold, I wouldn't have gotten as close as I had to Austin or agreed to the date with him. I would have waited for Ethan because we clearly needed to be together. Now, in order to be with Ethan, I had to hurt Austin. And if I hurt Austin, there was no guarantee Ethan wouldn't turn on me the second he thought he was putting my life in danger, instead of working through it. This was so frustrating, and I couldn't see any way forward that didn't lead to someone getting hurt.

23

We prepared for a tongue-lashing when we returned. There was no way Sonya would let us get away with the stunt we'd just pulled. The hall was bustling with chatter as everyone decorated for the dance. When I say everyone, I mean everyone, but the click of the door behind us created stale air, and suddenly no one was paying any attention to the decorations anymore. Instead, their attention fell on us. My eyes instantly locked on the ball of fire burning in the corner—Clover. However, it was seeing Sonya standing outside her office waiting for us that sent chills down my spine.

"My office. Now," she said through gritted teeth.

Whispers trailed behind us as we followed Sonya into the front room of her office. We shared one last glance as she shut the door behind us.

"What were the two of you thinking? You know how dangerous it is out there."

"Well, let me see," I said, my voice coming out condescending. "I needed my wallet. It may not matter to you, but it has sentimental value to me. You wouldn't let me go alone to get it, so I had to bring my trusty sidekick. Although, next time, can you just let Austin take me? The company would be much more pleasing."

"Yes, let Austin go with her next time. The two of them can run off into the sunset together." I wondered if he was still expelling pent-up aggression from me defending Austin at the coffee shop. "I'm done babysitting an ungrateful little girl." Then his focus turned to me. "You're so annoying."

"Maybe I'm annoying, but at least I'm truthful. I tell it like it is. You hide behind Sonya, acting like you're all high and mighty, when you are nothing but a big—"

"Enough, you two." There was a growl in Sonya's chest as she spoke. "Tasia, you may leave. Pull nothing like that again, or I will revoke all your privileges."

"Whatever." The door slammed behind me, causing an echo throughout the hall.

I could hear Sonya lecturing Ethan on how irresponsible he was. The several sets of eyes watching me scurried off the closer I got to my friends. Except for Clover; I thought she might self-combust from anger. I watched as she threw down the banner she was hanging and stomped away.

"How bad did she yell at you?" Lizzie asked.

Austin strolled over and hugged me. "Not too bad, I hope."

"It was fine. Ethan and I were yelling at each other, mostly. The typical—calling each other names until Sonya broke it up and threw me out. I'm sure he is getting the worst of it. So, what can I help with?"

They all stood there, watching me. What was I? A zoo animal? Austin spoke first. "You can help me hang lights. It will make up for the time stolen from me earlier today."

"Oh God, whatever you guys do, can you please do it far away from us?" Lizzie said. "I don't think I can handle you two right now."

"What do you say, beautiful? Want to play with my lights?"

"Sure, handsome, I'd love to."

"Gross, I have to go puke now." Lizzie walked away, gagging.

"Tasi, can you help me with one thing before you help Austin?" Emily grabbed my hand. Her grip was tight.

"Sure, lead the way." I gave Austin a wink. "Be right back."

We headed toward our room, but she pulled me into the bathroom across the hall instead. She must have realized the odd look on my face, because she let go of my hand and hugged me.

"Are you okay?" I asked.

"Yes, but I need you to tell me what's going on."

"What do you mean?"

"Tasi, you're doing it again. You can't keep hiding everything from me. I played stupid for a little while, but it was obvious something was up when you took off with Ethan. You didn't even have your wallet. It's in the room."

"Oh."

"That's all you can say to me? Tasi, you promised not to keep things from me."

"Sorry, Emily, I can't help it! Keeping you in the dark means you're safe. It's embedded in my head that way." I wasn't sure if she would believe me, but I was sincere.

"I get it, but no—keep your promise. It can't be you and me until the end if you don't talk to me and tell me what's going on."

"You're right." I hated when other people were right. Ethan had said the same thing. My leaving Emily in the dark put her at risk if something happened to me.

I dragged her by the hand into our room. I ran through everything, only leaving out Ethan's personal story, which I felt was his to tell. I told her about the blood testing, the Deity group, the story of how vampires came into existence, information Jelena was looking up for us, and how Sonya had told Jelena to keep details about the dhampyr transitions away from us. We talked about my theory that Sonya was hiding something big from us and that the dance was her opportunity to keep us busy while she covered something up. Finally, I told her everything pertaining to the three different transitions I'd read about in the book before it disappeared.

"We're going to die at twenty? That is, if I don't die when I change at thirteen? Is that what I heard?" Emily slouched forward.

"I don't know. The way it seems right now... yes. I'm scared that I... *we* won't be able to figure out how to stop it before my time is up. We have to keep researching and looking for answers until we've exhausted all avenues. There's just so much going on, I can't make the last transition my first priority right now. We need to figure out how to stay safe, and more importantly, I need to get you through your *first* transition, whenever it decides to begin."

"I'm not happy about holding off on the final transition, but I understand why we need to." A slow breath left her lips. "Okay. So, who do you trust?"

"You." I wiped my brow. "Sonya has been making an effort to keep me 'up to date,' but I don't trust that she doesn't have something up her sleeve. She's hiding something. Jelena, I think, is trustworthy, and Ethan is earning my trust too."

"Ethan? You two fight like you want to rip each other's throats out." She scratched her head.

"I can't explain it, but until today, I thought he hated me. Then, when we went to find my wallet, he told me he doesn't want Sonya aware that we're friends, which is why he is always so mean to me around others or avoiding me wherever there are cameras. He thinks it will keep us safer," I said. I wanted to add how it sucked, because I thought we would be together in a different situation, but I kept that to myself. Our kiss trickled back into my mind.

"What about Austin? You guys have been hanging out a lot lately. I mean, I saw you kiss him."

"He seems genuine. I'm not sure if he is trustworthy, but he has been helping me. The issue with him is he won't lie to Sonya, and that makes me nervous. So I'm not telling him. Not yet."

"So, what do you need me to do?" she asked, straightening up. She wanted to help, and she could do it. Keeping her in the dark wasn't right.

"I need you to stay safe, but keep your ears and eyes open for anything strange. We'll keep each other informed, and no discussing it outside of our room. The rest of the place has cameras."

"Okay. Thanks for trusting me."

"It's not that I never trusted you, it's that I can't imagine anything happening to you. You come first before any other, Emily." I wrapped her in a hug.

We needed to get back. I opened the door and collided with Ethan. He had a serious look on his face, staring between the two of us.

"Hi, Ethan," Emily said.

"Hey, kiddo. Can I talk to Tasi real quick?" The corners of Emily's mouth turned down as she tried to keep her composure.

"It's okay, she knows. I guess when I say things like 'I left my wallet,' then I should have it on me." I saw Emily's freckles darken as her cheeks burned red.

"Good. Emily should know everything." He put out his fist to do a quick fist bump with her. She blushed again. "What are you doing later? I wanted to stop by and try a little of the—"

"Sounds good."

"Great," Ethan said, walking away, not saying another word.

"I still say he's smitten with you."

I didn't need Emily confirming what I now already knew. "Come on, before someone sends out a search party."

We strolled back into the hall. I dropped Emily off with Lizzie and Cas. I heard Cas questioning her like a big brother, which made me laugh. Her reply was that we were discussing girl problems, and if he wanted a play-by-play, she would give it to him. Lizzie's laughter reverberated through the hall.

I headed over to Austin, who was wrapping lights around the railings. Watching him work so gracefully in his black button-down shirt and fitted jeans, I realized something was now missing. Now that I knew Ethan's genuine feelings, I was confused about my own feelings toward Austin.

He glanced up at me, giving me one of his crooked smiles, then winked at me like he always did.

"Your sister okay?" he asked.

"Yeah, girl issues—nothing a vampire could help her with," I said.

"No need to explain," he said, stopping me before I could add in details. "Hold this for a second."

With the lights in my hand, he swept me into his arms, pressing my body against his. The air moved swiftly around me, and before I could comprehend what was happening, we were alone in the media center. The lights crashed to the floor as I held on to him, steadying myself. He leaned into me, pushing me against the wall. His lips tickled the nape of my neck as he grabbed me by my waist, lifting me and pulling my legs up. I wrapped them around him just to keep from falling, and he nestled in closer. The butterflies that had recently flitted in my stomach when Austin touched me were now gone. Instead, my heart thumped violently, trying to escape my chest, making me unsure if I should let him go on.

His lips swept up to my chin, cooling my skin with each caress as he searched for my mouth. I was thankful for the darkness; only the dull glow from the lights outside the room lit our shadowed faces. He couldn't see into my eyes right now. They would be the first to tell him my heart wasn't here, with him, and that something had changed when I was with Ethan today.

Our lips finally met. There was hunger in the way he pressed his mouth against my lips and the way his tongue searched for mine. I tried to push the thought of Ethan to the side so I could give in to this moment. I kissed him with the same intensity I had the other day, when my gut had told me that Austin deserved a chance because Ethan didn't care. The only problem now was that I knew Ethan *did* care.

My head spun as I made my way through all the motions of physically being with Austin. I pulled back, and he kissed my lips one last time.

"I think I could get used to this." He brushed his fingers along my jawline, like he frequently did.

"Yeah, well, don't we have a date coming up soon? Shouldn't we be saving these kisses for then?" I rested my head on his chest, still trying to avoid his eyes, even in the dark.

"I guess. We probably should finish the lighting on the stairs before we get too distracted."

"Yeah, I agree." I intertwined my fingers in his and yanked him out of the media room, putting on the best facade I could as I tried my hardest to be in the moment and not think about Ethan.

"You guys are gross," Lizzie bellowed from where they were working at the bottom of the stairs.

"Don't be too jealous, dear Lizzie. I told you, blondes aren't my thing."

24

Bedtime couldn't come quickly enough. I appreciated the time I'd spent with Austin, but still struggled with how I felt. I was looking forward to seeing Ethan and hoping for clarity with my boy problems. Even more appealing was the compulsion I was about to try for the first time. I was trying to let that sink in—Ethan had volunteered to let me compel him, to control him, to become my puppet if I pleased. He was lucky I liked him, because the possibilities were endless.

We headed back to the dorms after a late dinner. It had taken hours to set up the hall for the dance, but I had a suspicion it was going to be worth it. Sonya had come out to announce that a few of the other covens would be attending the dance as well. This made Lizzie happy. The guy population in our coven house was slim, and Lizzie treated most of them like brothers or parasites.

"Sleep tight, guys," Emily and I said.

"You too," Cas and Lizzie replied.

Austin followed us.

"I'll see you inside," Emily said. She waggled her eyebrows so only I could see.

I peered up at Austin. "I guess I'll see you tomorrow." I pushed the hair away from his face.

"All right, Killer, see you in the evening," he said.

This was the part where I should want to dive in and kiss him; to fall into his crystal-green eyes. Instead, I gave him a meek smile and a hug before going inside.

In our room, I changed into my pajamas, making myself a little prettier than usual. I hoped Emily wouldn't catch on, but her face told me otherwise.

There was a knock at the door. Ethan had said he would take care of the camera in the hall tonight by moving it away from the view of our room. By the time Len or James came by to fix it, he would be safely inside. I sprinted from the bed to answer it anyway. I didn't want Ethan lingering in the hall and have someone pop out of their room and see him. I couldn't deal with the added drama that would cause.

Either way, I opened the door quickly, and to my dismay, Ethan wasn't alone.

"Jelena? What are you doing here? Hurry, get in."

"Sorry for not warning you. I stopped by to talk to Jelena after I talked to you this afternoon. I wanted to know if she had any other information that might help us out," Ethan said, an apologetic look in his eyes. "She insisted on coming."

"Yes, and finding out Ethan, Sonya's trusted watchdog, was aware of things that only Tasia should know was quite the shock. So, is it safe to say we are the only four who know any of this?" Jelena asked.

"Yes, we're the only ones," I said as they settled into my room.

"And Ethan is to be trusted?"

"Hello, I'm right here. You can ask me."

"Ethan is to be trusted," I said, with no hesitation. After our talk earlier, I had no doubt his heart was genuine.

"It's yours and your sister's lives, Tasia. If you trust him, I will too."

"Great, then what do we need to do?" I asked.

"I did some extensive research on compulsion, and everything I read was very vague. The one thing I saw in common in the various sources was that concentration is the biggest part of controlling it. So, let's begin with something simple." She strolled over to one of my books, took it off the desk, and placed it on the bed. "Okay, Ethan, you sit here, and Tasia, sit across from him."

We sat on the bed facing each other, the book lying between us. I tried to keep a serious face, but failed and let out a light giggle, which then made Ethan smile. Jelena's face was rigid.

"Sorry," I said.

"Relax and keep your heartbeat even," she said. "Remember, it's all about control. If you can't control yourself, how can you take control of another person?"

What she said was logical, but it was easier said than done. She wasn't sitting across from the most magnificent person alive. I sucked it up and took in some deep breaths, trying hard to keep them uniform.

"Now what?" Ethan asked.

"Ask Ethan to pick up the book, Tasia."

"Wait, that's it? Can't I ask him to rob a bank or buy me a diamond necklace? I mean, he might pick it up just to entertain me."

"Don't be so full of yourself," Ethan said. "If you want a diamond necklace, ask your new beau."

"Leave him out of this—and for the record, he's not my boyfriend."

"Can you two stop? You're bickering like an old married couple again," Emily said. Her face turned red as three sets of eyes fell on her.

"Sorry," Ethan said.

"Me too," I replied.

"Thanks, Emily. Now concentrate, Tasia, and tell Ethan to pick the book up," Jelena ordered. "Pretend you and he are the only two people who exist in this room, in the coven, in the world. Make him believe that his life depends on him picking up this book."

I concentrated on Ethan's face, trying hard not to focus on Jelena watching me from the left and Emily staring at us on my right.

I steadied my breathing and closed my eyes. The air was still, and Ethan's scent filled the space around me. My body relaxed as I made myself believe that only Ethan and I existed. Together, alone in the room, the building, the city, and finally, the planet. When I knew that to be true, I opened my eyes and looked deep into his. My breath caught as I studied his features. His full, soft lips stole my eyes for a split second. The corner of his mouth turned up, giving me a crooked smile. Fluttering filled my stomach as I pulled myself back to his eyes, focusing solely on him. I breathed in once more.

"Pick up the book."

Nothing happened.

I looked deeper into his eyes. In my head, I repeated, *You are mine, you'll do as I please*, over and over.

"Pick the book up."

This time I could see his pupils get larger, then become smaller. He still didn't move.

"I think this may be a bad idea. Tasia doesn't seem powerful enough," Jelena said, her tone laced with disappointment.

"I can do this," I snapped at her. "I need to clear my head."

My breathing slowed. With my eyes closed, I focused on myself first. My childhood, time with my parents, the rogue vampires I'd killed, my life with Eva and Emily, and the feelings I had for Ethan. I let my vulnerability come through by opening up my heart. With my eyes still closed, my head filled with memories and pictures. My eyes twitched, and my breathing tripled in speed. Drumming filled my skull until it became deafening. Vibrant colors inundated my mind and rainbows churned behind my vision, in and around the memories. Keeping my eyes shut tight, the images became more urgent. My mother, father, Emily, Eva, Ethan, and Austin. The people in my life continued to zip through my head. I was on a roller coaster that was wholly out of control.

I clutched my head as a searing spasm tugged inside it. It spun into a tearing pain, which continued to rip into my head until, finally, there was no more agony. When I opened my eyes, the room looked peculiar. Colors continued to whirl around, but they had muddled together. I realized Ethan's arms were around my aching body, and I saw tears rolling down Emily's cheeks as Jelena whispered a prayer for me.

"Tasi, are you okay?" Emily asked, wiping her tears away.

I blinked a few times and pulled myself away from Ethan. "I'm okay, Em, but that was wild," I mumbled. I was still a little breathless, but I thought I was okay.

"What?" Ethan asked.

"The pain was excruciating, but only for a few seconds. Before that, all my memories flashed before me as if they were holograms—colors and images floated wherever I looked. It was like I was reliving all my memories, speeding through my life. Then, when I thought my head was about to burst, something tore through: clarity." I smiled. "Weirder than that, you three lent me parts of you, which helped me come out of it. Ethan, I had your strength; Em, your love; and Jelena, your faith."

"I don't get it," Emily said.

"Tasia must have just broken open the ability to compel," Jelena said. "In the book, you said it mentioned that only the strongest are able to obtain compulsion. This must be how you gain the ability, and now you need to learn how to control it."

"Yes, and boy, did I break something open. But once it was over, there was nothing but relief."

"Let's try it again," Ethan said.

"I don't know—maybe we should let Tasia rest," Jelena countered.

"No way," I protested. "I feel great. If I didn't know any better, I'd think I could fly." I stretched my arms and let out a laugh.

Jelena watched me as I pleaded a little more. It was almost comical. She was only four human years older than me, but the respect I had for her mirrored what I had for my aunt Eva or any other elder. Well, at least, any other elder I didn't think had a secret agenda, like Sonya.

"Do you really feel all right?" she asked.

I stood up and did a perfect pirouette, causing Emily to snicker.

"Didn't know I could do that, did you?" I laughed.

"Well, I conclude she's fine," Ethan said.

"See? Doctor Ethan thinks I'm fine as well."

"Okay, we can try once more, Tasia, but if it doesn't work, you get some rest," Jelena said.

"Deal. One time."

Back on the bed, Ethan and I faced each other. This time there was no joking or sarcasm. I was there to prove I could do this.

I took a couple deep breaths and pulled Ethan's focus to me. "Pick up the book." Ethan's pupils grew. There was only a tiny trace of brown surrounding the black iridescent eyes that stared back at me. He picked up the book, still looking at me. "Turn to page twenty-five and tell me what the first word is."

He flipped straight to that page and said, "Determined."

"You can stop and forget what you did." Ethan's pupils slowly shrank, and his eyes were a warm brown again. "See, it works."

Ethan looked around. He seemed a little hazy, but he looked unharmed. "Did it work?"

Before I could answer Ethan, a sudden pain raged in my brain. Over and over, the hammering continued, banging so hard my eyes wanted to escape. Finally, after a few more seconds, something exploded in my skull. Liquid ran down my throat and out of my mouth, making me gag. It was my blood, but the sweet, metallic taste I often craved was not what I was gurgling at this moment. This blood was stale and wrong, and I immediately threw up.

Ethan held me as I, barely conscious, continued to spew blood and bile all over the floor. Emily rushed to grab a towel and wipe my mouth.

"Should we take her to the infirmary?" Ethan asked.

"No," I spat out, not knowing if they would understand my voice through the gurgle of blood. "Please, don't. Cameras."

"She's right," Jelena said, grabbing the half-filled water glass from the nightstand. She had me sip it slowly before the blackness took over.

When I woke up, my body was moving gently up and down. A dull ache still pushed against the back of my eyes, tolerable yet annoying. There was a dim light on in the room. Emily was sleeping, and Jelena was no longer in there. I tilted my head up, knowing who I would see. Ethan's eyes watched me as he held me against his body. That undeniable electric pulse between us calmed me.

"Welcome back," he said. "You scared us."

"What happened? Why did that hurt so much?"

"We aren't sure. Jelena is off doing some research, but she thinks that once you released me from your compulsion, you had trouble disconnecting from me and reconnecting with yourself," Ethan said.

"I guess that makes sense. The pain was so bad. I don't know if I want to do that again."

"You don't have to."

"And Emily? Was she freaked out?"

"Emily wouldn't let Jelena or me touch any of the blood you spewed up. She wanted to be the only one responsible for cleaning it, and when Jelena insisted, she told her if she touched it, she'd have to resort to restraining her."

That brought out a giggle.

"Emily sounded so much like you that no one was going to argue with her at that point. Then she pushed to stay up and take care of you. That's when I put my foot down and told her I would stay with you so she could rest. She's a great kid."

Emily continued to prove she didn't need me to take care of her. We were partners in this. She made me proud.

As much as I wanted to stay in Ethan's arms, I knew the longer I rested there, the longer it would take me to recover emotionally. So I sat up and stretched.

"What time is it?" I asked.

"Almost time to get up," he said, still watching me.

"Shouldn't you get going, then? I mean, not that I want you to go. I mean, I'm not trying to get rid of you or imply you aren't wanted, because I do want you." I stopped speaking. "My words aren't coming out correctly."

Ethan's smile grew as he pulled himself up out of bed. "No, you're right, I should get going, but I needed to make sure you were going to be fine."

He pressed his lips to my cheek. His cool breath brushed my skin. "If you're going to be in my life, never scare me like that again."

25

The Day of the Dead. It seemed quite ironic to attend a dance for dead people where most of the guests were undead. While I planned to have fun, I still had my suspicions that Sonya was up to something, so I would keep my eyes open for anything out of the ordinary.

The hall was bustling with caterers and a DJ setting up equipment. Sonya was talking to some of the hired help, and the conversation was intense. I watched her closely, but nothing seemed out of the ordinary with her actions. She appeared to be her bitchy self. Austin was at Sonya's side. He gave me a wink, then focused back on their conversation. A tightness in my chest formed. If he knew what I was doing with Ethan . . . no, Ethan and I were only friends. If I said it enough, it made it true.

It was early evening. The guests would start arriving in about two hours, so I had time to relax. Lizzie snuck up behind me as I headed toward the kitchen, unaware of anyone other than the strange people hustling around.

"Hey," she yelled, catching me mid-yawn.

"Not cool," I choked out.

"Not cool for you, super cool for me."

I gave her a sarcastic smile in return and stretched again. "I need something to eat."

"Just make sure it's human food," she said. My face must have told her how confused I was because she rolled her eyes and said, "You didn't notice them?"

"Notice who?" I asked.

Lizzie shook her head and glanced at two guys carrying in a speaker. "Do you think vampires need two people to carry a speaker?"

"There are humans here?" I asked, watching the two young guys, probably in their mid-twenties, attempt to put the speaker down.

"*Ding, ding, ding!* Someone give this girl an award," Lizzie sang out.

"Whatever. I don't get it, though. Why are humans helping?"

"There is something you may need to know about the way we party." She moved over to the stairs, patting the step next to her. I sat. "There will be humans here tonight, and, well . . ."

"Just say it. Not much can surprise me in this place."

"Fine. There will be vampires and humans interacting. Some will go off and have sex, others will hang out, and others will be available to . . . drink," she said with a huge grin.

"What!" My voice echoed through the hall. I brought it back down to normal level. "How can you? I thought you guys were different."

"We are different," she said. "I didn't want you to be shocked, that's all. So how come I can tell Emily, and she's okay with it, but you get all irrational?"

"Wait—you told my sister that there would be vampires taking unwilling souls out back to have a drink, and she was okay with it?" I asked.

"Maybe that's the part I left out." She gave me a wry smile. "These are all willing participants. If you asked any of them, they all know who we are and enjoy the intimacy they get from being with us."

"What?"

"Just what I said. We don't kill anyone or hurt any of them. It's very intimate. Humans say it's like getting a buzz, and for us, it's like having filet mignon instead of a burger," Lizzie said.

My face must have turned a shade of green because when Emily came out of the kitchen, she stared at me in concern. I observed the humans. They didn't seem uncomfortable about being around vampires. I then watched as Sonya went around to them, introducing herself and shaking their hands. My jaw dropped.

"She told you," Emily said, looking at Lizzie. "I told you I wanted to be around when you told her about the feeding part."

"Oh God, what have you done to my sister?"

Lizzie stood up, watching me closely. She then took a few steps away, leaving me to fend off the horrible visions swirling in my head before glancing back.

"Hey, Tasi? Gotcha." She laughed uncontrollably. "No one will be feeding on anyone. We aren't monsters." Emily joined in on what I slowly realized was a joke on me.

My eyes narrowed, and I stood up. As I walked by Lizzie, I shot her an evil look, only turning around right as I reached the kitchen. "Lizzie, you're lucky I like you. But remember: revenge is a bitch." I gave her a wide grin before heading inside.

Lizzie called out to me, "I can't wait, Tasi. Can't wait." I heard her laughter echoing through the hall as the door swung shut.

Emily followed me into the kitchen, still giggling at my expense. We were alone, and once she realized it, her amusement died.

"So, I was wondering how you're feeling today? You bumped your head pretty hard," she said.

That made me smile. She was clearly doing her best to disguise our conversations when we were out of the safe spots.

"I'm fine. I think the sleep helped. I also think I'll be careful not to do that again," I said. "Did you eat yet?"

"Yes, I had a bagel and an apple about an hour ago."

Picking up the blue mug and the coffeepot, I looked at Emily. "You don't have to stick around, you know." The whole blood thing made her nauseous, and I didn't want to make her uncomfortable.

"It's fine. I need to get used to it," Emily grunted. "My change is coming."

"Yeah, I guess you do. So, where is everyone?" I asked.

"Oh, Ethan, Clover, and Cas are picking up some last-minute supplies. Austin is helping Sonya sort out the guest list, the help, and security. Jelena had her nose buried in a book, and everyone else is getting ready for the dance or out somewhere," she said.

"I'm glad one of us is up to speed." I gulped the crimson liquid out of the mug I'd claimed as mine.

"I do my best."

She filled me in on the rest of the information. All the humans lingering outside were here to stay. They would handle coats, check invitations, and park cars. My back was to the door when I heard it open. Austin sat down beside me, kissing me on the cheek.

"Ready for our date tonight?" He waggled his eyebrows at me, which made me giggle.

"Date?" Emily asked. "When did this happen?"

"Austin wants to take me on my first date." I smiled.

"Aw, that's so sweet. Tasi's *first date ever*," an unpleasant voice joined in the conversation. "Next, you'll say you're a virgin." Clover walked over to the cupboard, back still to me. Cas and Ethan were right behind her. When I sighed, she spun around. "Oh my goodness. You *are* a virgin, aren't you? Well, maybe

Austin will change that for you." She looked me over again, staring me up and down. "Then again, maybe not."

My body trembled as I ignored her snide comments. The dance was starting in a couple hours, and I was looking forward to my date, since it was my first—even if it might be with the wrong guy. Though I was still working on convincing myself Austin was the best path for me.

The pounding started coming through my fingertips as I tried to calm myself. Then, just when I thought I'd lose it, another voice chimed in and shocked us all.

"Clover, seriously, get off her back. All you do is nag on her, and last time I checked, you and I aren't even together. Stop being so petty," Ethan said.

A smile grew on my face as Clover stood there, bewildered.

"Oh, snap," Lizzie said as she entered the kitchen and slithered into the seat next to Emily. "Damn, what did I miss?"

Emily quickly filled her in, and then Lizzie looked at me and mouthed, "Virgin?" Lizzie seemed just as surprised as Clover. I rolled my eyes.

"Petty? You think I'm being petty, Ethan? You have swooned over her since you brought her here. No one else may see it, but I do, and now you're going to throw what we have away for the mutant virgin?" She raised her voice and looked right at me.

"Throw what away? We broke up six months ago. You've somehow had everyone believing we were together when it was convenient for you, until you told people we weren't again—over and over."

"I see how it is. Well, I'm glad we cleared this up," Clover said, clenching her jaw. "You enjoy your virgin half-breed."

All Lizzie looked like she needed was some popcorn to make the show complete for her. Emily shrank in her chair as the conversation got louder, and even though Cas was pretending not to pay attention, I occasionally saw a smile or heard a chuckle. I sent Austin an apologetic look. He shrugged. Austin was always surprisingly understanding in these situations. A pang crept over me at the thought of what I was doing to him.

"You know what, Clover, you really have serious issues. Take a good look. *They* are going on a date tonight. Not Ethan and Tasi—Austin and Tasi. Get over yourself," Ethan said, leaving the room.

Clover stomped away as well. Fury burned behind her eyes. I couldn't very well miss out on that opportunity. I stood up and grabbed her arm before she was out the door. "Hey, I don't think you'll be getting any tonight either. Sorry."

The silence in the room erupted into laughter. Then, without warning, Clover swung at me, but I wrapped my hand around her fist and began crushing it.

"Ow!" she yelped, baring her teeth at me. "Let go."

"I guess you haven't learned anything. So, let's try a repeat lesson. I am and always will be stronger, faster, and smarter than you. Now go to your room, so I don't have to see you for the rest of the night. Got it?"

"Go . . . my room . . . got—" she said, folding under my gaze. Suddenly, something pulled me off her. Well, someone. Clover's eyes and mine had just locked when Emily kicked her chair out and jumped over the table, yanking me away.

Clover shook her hand out as well as her head. Everyone watched as Emily dragged me toward the door. "We need to get ready. Austin, what time are you picking her up?"

Austin stood up, staring at me wide-eyed. He slowly looked to Emily and asked, "One hour?"

"Sounds good. Tasi, move, before you stake her." She was trying to play off the fact that I'd almost compelled Clover, but I was fine now.

Thankfully, the others didn't follow as she pulled me out of the kitchen, through the common area, and toward our room. In the hall, a couple people moved out of the way as we hurried along.

"I'm fine. Really," I said.

"Ethan, go away," Emily said. "Someone will notice you following us."

I hadn't seen him right away, as I was still dazed from what I had almost done. "Act normal and go to your room. I'll pretend to head down to the security office," he whispered.

A few minutes later, we were standing in my room as Emily recapped what I had nearly done.

"Relax, I didn't do anything." I sat on the bed, still feeling a little dizzy.

"You have to control it, Tasi," Ethan insisted. "You saw what it did to you last night. That can't happen again. Plus, you cannot go around compelling vampires."

"At least if we see her doing it, we can stop it. Let's just keep all the people that piss her off away from her," Emily added.

"Might as well keep me in my room, then," I muttered.

Ethan, ignoring my failed attempt at a joke, reached out and touched my face. Then, sliding his fingers under my chin, he lifted it and looked into my eyes. "You look okay. Your pupils are normal. How's the head?"

"A bit foggy, but nothing else," I said, adamant that I was fine.

"You're all right because Emily stopped you. If she hadn't, this would have been bad," he said.

"I guess."

There was a knock on the door. The three of us froze for a moment. Emily took Ethan by the hand and hid him in the closet, keeping as quiet as possible. There was another knock, this one more urgent.

"Tasi, it's me, Austin."

After making sure Ethan was hidden, I opened the door.

"Hey," I said. "Sorry about that. Clover just makes me so mad."

"It's fine. I wanted to check on you. Are you sure you're okay?"

"Yeah, totally good."

"If you're *sure* there is nothing you want to share with me . . . then I'll see you in an hour, beautiful."

"Nope, nothing to share. See you in an hour," I said.

He kissed my hand before leaving. I stuck my head out into the hall and waved to Austin one last time. Ethan stayed hidden for several more moments, in case he returned.

"I think he knows," Ethan said, climbing out from the closet. "Dammit. I'm positive he knows."

"You think? But you were so quiet," I said.

"No, Tasi, he knows you can use compulsion." Ethan rubbed the back of his neck.

"How?" Emily asked.

"He wouldn't come out of his way to check on you if he didn't suspect something. He would have waited until—" The words broke off from his lips. When they returned, they were cold as ice. "Your date. Listen, I'll see you at the dance. Just stay out of trouble, and no more fights."

26

Over the next hour, Emily and I got ready for the party. Emily made an adorable black cat. She had on a bodysuit, which she wore with her Uggs, a black fuzzy tail, and ears. I also helped her paint her face like a cat. Lizzie, who did indeed dress up as a zombie prom queen, came by with Cas, who was dressed up as Dracula. That made me laugh. They offered to wait for me to finish, but Emily reminded them I was waiting for Austin.

The three of them left, leaving me alone to get ready. I slipped into my white minidress before yanking on my white thigh-high stockings and over-the-knee white boots. I was adding the finishing touches when there was a rap at the door.

I opened it and laughed. Standing there was Austin, as handsome as always. He was wearing blue scrubs, white shoes, a medical mask below his chin, and a stethoscope. His eyes took me in and he smiled, taking my hand in his and twirling me around.

"I see I have the right room. I wasn't expecting you to look so racy." He leaned in, kissing my cheek, then pulled one pink rose out from behind his back. He handed it to me before saying, "A date is not a date without a rose. Don't you agree, Nurse Tasi?"

"How did you know I was going to be a nurse?" I asked, eyeing him suspiciously.

"A doctor does not reveal his secrets, my dear." He pulled me in once more, looking deep into my eyes. "Beautiful, smart, and mysterious—everything a guy could ever want."

I reminded myself that I was on a date. I needed to put thoughts of Ethan aside and focus my attention on Austin to help me sort out what I truly wanted. Should I follow my heart and run into Ethan's arms, or should I build on the friendship with Austin and grow that into a happy relationship? I just didn't know. I silenced those thoughts and decided to live in the moment.

"Okay, first, a magician doesn't reveal their secrets, not a doctor, and second—" I paused, moving closer to him, closing the gap between us. "Would you tell me for a kiss? A mind-blowing, my-sensual-lips-pressed-against-yours-while-I-dance-with-your-tongue type of kiss?"

He leaned in, and wrapped his arms around me. "I told Cas to pick up a costume opposite to what you were wearing." He was so close to me when he spoke that his lips were skimming mine. He gingerly pulled me in closer, and we kissed for several minutes.

"Wait," I said, breaking apart from the kiss momentarily. "I think we are doing this wrong. Aren't we supposed to kiss at the end of the date?"

We pulled farther back from each other. I looked into his majestic emerald-green eyes and wiped the lip gloss from his lips with my thumb. He snuck in a kiss as I did this.

"We need to go." He picked up my stethoscope and wrapped it around my neck. "Now. Before I try to keep you here all night and get you out of that outfit." He licked his lips.

He took my hand and led me out. We headed to the party,

giving each other side-glances as we approached the hall. The rhythmic beats got louder and louder the closer we were.

When we reached the door, Austin looked back one final time and said, "Ready? It's your last chance to change your mind and tell me you want to spend the rest of the evening in my arms."

"Come on, goof. I've never been to a party before," I said.

"Okay." He sighed.

We stepped into the hall, where there must have been a hundred people on the dance floor. For the last few weeks, I'd become familiar with the twenty vampires in the coven—I knew all their names, and while many of them had steered clear of Emily and me, they weren't rude or mean—but I barely recognized any of the faces here.

The music pulsating through the hall was catchy. I spotted our friends and dragged Austin over to mingle. They were hanging out with two fresh faces. Lizzie doted over the vampire boy, who was dressed up as a sailor. The outfit outlined each one of his muscles. The other vampire was a girl who looked a lot like the boy who had Lizzie's attention. She was wearing a short sequin dress with delicate black wings. I didn't think she was anything in particular other than beautiful.

Still holding hands, Austin and I wriggled our way into the bunch. Cas and Emily were off to the side. I glanced at her for a long moment, waiting for her to look back at me. She was paler than usual, but with the lack of sleep from trying to take care of me, I brushed it off as her feeling overwhelmed.

"Hey, Tasi, I want to introduce you to some friends of mine." Lizzie took my free hand and pulled me in closer.

Austin gave her the evil eye and whispered in my ear, "Be right back with two drinks." I nodded as he headed off and turned back to the group.

"Tasi, this is Cora and Oliver. They are twins who live in a Brooklyn coven."

"Hi," I said.

"So you're the other dhampyr girl," Cora said snidely.

Oliver sighed. "Where are your manners, Cora?" Then, turning his attention back to me, he said, "Hi, you can call me Ollie. Nice to meet you."

Lizzie looked at me and said, "Twin vampires are rare. When they turn, one frequently kills the other. Usually, the one who completes the change first lives. No one knows why, but that's what they do."

Shock must have filled my face, because Ollie chuckled.

"I'm going to find Clover." Cora's voice still had an icy edge to it. Clover's friend—well, that explained the looks I was getting.

"Don't mind her," Ollie said. "Clover's her best friend."

I gave him a small smile and watched Cora walk away from the group, getting lost in the massive sea of vampires. Emily was nowhere in sight now. "Well, you guys have fun. I need to go find my date, and I want to talk to my sister."

Lizzie shot me a grateful look. But before I could get away, Ollie said, "Austin's your date?"

"Yeah?" It seemed like an odd question. "Why?"

"Austin never dates," he said.

Austin slid in beside me. "That's because I've been waiting for Tasi here to come into my life. I mean, look at her." He pulled my chin up and kissed my forehead. "Ravishing."

Lizzie was making her infamous gagging noises as Austin handed me a drink and wrapped his free hand around my shoulder. I took a small sip. Just what I had thought—it was the same wine from the other night on the roof. I would have to milk this drink.

"Come on." I yanked Austin away so that Lizzie could have some Ollie time. She smiled.

"Where to, Nurse Hot Stuff?" he said, leaning into my ear.

"Emily—I want to make sure she's all right. This is probably a lot to take in. You know, us homeschooled girls spent a lot of time alone. A roomful of people is overwhelming, let alone a roomful of vamps." I leaned back into him, trying hard to drown out the music.

He nodded and pointed upstairs toward the media room. "They went up that way."

We walked up toward the classroom. The music wasn't deafening, but it was loud enough to drown out the words once they left our lips. As we made our way to the stairs, I saw Ethan and Sonya come out of her office. Ethan was joking with her, smiling and laughing.

Austin noticed my eyes on Ethan and leaned in again. "They're closer than you think."

I kept moving. I didn't want to deal with that now. When we entered the media room, Emily looked paler than even a few minutes ago. She and Cas were joking around and laughing. Her mood did not match her looks.

"Emily, are you okay?" I said, sitting down next to her.

"Yes, sort of—I have a small headache," she said, still in good spirits.

"Yeah, this music is kind of distracting," Cas added. "I think we'll all have headaches."

"Are you sure you don't need anything?" I said.

"I said I'm fine. Jeez, Tasi, back off," she snapped. "I'm hungry. Let's eat something. Tasi, you and Austin stay here for a while and pretend you're on a date instead of bugging me."

Watching her stomp off was weird. She was never this rude —that was more my style. And I wasn't the only person who thought it was a little odd, as Cas shrugged at me on the way out.

"That leaves you and me, kid," Austin said, pulling me up from my seat. I wasn't particularly in the mood, but I followed his lead.

I hadn't noticed, but there was a slow song playing. He took my hands and placed them around the back of his neck, standing there looking at me for a few moments. He then put his arms around the small of my back and closed the space between us. He kissed me and, before I could protest, placed my hand in his and twirled me around, bringing me back to him and dipping me. As I hung there, lifting my head toward his face, our noses touched, making me laugh.

"Success—she laughs." He bowed.

"You are too much sometimes."

We finished dancing to the song, then headed back to the party. If we disappeared for too long, everyone would think we were somewhere *getting it on*, and the rumors would start.

When we reached the bottom step, Austin spun me out to the dance floor, and we danced again. It was another slow song. He was an incredible dancer, and the fact that I loved to dance made this date so much better.

"Thanks, Tasi," he said, looking into my eyes when we paused. "You have changed me into a better person. I think about you all the time, and I even seem to dream about you more often than I'd like to admit."

I laid my head on his chest, but he pulled me back again.

"What is it?" I asked.

"I just want to look at you a little longer. You captivate me." He was pulling me into another kiss when someone hard-faced and dressed in black stepped up to us.

I jumped. "Ethan?"

"What do you want?" Austin asked, gripping me a little tighter.

"Sonya needs you, and she said it's urgent."

"Fine." He directed his next question to me. "Want to come along?"

"Sure," I said with hesitation. I wasn't really sure if Sonya would want me tagging along.

"Yeah, she wants to see you alone," Ethan said.

Austin said nothing but gave Ethan a *what are you up to* look. "Fine, I'll be right back." He purposely put his body between Ethan's and mine as he planted a soft kiss on my lips. Then, turning back to Ethan, he smirked.

Once Austin was out of earshot, Ethan looked at me. "He's searching. Be careful."

"What are you talking about?"

"He's looking for any sign of compulsion, which is why he wants to stare into your eyes," he said.

"You're crazy. Is it too hard to believe that Austin likes me?"

"Stop being so naive," Ethan grumbled.

Staring at Ethan, I decided it was time to ignore him. I looked for another familiar face to talk to. I wasn't in the mood to listen to how stupid he thought I was. As I scanned the room, Ethan noticed. He walked away, letting out a sigh.

A tall vampire strolled over and put his arm around me. He wore a black outfit with a white ruffled shirt that peeked through the top of his vest, and the cape he had on was velvet, black on top and red underneath. I knew what his costume was the instant I saw the white mask covering half his face: Erik, or the Phantom, from *The Phantom of the Opera*.

"You look lost, little girl," he said.

"No, waiting for my date," I replied, ignoring him as politely as I could.

"As beautiful as you are, he shouldn't have left you alone." He then pulled me in so close, I could feel his icy breath on my neck. I pictured myself yanking a stake out of my boot, killing the vampire, then getting killed by the other ninety-nine vamps in the room. That wasn't what happened, though. Instead, Ethan pushed him so hard he flew across the room, gliding on the hardwood floor. He only stopped because the wall made him.

"Are you okay?" Ethan touched my neck, making sure there was no blood. We both looked back at the guy, who looked to be unconscious.

"I'm fine. You saved that toad's life as well as mine," I said with a smile. He looked at me curiously. "I was about to stake him." I pulled the stake up out of my boot, showing Ethan the top.

"Really, Tasi?" He looked at me, disapproving.

I shrugged. "I don't leave home without them." That made him smirk. "While you're here, want to dance?"

"And get on Austin's bad side?" He thought about it for a moment. "Oh yeah, I definitely want to dance with you."

Taking me in his arms, he twirled me around—even more gracefully than Austin had, which was shocking. When he pulled me back to him, his vanilla-woodsy scent tickled my nose, giving me goose bumps as he spoke.

"You look beautiful tonight. Costume or not, you're always so beautiful, Tasi."

That was when Austin yanked Ethan away from me.

"What are you doing?" Austin sneered at Ethan.

"Relax—I don't want her," Ethan said.

Ouch. Even though I knew he didn't mean it, my heart tumbled into my stomach.

"Romeo, on the floor over there, almost sank his teeth into her neck." He stood a little closer to Austin. "And between you and me, she's not so bright. So make sure she keeps those stakes hidden."

Austin turned his attention to me and smiled. "Is this true? You were going to stake one of us in a room *full* of us?"

"Yup, without delay." I scowled.

"You are one badass chick, Killer."

Ethan grunted something and walked off. I tried not to watch him go by focusing on Austin.

27

After dancing for what seemed like hours, Austin and I headed over to the kitchen to get refreshments. My eyes moved to Lizzie and Ollie, who were getting pretty cozy on the dance floor. Looking beyond them, I noticed how amazing everyone looked. Between all these strangers being gorgeous and their costumes so elaborate, it felt like I was walking through a very high-end fashion show.

The kitchen was empty, which made me happy. Austin stepped over to the fridge and poured a couple glasses of blood. He had lost the top part of his costume while dancing and was now sporting a fitted white tee. I had no objections. His black hair, which he had slicked back, was back to being disheveled, and his eyes were bright and focused on me, the way I was on him.

"What are you thinking?" he said.

I broke our gaze, remembering what Ethan had said. I didn't want to believe it, but what if he was right? "I'm thinking about how sweet you are to me."

"'Sweet'? That's a new one. Try not to ruin my reputation

with this talk of sweetness, Killer. I'm supposed to be the hot bad boy."

We were laughing when Cas burst into the kitchen with such force I thought the door would go flying off the hinges.

"Tasi, it's Emily." Before he could tell me what was wrong, I jumped over the table.

"Where is she?"

"Dorm room."

I took off running. Lizzie was still on the dance floor with Ollie, but I could see her mood shift as I pushed through people.

When I reached our room, Emily was lying bundled up under her covers.

"Emily!" I ran to her bedside.

"I told Cas not to bother you," she said before coughing so severely, she spit up a little blood into the garbage can.

That's when I knew what was going on. "It's happening." My voice was hoarse.

"'Happening'?" Her teeth began chattering.

I yanked the blankets off my bed and threw them on top of her.

"Cas, go find some more blankets. Austin, go to the infirmary and grab a thermometer, the strongest painkillers you can find, and an IV." Neither of them questioned my orders, they just ran out the door.

"Am I really transitioning?" Emily asked. Her bottom lip quivered.

I felt for her. I knew what it was like to go through this. When it happened to me, Emily was eight, and Eva wouldn't let her see me. The part I remembered most was feeling like I'd been attached to a torture device that stretched my body. The pain that was going to run through her would make her wish she would pass out.

"Yes, Emily, this is it. I'll take care of you, okay? But this won't be pleasant." I touched the side of her face, which was a raging inferno.

"Tasi, please don't let me die."

My heart plunged into my stomach at hearing her plea. I didn't know what to say. I knew I couldn't make that promise. I knew I could do everything right and still lose her. The only thing I could do was give her hope.

"You'll be okay, Emily."

She tried responding, which brought on another coughing fit. I was sitting on the edge of the bed, rubbing her back, when Lizzie ran into the room.

"Emily! Is she going to be all right?" Lizzie rushed over. "Can I help?"

"Actually, can you grab a pitcher of water?" I asked.

A few minutes later, Jelena entered with Ethan. "Do you need us to do anything? We ran into Lizzie and she told us about Emily," she said.

"I think we're good." I turned back to them, and a single tear rolled down my cheek. Jelena rushed over to the other side of Emily's bed and pulled up a chair. Religion wasn't part of something we grew up with, but right now, listening to Jelena whisper her prayers, I could do nothing but hope it helped.

Ethan came over to my side and placed his hand on my shoulder. "Emily is strong, Tasi."

I pressed my lips into a thin line. I knew she was strong, but was that enough to survive this change? That was what terrified me. My eyes met his, and they were empty. I thought back to Ethan's haunted face when he'd mentioned his sister's death from the change. He was standing by me now, but I wondered if being here was breaking his heart again.

"Blankets and water." Cas and Lizzie entered the room together.

I threw another blanket over Emily's shuddering body.

"Tasi, I'm sorry for snapping at you earlier."

"Stop, it doesn't matter. I love you, and all that matters is that you get better, and that you survive this. I know you will, Emily." I tried to sound reassuring, but I'm not sure I pulled it off, based on the sound of my shaky voice.

Her eyes still searched mine for assurance, and when she confirmed I wasn't lying, she acknowledged me with a smile. That was until she let out an ear-piercing scream. Jelena held Emily's hand tightly.

"Cas, find Austin and the medical supplies, now."

He bolted out of the room. I hadn't even noticed Ethan leaving, but he brought Jelena a bowl with cool water and a rag. She dabbed it along Emily's forehead. I gave him a grateful smile as I knelt next to her bed, trying my hardest to keep her calm. A crackling and popping noise came from under the covers. She screamed again as Austin ran into the room.

"Hook up the IV—she needs constant hydration. Were there any pain meds?" I asked.

"Yes, I found a morphine drip," he said as he hooked everything up.

"Oh, that's perfect." I grabbed the thermometer and placed it on Emily's head. "She's seven degrees above her normal temp."

Emily continued to shiver uncontrollably, but when Austin finally finished hooking up the IV and drip, I saw her body ease a little. I knew the medication was working.

Over the next hour, Emily fell asleep. Cas went out to round up the blood we would need for the last day, and Lizzie and Jelena offered to stay with Emily while I checked out the infirmary for more supplies. We would need a lot more fluids and morphine to make it through the next few days.

"I'll get Sonya and meet you at the infirmary," Ethan said.

The infirmary was colder than usual; it made my cheeks burn. I wasn't sure when I'd started to cry, but I noticed it now. Austin was with me. He took my hand and pulled me closer to him.

"Hey, she's going to be all right," he said.

He didn't know if everything would be okay. There was no way to know.

I stared at my boots as he closed the space between us.

"You aren't alone in this. I'm here to help." He looked into my tear-ridden eyes. "You're stronger than this. You'll have to be for Emily."

He was right. I wiped away my tears before taking in a deep breath.

In came Ethan and Sonya, and I stepped away from Austin.

"How's Emily?" Sonya asked.

"She's fine right now, but she's in a lot of pain. We need more morphine. There isn't enough to last through tomorrow."

"Ethan or Austin will run out first thing tomorrow and get some," she said. "Anything else?"

"Yes, she needs to be left alone. Lizzie and Jelena offered to take turns watching her with me. Everyone else needs to stay away unless I tell them it's okay. This is going to take a lot out of her, and she needs calm."

My eyes stayed on hers for a moment. Ethan interrupted my gaze.

"How many days should we get pain medicine for?"

I dragged my eyes to him, which desperately tried to tell me to be careful. He knew my emotions were all over the place, and he probably thought I would lose it and start compelling everyone around me.

"Get enough for a week to be safe. I need to get back to her," I said. "And thank you for all the help."

"Whatever you need," Sonya said, leaving the room flanked by Ethan, who shot me one last look of concern.

Austin came up and touched my hand. "That's the Killer I know and love. Let's get you back to your sister."

Did he say *love*? He couldn't possibly mean that. But why

would he say love? I couldn't think about that right now, so I nodded and headed back to the room, my mind whirling.

Stopping at my door, I listened to see if any noises were coming from the room, but all was silent.

"Thanks, Austin. Thanks for being there for me whenever I need you."

"Well, that's what people do when they love someone." Austin pulled me into a hug. "If you need anything for Emily or yourself, call me. I'll be here."

"You're an amazing guy."

"Only because you're an amazing girl." He kissed me on my forehead.

"Go enjoy the rest of the party." I pushed my hand against his chest. "Sorry about the date."

"First, I will start cleaning up. The party is dwindling. Second, don't be sorry, love. It's only postponed. We'll do this again once everything gets back to normal. Once your sister is better, okay? This time, though, we'll do it right: limo, dinner, Broadway show."

I wasn't sure there would be a next date, but this wasn't the time to tell him that, nor was it the time to make any decisions on my confused love life. Emily needed my full attention.

He graciously bowed and headed off toward the hall.

28

Emily lay there, her breathing steady, as I double-checked the IV. It had been a few days of monitoring her every hour. Lizzie had been camping out in our room since Emily's change began. Her concern for Emily tugged at my heart. She tried staying up with me, but failed miserably, so I left her asleep in my bed while I sat by Emily's side with my head buried in my hands.

"Tasi," Emily said, her voice hoarse. Her hand slowly reached out to touch my face as I looked up at her.

"Hey, Squirt, don't try moving. Do you need anything?"

"No, I'm just glad you're here," she said. Lizzie stirred in my bed. "Who's over there?"

"Lizzie. She was worried about you. We have shifts set up between Jelena, Lizzie, and me. So if I'm gone, it won't be for too long, and I'll be close by," I said. "Is that okay?"

"Yes, I trust you to do what's best." Emily coughed.

"Okay, no more talking. You rest. It'll be over soon enough." I tried my best to comfort her as she drifted off again. Saying it would be over soon enough meant . . . what, really? Over as in she'd survive, or over as in she was going to die. I continued to weigh both outcomes in my head. There was no in-between in this situation. My sister would either make the change, or she'd die.

There was a quiet knock, and I heard Jelena outside talking to someone. When I opened the door, she was standing there with Ethan.

"What's going on?" I asked.

"We need to talk, and not in front of Emily. Ethan can fill you in. I'll stay here," she said.

Ethan wasn't looking at me. "We can go in my room. No one's there."

"You two figure it out. I'm going to see Emily. I'll make sure she is well taken care of."

We headed to his room, which was about half the size of mine, but then, it was a room for one. He had a full-size bed in the middle of the space, and to the left was a wall of bookshelves filled with a rainbow of books. A big comfy chair sat in the room's corner.

"Wow, have you read all of these?" I ran my hand along the book bindings.

"Most of them, but some I haven't gotten around to yet."

"It's an impressive collection. Maybe one day I can read them." I turned back to him. "So, what's going on? Jelena made it sound like it was important."

"Your blood's gone. Jelena said she stopped by Sonya's office to ask where your blood was because she thought if she did some testing, maybe something in the results would help Emily through the transition. Sonya told her the blood was gone and she hasn't told anyone yet because she's trying to track it down or see if it got into the hands of the Deity."

"What! That's not supposed to happen. We were the only ones who knew where it was, and Sonya promised me it was safe, or she would come after our heads."

I was emotionally overloaded, but I couldn't stop the anger flooding through me now. Ethan looked at me as if he knew the news of my missing blood would trigger something. He tried to put his arm around me, but that didn't happen.

I took off before he could stop me and scrambled into the main hall. Fury must have filled every feature in my face because anyone who was in my way moved as I passed. I grumbled under my breath over and over as I headed to Sonya's office. Not even a freight train could stop me. Ethan gripped my arm.

"Stop, Tasi. Don't do this right now. Think of Emily," he said.

Ethan's words lingered in my head. Emily needed me, and needed me to be safe. As angry as I was, I wouldn't put her in danger.

"Ethan, I am thinking of her. If someone finds out about our blood, or it gets into the wrong hands, it will be open season on dhampyr girls. No bloodsucker will want us alive, knowing our blood could be the cause of their death." I yanked my arm out of his grip. "Sonya won't kill me, 'cause I'll kill her first. So I'm still going into this office. Please don't follow me or try to stop me."

Then, the door opened, and Sonya stood there staring at us. She might have heard the entire conversation.

"Come in." Her voice was cold, her face humorless, as if we were about to be put in our place. "Both of you."

I stomped into the room and crossed my arms tightly over my chest. Ethan slumped forward as he stepped through the doorway. He looked at me with irritation in his eyes.

"Where's my blood? You said it was safe. You lied."

"Hello to you too, Tasia," Sonya said as she sat down in her chair. "Both of you, sit down, please."

Ethan didn't hesitate as he sat in the chair across from Sonya. I faltered for a few moments before following her simple direction. You know me; anything to be complicated.

"How about you explain yourself?" I said.

Ethan shook his head.

"Because of your emotional state, I am going to ignore your poor manners and bad attitude. I am not sure what you have heard, but your blood is safe. It was sent out for testing to someone I trust more than Jelena, or anyone, for that matter."

"Are you lying?"

"Careful, Tasi."

"Now is not the time to be careful," I said.

Her lips were pursed as she took me in. She let out a long breath. "I understand we had agreed Jelena would handle the testing, but plans changed. I had an opportunity to have someone test your blood who has a previous blood sample from when you were younger. I didn't share this information with anyone because there was no need to. When I receive results, we can then discuss any findings, including comparing them to your results from when you were younger," she said. "If you had asked me, I would have told you what I am telling you now."

"But—"

"You need to put all this energy into caring for Emily. Your blood can wait."

Before I could jump down her throat, Ethan stepped in. "But we were told someone did come to you and asked about it, and you said it had been stolen."

"If that someone was Jelena," Sonya said, "she must have misunderstood when I told her I did not need her to test the blood, days ago, or she blatantly lied to you. Don't worry, I will discuss this matter directly with Jelena. I am not sure why she would rile you up this way."

Ethan and I looked at each other. I was becoming more and more confused as this conversation continued.

"Okay, so Jelena was mistaken. So then, where is my blood?"

"You're not listening. It's with someone I trust. She picked it up the night of the dance. It was the perfect time to hand it off to an ally without anyone being suspicious or knowing who is helping us. It has been with her ever since."

I knew there was something up with that dance. "So the dance was a ruse to keep us preoccupied while you went ahead and handed off my blood."

"Trust me, Tasia, no one wants to keep that blood safe more than I do. Do you think I want to start some major outbreak if it falls into the wrong hands, or have two dhampyr girls under my care go missing or end up murdered? No, Tasia, I don't. It would be best if you took down whatever wall you have put up with me before someone gets harmed. I wouldn't hurt you or Emily."

She had a point. From what I knew of Sonya, she was in favor of keeping the species safe. I couldn't see her selling my blood on the black market to make a buck or two when she had everything.

"Fine, I believe you. If you say it is safe, it's safe."

"Thank you, Tasia. I appreciate your trust in this matter. I promised to keep you informed, and I plan on keeping my promise."

Ethan stared at me in disbelief, but quickly reverted his face to indifference. "Okay, so this is settled," he said.

"Almost. Tasia and I have settled our business. She knows my door is always open to her, and that she can come to me with whatever questions or accusations she may have. Even if the accusation has no backing." She stared straight at Ethan, no longer even acknowledging I was in the room. "But you and I need to talk."

The discussion from the coffee shop of what would happen if Sonya knew Ethan was helping me played in my head. "Please, Sonya, he was trying to protect my sister and me," I blurted out, briefly pulling her attention.

"Tasia, you go. Ethan, you stay."

"But—"

Ethan turned to me and placed his hand over mine. "Go,

Tasi. I can handle myself." He looked at me, digging into my eyes for understanding. "You'll make it worse. Please go."

There was a bang on the door. I leaped for it as Sonya and Ethan stood. Lizzie fell to the floor as the door opened, tears in her eyes, hands shaking uncontrollably.

"It's Emily."

29

My shoes pounded against the floor, and vamps scurried out of my way as I barreled through the main hall. Upon entering the room, I saw Emily lying in a pool of crimson liquid. The sight of the scarlet blood flowing out of her mouth, her eyes, and trickling down her cheeks made me wince. That didn't happen to me. I turned to her IV and realized it was no longer in her arm. She was choking and thrashing around uncontrollably.

"Ethan, help!"

He held her arms down long enough for me to insert the IV again. The morphine slowly seeped into her body. Within a few minutes, a calmness came over her. The flailing stopped, but the coughing did not.

"Prop her on her side so she can spit out the blood," Ethan said.

Sonya and Lizzie stood there. Lizzie was crying like a child.

Finally, Emily completely relaxed. The coughing subsided, and her body eased as the bleeding stopped. I wiped the blood from her face and watched her as she continued to settle down. That's when I noticed her length. She had grown what looked like four inches, which meant the change was almost over. If it was anything like mine, I remembered feeling rejuvenated after. Ethan and I rolled her onto her back again, and I tucked her hair behind her ears. He was straightening out her blankets when I noticed her neck.

Less than two seconds passed from when I was sitting next to Emily to when I had Lizzie up against the wall, my stake inches from her heart. She yelped in pain as the tip burned into her skin.

"What are you doing, Tasi?" Lizzie screamed.

"What happened? Where is Jelena, and why was Emily left alone? Did you do that to her?"

No one existed in the room at that moment except for Lizzie and me. That was, until Sonya and Ethan began jerking me off her. Sonya, who was stronger than me, pushed me back against the wall before grasping my hand that held the stake and slamming it over and over again. Finally, the stake fell to the ground.

"Calm down, Tasia. Attacking Lizzie will not get you the answers you seek," Sonya said.

I turned my focus on Sonya, and my voice dripped with venom as I growled, "You don't get it. Someone tried to kill Emily. Look." I strode over to her, glancing once at Ethan and Lizzie on my way, then pulled her blankets down to show her neck. Her skin was bright red with what looked like burns, and blue and deep purple marks were forming in a perfect half circle around her neck. "Her IV didn't come out. Someone wrapped it around her neck!"

Ethan stepped back, still holding Lizzie. "What happened, Lizzie? I know you didn't do this."

She was shaking her head back and forth. The girl I knew to be a kick-ass, sarcastic jokester was as docile as a day-old kitten.

"I didn't. I would never . . ." Lizzie began with a quivering voice.

Finally, Sonya stepped forward. "Calm down, Lizzie, and tell us what happened."

Lizzie sat on the bed next to Ethan.

"I woke up and found Jelena sitting next to Emily, holding her hand. I asked her where Tasi was, and she said she had to talk to Ethan about something." Her eyes focused only on Sonya as she spoke. A sob escaped her lips every few words. "I waited for Tasi, to see if she needed me to do anything, but Jelena turned to me and told me I didn't need to stick around. I told her I had nothing better to do because Austin and Cas had already left to get more morphine, and I preferred to wait for Tasi. She then asked if I could get some more warm water and fresh towels. I thought it'd be okay because she had been alone with Emily before. When I came back, Emily was choking uncontrollably, and the IV was strung around her neck. I pulled it off and ran to get Sonya because I didn't know where you were."

Fresh tears streamed down her face, leaving bright red marks along the way. "I'm so sorry, Tasi."

Ethan said nothing, only nodded toward Sonya and bolted out, almost as if they had an understanding.

I sat on the side of Emily's bed and buried my face in my hands. "I'm sorry, Lizzie. I lost control and overreacted. All I could see was that Emily was hurt."

Lizzie sat next to me at the foot of Emily's bed and wrapped her arms around me. "It's okay, Tasi. I know what she means to you. I wouldn't let anyone harm her. I'm so sorry for not being here."

"No, it's me who should be sorry for that. I should've been here, not losing my temper over something stupid," I grumbled.

Ethan was back in a few minutes—without Jelena. "She's gone."

"What do you mean, she's gone?" Sonya's voice was bitter.

"I checked her room. It was empty, so I ran to the security room and examined the main camera. While we were in your office, she escaped through the front door and straight into a black van. I recognized the driver from the fight we had with the humans in the alley," Ethan said.

The Deity.

My face must have shown a multitude of colors—baby pink, bright pink, tomato red, and then fiery red as the heat rose within me, getting hotter and hotter as what Jelena had done settled in my stomach. "I am going to hunt her down and kill her. I'll rip her throat out and watch as she slowly heals herself and then do it again, body part after body part."

Sonya walked over and knelt in front of me with kindness on her face. "We'll find Jelena, Tasia, and she will pay, but you can't go starting a full war when you need to be here with Emily. She's going to need you more than ever, and I don't think you should leave your room until she finishes her change."

Sonya was the voice of reason, and I forced myself to calm down and listen. "Fine, but if you find her, I want to be there." My voice was still trembling, hot with anger.

Sonya acknowledged my request, and before heading out of the room, she addressed all of us. "One more thing: what happened here stays between us. I do not care who they are and how close they are to you. I need to figure out what is happening and decide how to handle this."

On her way out, Lizzie turned back to me. "Tasi, can I come back after I clean up? I want to help with Emily, if that's okay."

Today's events had me drained. All I wanted was to forget everything. The problem was that I knew it would be fresh in my mind for days to come. "Sure, Lizzie, I would like that. If you want to bring over sleeping bag, you can stay the night. The company would be nice. And again, I'm really sorry."

"It's okay." As Lizzie left, Austin came running in.

"Are you okay?" he asked, pulling me into his arms tightly. "All I heard was Emily was coughing up blood."

I watched as Ethan, who had been waiting to talk to me, left.

I didn't want him to go, but I knew pushing away Austin would be a bad idea right now.

"Yeah, she's resting. Somehow, the IV came out. Lizzie was here, thankfully, and ran and got me while I was with Sonya," I said. "Now I'll stay with her until she's done. I think the change is almost complete."

"If there is anything I can do, let me know. I mean it, Tasi. I know you like to take care of everything yourself, but I'm here for you. No need to do it alone." Tears filled my eyes. He ran his finger across the corner of one of them, urging the tears pooling there to run silently down my cheek. He wiped them away and brought me into his arms. I appreciated his offer, but the last time I'd trusted someone to help me, it almost cost me my sister.

30

The next couple days consisted of me taking care of Emily. I wouldn't even leave her side to shower. Luckily, I had Lizzie. There were no hard feelings, and she stayed with me, helping me out as much as she could. I filled her in on Jelena and the Deity, on how our blood in the wrong hands could be a dangerous weapon against vampires, and how if vampires caught wind of it, we might end up dead because we were a liability. She was sympathetic, and we bonded over those two days, becoming closer than before. Lizzie even offered to leave the coven with me if Emily and I ran.

Outside of Lizzie, I refused to see anyone except Sonya. Not even Ethan or Austin. I needed a clear head. Sonya had been coming to see us daily, giving me updates about what had happened with Jelena.

Jelena had sided with the Deity. She'd been working undercover for a long time, and when she'd found out two dhampyr girls might be coming to Sonya's coven, she took advantage of their relationship and transferred. The meek girl who sat in the back of the hall reading and learning had been plotting and scheming.

The conversation about her religious fervor came back to me. She must have hated being a damned creature, and living among the same people who took her life from her. To me, it gave her no excuse to do what she did. I agreed that vampires were unnatural, blood-drinking creatures of the night, but so was I. As much as I tried to separate myself from them, I couldn't. We both drank blood. Maybe I couldn't take it directly from a human, but it was still blood. We both had super strength, incredible grace, and sharp senses. And all the vampires I had met along the way that didn't attack me had wanted the same thing as me: to be accepted.

When Sonya came in for her daily visit, she sat down to talk. Lizzie graciously waited in the hall, giving us some space.

"So, any news?" I asked.

"No, my guess is they are keeping her on lockdown at their facility to keep her safe. I contacted the coven I told you about, the one with the intel on the Deity, and told them to keep an eye out for her. I kept the details to a minimum and told them we caught her spying, so she is now on their fugitive list," she said.

As much as I wanted to be the one to kill her, I didn't care right now—I just wanted her dead.

"Everything she told me was a lie, wasn't it? How you didn't want me to learn anything about dhampyr transitions, or how you asked her to lie to me about certain information, and how she asked you about the blood and you told her someone stole it?" I sighed.

"You guess right. Tasia, I know we haven't seen eye to eye this entire time, but I stand true to my word—I won't lie to you." She caught my eye. It was the first time in a while that I had looked at her face in great detail. The dark eyes and brown hair, the thin lips and full eyebrows, even the skin tone—it all reminded me so much of someone. But before I could say anything, she continued, "I wanted to add—on the day she told you about the blood going missing, when she attacked Emily, I checked all the video cameras for the previous week. She was in the infirmary looking for your blood the same day I told her I no longer needed her to test it. I had moved it into my office to keep it close. She knew it was gone days ago, but she waited to say something to you."

"So her trying to kill Emily was all because she couldn't get my blood? That doesn't seem like Jelena. We must be missing something."

"Maybe, but I'm not sure what her intentions with Emily would have been. The only thing I can think of is that ending Emily's life would give the vampires a disadvantage because we would no longer have two dhampyrs to learn from. This entire thing is my fault. I should have questioned Jelena's intentions. She only ever came to me when she wanted to discuss your blood, but I never would have thought she was working with the Deity. I just thought she was overzealous . . ." Sonya's brow furrowed.

"It's no one's fault but Jelena's. Plus, if she had gotten a hold of my blood, it would be in the Deity's possession now, and they might have been able to figure out how to mutate it into some sort of virus. Sonya, I swear she'll pay. One question—in searching her room, did you find a dhampyr book? I want to finish reading it."

"I'm not sure. Ethan and Austin stripped her room down looking for any clues, but neither of them found anything they thought was worth mentioning."

"I can ask them."

"Again, if you need anything, please find me. If you trust only one of us, let that person be me. I'll let nothing happen to you or your sister." Her voice was commanding and strong.

In that moment, I realized I did trust her—and that's when our relationship truly began. It was a connection I thought could never be possible with Sonya, but the leader everyone feared was attentive and caring toward us. If I would have let my guard down earlier, none of this may have happened.

Emily shifted in her bed. "Tasi?"

I ran to her side, my heart pounding against my chest, and took her hand. "I'm right here."

"She tried to kill me." Tears formed in both of our eyes as I thought of the terror Emily had endured.

"I know, Em, and when I catch her, I'll kill her, painfully and slowly," I grumbled.

"No, Tasi, she's dangerous. She told me she would stop at nothing..." Her voice trailed off as she coughed.

"It's okay, Em. Let's talk about this when you're better."

Just as the words left my lips, her eyes rolled to the back of her head, and she began gasping for air as if she was choking. Then, her lips changed color, first to gray, then to blue. It was happening so quickly that I seemed to move in slow motion compared to her.

"This is it, Lizzie. Blood!" I called through the door.

Lizzie, who had been waiting in the hall, was ready for what came next. We'd preplanned who would do what as Emily finished the transition. We needed two pints of blood—one that Lizzie would stick into the IV, pumping it into her veins, and one that I ripped open and poured directly into her mouth.

I lifted her head and slid behind her as she continued to gasp. "Please be strong enough. I can't do this without you," I mumbled as I pressed the bag to her lips and forced the red liquid down her throat. I remembered going in and out of consciousness when Eva did this for me. The blood had dripped inside me, slimy and cold.

Lizzie ran back to where the blood was, grabbed another pint, and placed it next to the bed for when Emily fully woke up.

"Thanks," I said.

"Anything else?" she asked.

"Yeah, go grab some towels."

"Got it." She scrambled to the door.

I focused back on Emily, pressing more and more blood against her lips, forcing her to take it in. Her breathing still seemed strained, but it was at least a steady pace now. I watched as the color, which had drained from her face, slowly returned. When I wiped the blood from her lips, I saw the pink hue filling back into them. Only the corners of her lips were now blue. Her eyelids fluttered open, and her big aqua eyes stared at me.

"Tasi?" Her voice, still a little hoarse, sounded so much better than it had for days.

"Welcome back, Em," I said. Tears streamed down my face. In the last few days, I think I'd cried enough to fill a bathtub, maybe two.

She slowly sat up. When she glanced at the IV, she frowned. "Was that necessary?"

"Yes. It's so great to have you back. Not knowing if you would make it through the transition—I never want to go through that again," I said.

"Me either." She mustered out a wholehearted laugh as I handed her a cup filled to the brim with blood. "Down the hatch, I guess."

"Down the hatch." I watched Emily as she carefully gulped down the crimson liquid.

"Not bad, though it has quite the metallic bite to it. I can get used to this."

I laughed as she finished the cup. She survived. She was strong enough.

Sonya and Lizzie watched as Emily returned to herself. Relief flooded the room, and the two of them smiled at her.

"Welcome back, Em," Lizzie said. There was so much relief in her expression, and I wondered if she would have held herself responsible if Emily had died.

"Yes, welcome back. How do you feel?" Sonya asked.

"I'm fine. Actually, I feel great."

"That's wonderful," said Sonya.

"Um, Tasi? Can we talk a minute?" Emily looked lost.

I knew where she was going with this. Before she'd changed over, we didn't trust Sonya, and Lizzie had been oblivious to what was going on. Now they were here, in the thick of it.

They started to leave, but I told them to wait a minute.

"Is it because of Jelena?" I asked quietly. Emily's eyes were still on the two of them, clearly unsure of what had happened or how to answer. "If yes, it's okay. They know it all. We were wrong about Sonya, and well, Lizzie probably saved your life when she untangled you from the IV."

"Let me shut the door," Sonya said in a kind voice. I was still getting used to the sweetness she was exuding lately. Of course, I figured that would change once things returned to normal.

"Do you want to talk about what happened so soon?" I asked, watching her for any sign that I needed to kick everyone out and let her rest.

"Yes, I'm okay," she claimed. "There isn't much to tell. I remember Jelena and her hands around my neck, then when I started moving around, she grabbed the IV and used that." She paused a moment, and I slid my hand into hers, knowing it would calm her down. She gave me a warm smile. "Then she took my blood and ran out of the room, leaving me here to die. She may think I'm dead, for all I know."

"She took your blood?" I said. Of course she took her blood. "How did I not think about that? When she couldn't find my blood in the vault, she decided to get the Deity what they wanted while you were incapacitated. Oh, I'm so going to kill her."

"The Deity?" Emily's eyes widened.

"Jelena was lying to us the entire time. She was working for them," I said.

"Oh." Emily took this all in with a new understanding. "Am I going to be the reason vampires become extinct?"

Before I could answer, Sonya moved in closer. "No, Emily, I don't think the blood you had within your body at the time had enough vampire blood in it to do anything."

"What do you mean?" I asked.

"Think about it—for the first thirteen years of your life, outside of the agility, you were mostly human, with a normal, healthy appetite for human food only, normal growth, and nothing that showed you had vampirism in you." She paused. "Now, look at Tasia, who underwent her first transition five years ago. She can easily match a vampire in a fight. She craves blood, but can still eat small amounts of food. Her blood makeup is more advanced, as is yours now. I think what Jelena took from you, since it was before your transition completed, won't be enough to work with."

"Are you sure about that?" I asked, still baffled about our genetics. "I mean, how do you know that for sure?"

"I was waiting for Emily to wake up to talk about this together." She glanced at Lizzie.

"I'll get Emily some food. Be right back," Lizzie said.

My attention fell back on Sonya.

"I received a call from the person testing your blood. As I said before, she had a sample from when you were younger, and she tested the new sample against the old. Your blood now is truly half-vampire, half-human. The other sample showed you as eighty percent human, twenty percent vampire."

I sat on the bed, taking in the information. "I never asked before, but how does this person have an old sample?"

"Your mother sent it to her when you were young. No one knew what you were, and they used it to find out whether or not you were human." Sonya's words were cautious as she laid this on me.

Emily decided it was her turn to speak up now. "She went

through the second change; I think they call it the mind transition. Do you think her blood is different now?"

I glared at Emily, not to be mean, but I wasn't fond of the way she was offering me up as a guinea pig.

"Is this true? If it is, you can compel," Sonya said.

"I should have known you would know all about that," I said.

"Yes. How are the headaches?" she asked.

"Painful."

"We can work on it later, but for now, we should probably take a break and let Emily rest."

"I need to get out of bed and stretch my legs," Emily said, squirming her way off the bed and moving her feet to the floor. She wiggled her toes as if it was the first time she had ever seen them.

I no longer needed to look down at Emily. My little sister now stood as tall as I did. She looked less like a child now that she was almost five-foot-eight. Even her facial features looked less round and more defined. I bet at a fast glance, she could be mistaken for me.

She strode over to the mirror, as graceful as a gazelle. She pulled at her features, smiling at herself, occasionally letting out soft giggles that reminded me of her actual age. She stared down at her pajama bottoms and then frowned slightly. I caught her expression and laughed a little. She eyed me through the mirror, giving me an exasperated look.

"I don't know why you're laughing," she said. "It's your clothes I'll steal now that I don't fit into mine."

31

Before leaving, Sonya asked us to meet her in her office before bedtime. It must not be great news, because she always relayed the lousy kind before bed—maybe so we could sleep on it. We agreed, then headed toward the kitchen. I desperately needed a refreshment, since I had barely eaten in the last few days.

When we entered, stares and gasps trickled out from the onlookers. Once they were over the initial shock, I heard whispers as the vampires scattered like cockroaches. Lizzie and Ethan were sitting there, clearly relieved to see Emily doing so well. I grabbed my blue mug and a red one for Emily, just in case. The usual carafe on the table meant the blood would be warm, just how I liked it.

"Wow, you two looked similar before, but now you're like twins," Lizzie said.

"Don't worry, only one will still be a bitch, I bet." Ethan bumped me in the shoulder as I sat down next to him and gave me a crooked smile.

"Hey, I've perfected my bitchy status. I can't let anyone steal my crown." I bumped him back, smiling at him for a longer time than I should have.

"What's this?" Lizzie joked. "Did I just see Ethan and Tasi tease each other without any underlying hatred? I don't know what's more shocking, Emily's new model hotness or Ethan and Tasi getting along. I guess the world truly is ending."

I stuck my tongue out at her, then snatched the carafe out of her hands before she could pour any in her glass. "Ladies first," I said.

Emily then took it out of my hand, giving me a devious smile. "In that case, I go first."

For a second, life felt normal.

When we were all done, Emily insisted we go to the training room. She felt so good she was sure she could take me on.

"Come on, are you chicken?" Emily asked. She flapped her arms around me, making demented clucking sounds. "I want to see what I can do."

"I'll fight with you," Lizzie said. I watched as she put her fists up to her face and made jabbing motions.

"No way. I'll do it," I said, letting out a tremendous sigh. At least if I fought her, I could control the fight. She might be feeling better, but I planned to take it easy on her. Maybe.

Emily clapped her hands and jumped up and down. She looked so much older now, yet still acted like my thirteen-year-old little sister.

The training room was empty, so Emily tossed a few of the floor mats toward Lizzie and Ethan.

"Take a seat. We won't be needing those." Emily let out a devious chuckle.

Lizzie and Ethan both shrugged. This made me shake my head. When Emily was training before her transition, she was strong, but nothing like it would be now.

"Rules?" Emily asked, stretching out her fingers in front of her.

"Yeah, one: wreck nothing we can't fix. I don't want to pay for damages," I said.

This made Emily laugh more.

We stood across from each other, studying one another's movements. I knew she would make a few mistakes, not knowing her body yet, but I was shocked when she leapt for me. She extended her arm as if she was ready to decapitate me. The move was messy. I laughed, gripped her, and slammed her down. The floor vibrated. Emily jumped up on her heels, steadying herself as she eyed me.

"Nice," she said.

I smirked. "Distract me, you will not."

I heard Ethan laugh. I looked at him as his melodious voice traveled to me and brushed my skin. That did it—so much for not getting distracted. There was a throbbing pain where my head crashed on the floor. Emily pushed me onto my stomach, trying hard to crush me under her weight. I could've thrown her off me, but she did good, so I wanted to give her this one.

"Round one, Emily," Lizzie said.

We stood up. Emily's face lit up. My grin was from ear to ear.

"Tasi, you might want to watch those distractions," Emily said, before turning to Ethan. "Thanks for the help."

I rolled my eyes at her as my cheeks burned. Of course Ethan distracted me. Who else's voice could draw me in like that? I refocused myself.

"Don't worry, I won't make that mistake twice."

I lunged for Emily. Upon impact, she let out a loud grunt before hitting the floor, which rattled beneath us. Standing up, she spun around and connected with my ear. A piercing hum filled my head. I grabbed her heel. *Boom.* Her body sprawled out on the floor as she gasped for air. She wriggled around under my hold.

"Round two, Tasi," Lizzie said.

I helped her up. We were both panting a little from all the

laughing we were doing. Sparring with Emily was the most fun I'd had in a while.

"Ready to fold, Tasi?" she teased.

"Never will I abdicate," I said with conviction.

"'Abdicate'? This isn't a vocab quiz. Big words won't help you in a fight."

We again danced around each other, waiting for the other to make a mistake. I started with a flurry of jabs and kicks. She stumbled. I pounced, my hand wrapping around her neck before lifting her and thrusting her to the floor. She flailed about.

"Do you give in?"

"No way," she replied as she squirmed out of my grasp and landed a blow to my gut. Pain rippled through me. I grabbed her ankles. She squealed as she whacked her head. We sprang to our feet and began the routine again. This time she threw the first punch. It whizzed by my ear like a buzzing fly. My palm thrust into her nose. Blood gushed down her face.

"My nose, Tasi! Why would you do that?" she said.

I ran over to help her, yanking my T-shirt off in the process so she could use it to stop the bleeding. As soon as I was close enough, she threw a punch. Fire blazed through my stomach. I crumpled to the floor, gasping for air as she pulled my hands behind my back. This time, I didn't let her hold me. If she was going to play dirty, I wasn't going to let her win. I wrestled my body out of her grasp. Her eyes widened in surprise. We danced.

"Thought you had me, didn't you?" I asked.

"Yeah, what's up with that? Did you throw that first round also?"

I laughed.

"That's it—no more Miss Nice Person," she bantered. She was concentrating so hard, it made her a sloppy fighter, and all her attempts to take me down failed. In one swift movement, I knocked her down, giving her the same blow to the gut she'd landed on me earlier. She keeled over.

"Tasi, you suck."

"Round three, Tasi. *Ding, ding, ding!*" Lizzie exclaimed.

Emily was now laughing so hard she could barely stand upright. She lay on the floor, using my shirt to wipe up any excess blood from her face and body. I flopped down next to her.

"Tasi, I almost had you." She lifted up into a sitting position.

"No, you didn't, not even close. You may almost have the strength and speed, but you need to work on the skill and control." I rolled onto my side, facing her, then pushed her, making her fall back. We exploded in laughter again, wrapped up in our perfect little world. That was, until Austin came over with Cas.

"Damn, two badass Vasile girls. The world better be on the lookout." Austin sat down next to me on the floor, sliding in as close as he could.

I looked over to where Ethan was sitting, but he must have left when Austin came over to me. I watched as Cas helped Emily up.

"I'm going to the infirmary to clean up," Emily said.

"Do you want me to come?" I asked.

"No, I'm fine. Let's meet up before bed at Sonya's." She gave me one last brilliant smile. Cas and Lizzie followed her out.

I shook my head. I knew she was leaving me alone with Austin because it had been days since I'd spent any time with him.

"So, how are you, love?" Austin lay on the floor beside me.

"I'm okay. Sorry I haven't talked to you much. I was busy with—"

"No need to explain. I'm glad Emily's okay." Austin ran his fingers along my jawline, pushing back the hair that had fallen out of place. "I'm also glad you're okay. I was worried for a while there."

I'd be lying if I said I hadn't been worried as well. I kept that to myself. "It all worked out. I hope things can go back to normal now."

"'Normal'? There's no such thing as normal with you involved." He reached his hand to the back of my neck, kissing me along my jawline. Once he reached my mouth, he pulled me in for a long, passionate kiss. His tongue pushed against mine as he pulled me in closer. Finally, we broke apart.

"Oh, how I missed that," he said.

I forced a smile. It was in this moment, this very kiss, that I was positive who I wanted—and it wasn't Austin. All I could think about while kissing him was wondering where Ethan had gone after my brawl with Emily, what he was doing, and whether I would get to see him later. I had been fooling myself since our talk at the coffee shop. Ethan was the only person I wanted, the one I knew was meant for me. Even if he wouldn't be with me, I had to tell him.

I chose him.

I couldn't stop the awful feeling in the pit of my stomach, and I knew I had to tell Austin I couldn't be with him. Even worse was that he kept calling me "love" and saying things about me being the girl he loved. I was going to hurt this great guy, but if I kept pretending that I thought I should pick him, it would make things worse in the long run. I couldn't do this right now.

"Did you hear me?" he asked.

"Sorry, I was thinking about Emily," I said.

"Why are you meeting with Sonya later?"

I watched him closely. Since when did he care about me meeting with Sonya? After a moment, I stopped reading into it. He was probably just making conversation, since it wasn't like I was talking much.

"My guess is to go over the last few days. It would be wise to document it all, especially if there may be others like us in the future," I said.

"That's a great idea. Let me know if I can do anything to help." He rested his head back against me.

Lying on the floor, I stared at the ceiling. I had become a terrible person. I was pining for one boy while leading on another kind, sweet guy who loved me. Until I told Austin the truth about the way I felt, just call me despicable.

32

We showed up at Sonya's office right as the rest of the vampire world headed off to bed. Emily's nose only showed a little greenish-yellow color around it. The bruise I'd given her was healing up nicely. Hopefully, Sonya wouldn't give us the third degree about our minor battle.

When she answered, she looked tired, almost defeated.

"Take a seat. We have a few details to go over, and it may take a while," she said.

We sat in seats across from Sonya and gave each other a quick look of confusion while doing so.

"Is everything okay?" asked Emily.

"It will be. We're going to endure some changes around here." I tried to read her expression—was it sad, angry, or annoyed? I couldn't tell which, but it wasn't good. Somehow, I knew I was about to kiss the bit of freedom we had goodbye. "We're moving you away from New York City," she said.

That was not what I was expecting. "What do you mean? You're sending us away?" I asked.

"Tasia, please don't get upset. It's for your safety. There is a coven that I trust. No one else knows of its existence, except for me and the few vampires living there, so I know you'll be completely safe," Sonya replied.

"Just like Aunt Eva and my mother sent us here to be safe, right?" I threw my hands up in exasperation.

"Why are we really being sent away?" Emily asked. "Is it because of Jelena?"

"Mostly," Sonya began. "With Jelena knowing everything about this place, I'm sure they will plan an attack of some sort soon enough. So we need to get you somewhere safe and with people I trust."

"People you trust. How do we know we can trust you?" I asked.

"Have I ever given you a reason not to trust me? The first day you came here, I told you I would protect the two of you because I made a promise to your father. I'll never go back on that promise." Her voice trembled as she spoke. There was something that she wasn't saying. Emily knew it too.

"No offense, Sonya—you have been wonderful to give us a home and provide for us when no one else could, but Tasi's right—why should we trust you with something this big? We know you are hiding something from us." Emily's face turned pink as she questioned Sonya. She usually left these types of conversations for me to handle.

Sonya tapped her fingers on the desk and watched the two of us closely. Finally, the tapping stopped, and her face looked paler than usual. She let out a long sigh before she spoke again.

"Do you want to know why I promised your father I'd take care of you if something happened to them, and why Eva sent you here? My real name is Andreea Vasile. I am your father's sister; your biological aunt." Silence settled in the room. She continued again, probably trying to break the stupor that Emily and I had fallen into. "When you were born, we knew it wouldn't be safe for you anywhere, so this was to become your home only as a last resort."

"Why didn't you tell us? Why didn't you tell me when I asked you about her?" I asked. My voice grew cold. "When I asked if Andreea was alive?"

"Safety, Tasia—I tried my hardest to keep you two safe, and the only way I knew how was to keep this a secret from everyone, not just you." She moved restlessly around in her chair. "I still don't know if telling you now is the right thing. This information cannot fall into the wrong hands."

Emily stood up and rushed around the desk, straight into Sonya's arms. Tears ran down her cheeks as she buried her face into Sonya's shoulder. I, on the other hand, saw red. I was pissed.

"You said you would be completely honest with me, but you lied," I said. "Just like my parents lied and Eva lied. Why does everyone lie?"

"Tasi, don't be mad at her. She was trying to protect us," Emily said.

"I was, Tasia. We all had good intentions. If they had known I was your aunt, they would have come after me just like the others, and then you would have had nowhere else to go." Sonya's eyes were on me. I could see them pleading with me to forgive her.

With my head hung low and my voice but a whisper, I said, "I'm sorry, but I can't forgive you right now. I can't forgive being lied to repeatedly." All the trust issues I had resurfaced, making me feel alone. "Can we finish discussing the plan so I can go get some sleep?"

It wasn't easy, but I refused to give in, even if all I wanted was to run around the desk and throw my arms around her, knowing now why she was so familiar to me. She looked just like my father—I could see it now.

"Antanasia." Emily turned to me, crossing her arms against her chest.

"It's okay, Emily. She has every right to be upset," Sonya said.

Emily sighed, then came back and sat down, more attentive than before. She was always the more forgiving one.

"Here is what's going to happen. We'll leave the day after tomorrow, right before the sun comes up. It'll give us enough time to get out of here with no one else knowing. Well, until evening, that is. We'll be safe by then. Len will be in the security room. He doesn't know where we are going, but I know he won't tell anyone we left together. I left him in charge while I'm gone, since I know people will follow his orders. Other than that, I'd say pack as light as you did when you first arrived."

"Sounds outstanding," I said. Unfortunately, my attempt to not roll my eyes failed miserably.

"Tasi, let's make the best of this, okay?" Emily said.

Great, I'd lost Emily. No matter what I said now, it wouldn't make a difference. She was Team Sonya.

"Fine, I guess I'll go say my goodbyes, then." I got up to leave. I couldn't look Sonya in the eyes right now. It hurt—not only because she'd lied, but now I couldn't stop thinking of my dad when I looked at her.

"No, Tasia."

I stopped, turning to Sonya. The eyes I had been avoiding looked back at me apologetically.

"No, what?" I asked.

"No, you can't tell anyone you're leaving, that we're leaving. And again, no one can know about us being family. So I suggest going straight to bed and acting like nothing has changed until we leave," she said.

"Unbelievable," I grumbled, before heading out the door, leaving Emily behind.

As soon as I was alone, the space around me collapsed. I breathed in stale air. Sonya was related to my father. She was related to me. Comparatively speaking, I could say Sonya was the equivalent of my aunt Eva. My stomach twisted in knots, and my legs trembled with each step I took. The world closed in on me, and I needed to escape.

I started to head to the rooftop, but then I remembered the cameras. Right now, I wanted no one spying in on me or my life. If I went to my bedroom, then Emily would find me, and I was not in the mood for a motherly lecture on how wrong I was, especially when I was already aware. I made my decision and began heading outside. I remembered that there was an alley behind the school where all the deliveries came in for the party. Whether the cameras would catch me was another thing, but I was ready to risk it.

I snuck through the kitchen and headed through the back pantry. There was a chain on it, which I quickly removed with a flick of the wrist.

The cool air chilled my skin, and being outside allowed me to inhale some normality back into myself. The alleyway was spacious enough for a small truck to haul in necessary supplies. I walked to the opposite wall, where there was a small ledge, and hopped up onto it. There was one camera, but they'd set it to watch the entrance of the alley, so I should be in the clear.

I lay down and stared up at the sky, which wasn't a dark midnight blue anymore. It was streaked with brighter hues, indicating the sun would be up soon. When I was younger, before I knew of vampires or thought my life was any different from the kid next door, I would climb up to my roof and study the stars, wondering if my parents were dancing among them. Life was so simple and dull then, and I wished I'd appreciated it more.

There was a peacefulness out here. Yes, I could hear the faint honking of all the horns as cars sped by and the chuckling and babble of people in the distance, but it only added to the tranquility. A few more minutes, and I'd go to bed. I didn't need the search party to find me out here. Maybe tomorrow I could talk to Sonya and apologize. I closed my eyes.

"Grab her."

That voice... *Jelena.*

They were too fast for me. Two enormous men dragged me off the ridge and had me kneeling on the ground before I knew what had happened. They each had one hand on my shoulder and the other pulling my arm back. The man to my right had blond hair, while the man to my left was bald. I didn't fight back, only studied them. I needed to plot this fight strategically; I couldn't count on anyone showing up to help me. But in typical Tasi fashion, that didn't stop my mouth. Plus, I needed to buy some time.

"Bitch, I am going to murder you."

"Oh, sweet Tasia. Dear, sweet Tasia. I'm not sure you've noticed, but you'll do nothing I don't want you to do. And thank you for making my job simple. I had disabled the alarm because we were going to break in and find you, but this makes it so much easier."

I scanned my surroundings as she talked. The two men holding me I could easily take out. Another three guys stood behind Jelena, and the wicked bitch herself made six. One man was tiny compared to the others. I wasn't sure what the little man's deal was, but I could tell he wasn't a fighter, so technically five. Depending on their weaponry, I had a chance. I was less concerned with the humans. With Jelena, I was going in blind. She had put on such a good front as a holier-than-thou bookworm that I worried she might have some crazy secret abilities.

"Didn't you take enough of Emily's blood the last time, you evil witch? You almost killed her!"

Jelena raised her brow. "Almost?" She shrugged, then continued, "The properties in Emily's blood were all over the place, but we found an oddity that we hadn't seen before. Although it was weak, there is an interesting life energy in the blood of you dhampyrs. If we can extract the living essence from your blood and mutate it, I believe we will have what we need to rid this world of the malevolent creatures who roam it. I just need more of it, and that is where you come in." She inspected me curiously. "You could join us. Side with the Deity and aid our takedown of the vampire world. Then you and your sister could live a normal life. Think about it—no more running or fighting. You'd be free, and all you would have to do is supply us with a little blood."

Not too long ago, I would have welcomed Jelena's offer. But the thought of no more Ethan, Lizzie, Cas, or Austin? And even Sonya? No, they had become my family, and I protect my family. "Not all vampires are evil, Jelena. Plus, aren't you breeding your own dhampyrs? Why do you need our blood?"

Wonder flitted through her face. She clearly wasn't expecting me to know that.

"If you must know, then yes, we are trying to create dhampyrs to farm their blood. Whether we have been successful, I'll only tell you if you join us."

She was a seriously troubled woman. "I will never help you. You'll have to kill me."

"So be it, Tasia."

Before she could order my death, I needed to know what her deal was.

"Answer me this: why are you doing it? If you help them, you die too. Unless that is your plan for getting into God's good graces again? You kill all the evil, immoral creatures, and you become a martyr?"

"Tasia, I'm not selfless. If I help kill all the vampires, the Deity will provide me with an inoculation, and all the disgusting vampires will die—except me." She leaned into me, making certain that only I could hear what she said next. "Then I will be the original and conceive a line of vampires who will be devout only to me."

"You're a true psycho, you know that? I think you have been

sniffing too much frankincense over the years, and now you've lost your damn mind."

"Be quiet, you stupid, stupid girl." She looked at the men behind her. "I'm finished with her. Take her blood, as much as you can, then execute her." She looked to the small man. "They will drive you back to the hideout when you're finished. Don't screw this up." She focused back on me. "Sorry, Tasia, you chose your destiny, and now you have to die. Too bad I won't be here to witness it."

She was leaving with one of her thugs. No, she couldn't go—this was my chance to kill her for all the things she had done, especially hurting Emily.

"Hey, Jelena, why are you running? Stay here and fight, you cowardly, sinful bitch." But no matter how much I provoked her to come back and fight, it didn't affect her. "I'm going to come for you, and when I do, it's going to hurt. I promise you," I said.

"Shut up," said one thug. He punched me in the face. Warm liquid dripped from my nose and onto my lips. "Don't give us any trouble."

"Oh boy, a tough man beating on a little girl. Do you feel stronger now?"

The guy preparing to drain my blood was busy hooking up his equipment.

"Wait until you feel my blade, little girl."

"Promises, promises."

Down to four measly humans. Getting away should be straightforward. I stood up with the force of a high-speed train, shocking my abductors. The man in front of me was the biggest threat. Grabbing him by the collar, I yanked him down to the ground and put him in a choke hold. Holding him there seemed to take an eternity as the other two guys tried to seize hold of me but couldn't. I used the man as a shield to guard my body. Once he fell unconscious, I shifted, smashed his head into the ground, and shoved him into the blond-haired attacker.

Without taking a breath, I propelled my body upward, wrapping my legs around the neck of the bald man still standing, who had pulled out a knife. He reached up to unravel my legs from him, slicing the icy blade along my thigh. I gripped tighter, unfazed by his attempt to make me release him from my grasp. I crushed his neck.

Two men down; two remained. The small man looked terrified and unsure what to make of the situation. His behavior made me question my next move, which was poor form. The blond guy was back up and reaching for me. His arms slithered around my body, squeezing the air from my lungs.

"Get her blood, you simple fool, so I can kill this little bitch."

The frightened man stood there with his large needle. I watched as he crawled closer, moving his shaky hand toward me. He was too close. It was now or never. I closed my eyes and slammed my head back into my blond captor's face. As soon as my head made contact, my entire body jolted and my eyes quaked in my skull. I whirled around and saw blood covering the man from the blow to his head. My fist connected with his throat. Then I swiped his feet out from under him, forcing him onto his back. My fury burned through me like lava. The crackling noise continued each time I connected with his face. He stopped moving.

I faced the small man now, who was crouching on the ground.

"I'm sorry, miss. Please don't hurt me. I'm only doing what the Deity told me to do. I won't hurt you if you let me leave." He rambled on incoherently for a few more seconds.

"You're coming with me."

33

Looking around, I knew I needed help cleaning up my mess. Vamps could turn into ash; humans, not so much. Also, now that the adrenaline was wearing off, my leg burned. I hated the Deity and their stupid delayed-healing crap. I left the alley, small man in tow, and headed for Sonya's office.

When I reached the office, I hoped she wouldn't be angry with me for my mess or for bringing this human into the coven. I mean, I didn't do this on purpose, but I did go outside alone, so I guess some of it was my fault.

After one more big breath, I knocked on her door. I didn't realize it at first, but there was someone else in there with her.

"Tasia, what—" Sonya scooted me into her office.

"Where's Emily?" I asked.

"She left with Lizzie. She was going to sleep in Lizzie's room. I believe it was to give you some space," Sonya said.

"As long as she's safe."

"What is going on, and why do you have a human with you?" Sonya asked as she took hold of him and sat him in a chair.

Sonya eyed me, waiting for me to tell her what was going on. Ethan was with her, staring at me with wide eyes. I wondered what I looked like—a bloody mess, probably. I swear he looked at me like I'd come out of a gladiator's arena and whether I was the victor was still up for debate. He walked into Sonya's bathroom without saying a word and came out with a small medical kit, then looked over my injuries.

"It's not too bad," Ethan said as he wiped my face. I recalled the punch to my nose. "Sit, Tasi, and tell us what happened while I clean you up."

"Deity, Jelena—I killed a few people, and I need some help cleaning up. I don't know what to do with human bodies. I'm hoping someone here does. As for this guy, I thought maybe someone could convince him to tell us where Jelena is. He knows, because he was supposed to drain my blood and bring it to her."

I ran through the events, starting with Jelena deactivating the alarms to her coming back for blood. Sonya's face grew more and more concerned as I spoke. Ethan finished mending me and left the room.

Sonya stood before the small human. "If I ask you where Jelena is, will you tell me?"

"No—no, ma'am. I cannot tell any details of her whereabouts. Even if I wanted to, I don't know anything. The driver—the one the girl killed—was the only person who knew the exact location."

"Great, I kept the wrong one alive."

"Jelena compelled him not to say anything," Sonya said. "She's smart. If she is compelling the Deity humans, then vampires will have less of a chance to capture and torture them for information."

"Can we put a transmitter on him or something to track where he goes? Saving him couldn't have been all for nothing," I asked.

"No, Tasia, it wasn't all for nothing. If my theory is correct, you should be able to do this as well. Watch and learn." Sonya looked into the man's eyes and smiled in a way I had never seen before. Her voice became melodic. "What is your name, human?"

The man looked at Sonya and his lips curved upward. "Fredrick, ma'am."

"Fredrick—what a pleasant name." His smile grew wide. "I want you to forget what Jelena said to you about keeping secrets. You will tell me where the Deity has Jelena hiding and what they are doing with the blood."

"Jelena." His voice was even.

"Yes, Jelena," Sonya repeated. "Tell me where she is hiding."

"Jelena is staying in a compound in upstate New York. I am to bring her the blood, help the doctors run tests, and find the properties that may help them create a mutated virus."

Sonya's lips twitched upward, and I wasn't sure why.

"Fredrick, what you are going to do when you leave here is call Jelena. Tell her that the humans she sent with you are dead. You escaped before the girl could kill you too. Any tests performed from here on out, you will sabotage them discreetly. You will tell no one we had this conversation or what you are doing. You will only remember the girl in the alley. You will not remember coming into this house. You will not remember me. Do you understand, Fredrick?"

"I understand."

I watched Sonya's dark eyes glisten with an iridescence that reminded me of all the colors I saw when I broke through the barriers and gained the ability to compel. I looked at Fredrick, and he had the same iridescent colors in his eyes. The truth clicked for me—she could lift the compulsion of another vampire. *I bet she can also compel other vampires, like I can. It must be because Sonya is an original.*

"Good, Fredrick. Go with Tasia, quickly." She closed her eyes for about five seconds, and it released him. She then turned to me and had me take him out the same way I brought him in, still dazed from the compulsion.

When I returned, Sonya was leaning against her desk with her face in her hands as she massaged her head.

"Sonya," I said. "I'm sorry for getting upset with you earlier. I only went outside to clear my head because I knew I was out of line."

"Tasia, what you did was unbelievably irresponsible. Going outside and staying out of the line of sight so the cameras wouldn't pick you up was reckless." She was right. Then she surprised me as she strode over and took my hand. "But all I care about is that you're okay now. Promise me you'll never do that again."

I nodded.

There was a knock on the door.

"Come in," Sonya said.

Ethan and Len came into the room. Both of them looked at me.

"Little miss," Len said, "those were three big dudes—not an easy cleanup."

Ethan looked me over again.

"I'm fine, Ethan. Really," I said, giving him a warm smile.

Sonya was looking at Len's phone—most likely at the photos he took of the bodies I left in the alleyway.

"I think Tasia should get some rest. She has had a long night," Sonya said. Her tone made it clear there was no arguing about that.

"I'll walk her back to her room," Ethan said.

Before I could protest, Sonya agreed it was probably best.

"Can we peek in on Lizzie and Emily, please?"

"Sure," said Ethan.

I stood up. My body was achy, but overall, I was okay.

Lizzie and Emily lay undisturbed on their beds. I realized this was her first actual sleepover with a friend, as silly as that may sound. The thought of us leaving again made my heart hurt. I was going to miss Lizzie tremendously.

Ethan and I said little along the way, but he watched me as we headed into my room.

As soon as we stepped in, Ethan pulled me close.

"What's wrong?" His voice brushed my skin the way the cool breeze had earlier tonight.

"Nothing, Ethan."

"You know I can tell when something is wrong with you. Others may buy into the fakeness, but not me."

"What do you want me to say? That I had a tough night? That Jelena won't stop until she gets her hands on my sister or me? How about I am tired of everyone asking me if I am all right all the time? Or maybe you want me to say that everything is awesome, and since we're alone, we can have a heartfelt talk?"

He watched me incredulously as I ranted, though I left out the most significant point of all: how much I was going to miss everyone once we left.

"Do you want me to go?"

There was no malice in his voice, and his eyes were so beautiful. Some would say brown eyes weren't unique or intriguing, but Ethan's eyes were so inviting. They took me away from everything happening in my life and made me feel safe.

"No," I said, plopping onto the bed. "I want normalcy in my life."

"Can I ask you something?" I could see his inner struggle. "Why were you outside alone? You could have called me, or even Austin, to go with you."

"That defeats the purpose of trying to find clarity," I said. "But honestly, Sonya and I got into a fight, and Emily took her side. So I wanted some time alone for once. When I was in Maine, I had all the time alone I needed, and here I feel suffocated sometimes. I thought a few minutes outside would be safe enough. Obviously, like with most other things, I was wrong."

"What do you mean, like with most other things?"

"Let's tick down the list, shall we? I was wrong to stay in Maine for so long. I was wrong to run from you and Lizzie when you found us in Boston. I was wrong thinking all vampires are bad and humans are good. I was wrong about the people I trusted. I was wrong about Sonya . . ." I said, my voice trailing off. "And I was wrong to pick Austin over you. I should have fought harder for us to be together, even when you pushed me away. Instead, I turned to a boy who gave me what I wanted from you. Which resulted in a boy who told me, more or less, that he loves me, and I know for a fact I can never return that favor because of you. I want the feeling I get when we're together—the electricity, the quickening of my heart, the way you make me feel when all you say is hello. I should have been patient." Ethan's face was unreadable as I dumped all these things on him.

Before I could tell him I was sorry for being such a brat, Ethan pulled me onto his lap. Our eyes met, and I knew there was no going back from this moment. His mouth met my neck, where the kisses started gently. I gasped. His lips were cool against my skin as he moved to my chin until, finally, our mouths formed a bond. Time stopped. Our tongues found each other's, his soft against mine. That woodsy, vanilla scent that always lingered on Ethan hypnotized me. I wanted more of him.

I shifted from sitting on his lap to straddling him. If my legs caused me pain as I draped them around him, I didn't notice. All I could feel were his hands caressing my back, pressing me into him, and squeezing the air out from in between our bodies. His hands drifted down until they reached my waist. That sense of electricity intensified as his hands no longer touched the fabric of my shirt but the skin on my back. Grasping my waist, he drew me in tighter, before tugging at the shirt in a way that let me know he preferred it off. There was urgency, but also a sign of waiting for my approval. I leaned back from the kiss and lifted my arms straight up in the air. His smile was hungry as he pulled the shirt over my head. I returned the smile and found his mouth again.

In one swift movement, I interlaced my hands around the back of his neck, before pulling him down to lay on the bed with me. Never once did we tear away from the kiss. He lay there, his body heavy against me, as he pressed his lips harder and harder against mine. He pulled back for a second, wiping my uncooperative hairs from my face. The corner of his mouth turned up. But before he could kiss me again, I yanked at his shirt to come off. It was less graceful than the way he'd taken off mine, but with the same result.

His bare chest was cool as my fingers traced his smooth muscles. Our eyes met, and there was a hunger in his eyes I'd never seen before. He leaned in, finding my lips once again. Our bodies melted into each other the minute our skin touched. The weight of him on top of me sent tremors through me. The kiss was feral, and the once-gentle touch of our lips became fierce and downright sexy. My tongue searched for his fangs. I brushed it against them, allowing some of the venom to drip into my mouth. It created a tingling sensation on my tongue.

"Careful, beautiful," he said. "You don't want to cut your tongue on those."

His face brimmed with desire. But how far I was willing to go, we would not find out right now. With one last kiss, I relaxed back onto my bed. Ethan shifted, lying on his side, still moving strands of hair from my face and stroking my body with his fingertips.

"This is the most naked I've ever been in the presence of a guy."

This made him laugh. "I guess I'll need to see if I can get you to say that again next time."

My face burned at the thought of us more naked next time—

would our pants come off?—until reality hit, and I remembered that there would be no next time.

"I need to talk to Austin tomorrow." His hand stopped, leaving an icy feeling on my skin. "I have to tell him I can't ever love him. I can't ever love him because there is a boy who stole my heart on the train platform in Boston."

Ethan pulled me in for one last deep kiss. "I thought staying away from you was for the best. I'm quickly realizing that was stupid. We need each other, Tasi. Tell me you saw me on the platform at the train station. You saw me in fog-ridden vision. You and I together in some capacity. I didn't know if it was friends, lovers, enemies, but our lives were intertwined."

My heart shattered. I sat up, not looking at him, fearful I would cry.

"What's wrong?" His hand grazed my back, tingling the skin beneath his touch.

"I have to tell you something—something that is going to get me in a lot of trouble with Sonya if she finds out I told you, but it's something you deserve to know."

Ethan sat up, sliding his arm around my waist and forcing me to look at him. "Tasi, what is it?"

My finger followed his lips before moving my hand to his chest, resting it on his heart. I'm not sure if I was expecting a heartbeat, but there wasn't one. My eyes looked back to his, which were staring at me anxiously.

"I went outside tonight to clear my head because . . ." I took in a deep breath, locking my eyes on his. "Emily and I are leaving tomorrow morning when the sun comes up. Sonya is taking us somewhere safe, and after this last attack, I'm guessing there is no changing her mind."

The space around us remained still for too long.

"I want to go with you. I can help protect you and Emily." He was serious. "You don't even have to tell Sonya. I'll meet you outside when you are ready to leave, and the three of us will go together."

"Ethan," I said. "Sonya is coming with us, and Lizzie can't lose us all in one day."

"Then Lizzie can come too. I don't care if the entire coven comes along. We just found each other." Ethan's hands were trembling.

"Ethan . . ." I looked away from him. The tether between us loosened.

"No, Tasi, look at me." My eyes finally met his and tears welled up. When I blinked, a river began running down my cheeks. "You feel it too. Please don't deny it. We need each other. We need to be together."

"I don't . . . I can't . . ." I covered my eyes with my hands. For the first time, I didn't know how to fix this. My heart was crumbling into a thousand pieces, and nothing would put it back together after this.

"Tasi, don't push me away." His voice was a low growl.

I didn't know what to say to him. This wasn't me pushing him away. Did I want him to come? Yes, more than anything. Would Sonya let him come? Doubtful. I let the silence linger too long, and then Ethan was standing up, putting his shirt back on. He didn't make eye contact with me until he reached the door.

"Have a nice life, Antanasia."

34

Sleep came and went. My make-out session with Ethan had lasted a while, plus, with all the drama before and afterward, I was functioning on only a few hours' sleep. One would think I would have stayed under my covers crying over Ethan, but I grew angry instead. How dare he walk away from me after last night? He was the one who always hurt me. He was the one who'd decided to pretend we couldn't be friends. I guess it didn't matter; soon I would be far away.

The one thing I knew I had to do was tell Austin I only wanted to stay friends with him, after I told him I was leaving. Man, Sonya was going to be super angry with me for blabbing about our secret trip—first Ethan, and now Austin.

The first step was to hide what remained of my sliced-up leg from yesterday, and the second was to check and make sure my messed-up face had healed. Remarkably, it had, so I headed to the kitchen. It was the typical hangout, and I figured it was the place I was most likely to find Austin.

In the kitchen sat Lizzie and Emily.

"Hi, guys. How was the sleepover?" I asked.

"Stellar—we braided each other's hair and talked about boys

all night," Lizzie mused.

"How are you, Tasi? Did you have time to talk to Sonya?" Emily asked.

"Yes, Emily, we can talk later about it, but I spoke to Sonya. I get it, she protects us, so we are on the same page."

"Do you two need time alone?" Lizzie said.

"No, I'm looking for Austin. Have you seen him?"

"Check the media center. Last I saw him was on my way to training with Cas," Emily said.

"Thanks. Catch you guys later," I said. I crinkled my brows. This wasn't going to be easy. My gut fired up, bile bobbing in and out of my throat.

The media room was empty, but our door was cracked open. When I reached the rooftop area, Austin was looking out into the sky, relaxed and unaware of the bomb I was about to drop on him.

"Hi." I reached for his hand, my fingers grazing his.

Austin turned toward me, pulling me into his arms. "Hi to you, love." His lips met mine, and for a moment, I wanted to die. I pulled away from him. "You're beautiful, you know that?"

"Thanks," I replied. How was I going to say goodbye to him? He searched my eyes. "Austin, I have to tell you something."

"Let me guess. You love me. You can't live without me. Am I close?" He waited, watching me with desire.

"Actually, can we sit down?"

We sat on the bench, our knees touching as he studied my face. "What's the matter?"

"I'm not supposed to tell anyone this, so you can't either, okay? Sonya's going to kill me if she finds out." All the confidence I had in telling Austin was dwindling. If I didn't tell him soon, I wouldn't tell him at all. "Emily and I are leaving."

His face fell. Those beautiful green eyes of his immediately looked dull and worn.

"You can't be serious," he said.

"I'm very serious. Since the Deity knows we are here and it may trigger further acts of violence against us, Sonya has found us a new place to go, somewhere safe."

"When are you leaving?" I watched as he stood up, not looking at me, only pacing back and forth.

This was not going as I had hoped. I watched Austin more closely. Anger and frustration were filling every part of him, making me already regret what I had to say next.

"We're leaving in a few hours, at sunrise." The words were barely a whisper as they left my lips. Austin stopped pacing and stared into the distance. I walked over to him, touching his arm.

"Do you love me?" His pleasant attitude returned as he pulled me around and lifted my chin to his. His words were rushed, and his eyes caught mine.

My fingertips went cold. Chills crept up the back of my neck as he asked the question. *No, Austin, I don't love you, and actually, I don't even want to be with you because I want to be with your archenemy, Ethan.*

"That was something else I wanted to talk to you about," I said, looking away. "You're an amazing guy, Austin, but the truth is—"

He put his finger over my lips. "I want to run and get something. Wait here—I'll be right back," he said. "Then we can continue talking."

I nodded, and he ran down the steps and out of sight.

Standing there looking out into the night, I embraced the gentle wind washing over me. This was my goodbye to the city I'd learned to call home. My goodbye to friends I called family, a boy who loved me, and a boy who I might love.

I heard the bottom door click and the stairs creak slowly. When Austin reached the top, he held one hand behind his back. With the other free hand, he took mine in his and pulled me once again into him.

"Tasi, I can't tell you how long I have waited for an opportunity like this," he said.

"Austin," I said.

"No, Tasi, let me finish. I need to say a few things, and since you are leaving, I need to get them out now. We have spent a lot of time getting to know each other, but I feel you don't know one of the most important things about me: the way I became a vampire. It's not something I tell many people because it still hurts me."

He ran his hand along the side of my face, looking at me eagerly.

"I was a painter. I loved to paint portraits of people, so that's what I did for a living. My name was Augustine, and I later changed it to Austin. Anyway, I was married to the most beautiful woman in France, Madeline Pascal. Men would fall all over her whenever she walked by. Her beauty was one of a kind, and she only had eyes for me. One day, I was painting her wearing very little. It was a birthday present for me." Something about this thought made him smile. "When I finished the painting, she was so delighted that she gave me the only other thing I had wanted from her: eternal life."

"She was a vampire?"

"Yes, and she chose me. We had planned to spend our lives together—forever." He sat down on the bench, eyes fixed on the floor.

I hurried to sit next to him. "What happened?"

He stared at me expressionlessly. "After a hundred years of happiness, we moved to Italy. It was my idea, and she did it for me, for my love of painting. In Italy, I painted even more beautiful portraits. It was my passion, and she was my muse. My life was perfect." His body shifted uncomfortably. "One day, I was painting her on our bed. She lay there, intertwined in the sheets, and it looked like someone had poured liquid gold all over her body. The sheets clung to her, puddling onto the floor, her long blonde hair flowing down the sides of her face."

I wondered if this was why he never dated blondes. "She sounds beautiful," I said.

"She was. It was a perfect painting—appropriate considering it was the last portrait I would ever paint. Right as I finished, a man barged into our room. He lunged for her so fast, and when I ran to help her, he backhanded me. I flew across the room. It took me a minute to get back to her. We struggled for some time, and he threw me again. Finally, he said to me, 'My problem is not with you, but with her. She owes me her life, and now she will pay.' I watched as he bit into her neck and ripped her throat out. He then plunged his hand into her chest and yanked out her heart. Blood filled the sheets, and the once-golden river of silk ran red. She tried to scream and call me to her, but I couldn't help. The man left me with her, dead and tangled in the sheets. I wanted her to wake up. I lay with her for days before I could bring myself to move on. I kept telling myself it was all a bad dream, but in reality, it wasn't."

Horror was filling my face now. Why was Austin telling me this? I could feel him hurting, and reached to touch his face to say it would be okay, but as my fingers made contact, his eyes looked up to mine. Hatred and anger were flowing through them.

"Austin?"

His eyes quickly shimmered from green to black, and he pinned me against the wall before I knew what was happening. The thing Austin had hidden behind his back plunged into my neck, and suddenly, I could barely keep my eyes open. Whatever he had put into the syringe tingled inside me like pins and needles, making me sleepy.

His face was an inch from mine, his hand still wrapped around my neck. Disgust was all I could see in him now. "His name, Antanasia—the name of the vampire who took the only reason for me wanting to spend eternity as an evil creature—was Adrian Vasile."

35

When I woke up, my head was pounding. Even worse than the headache was the burning itch coming from my neck. Realizing none of this was a dream, I blinked to focus on where I was. I saw that I was still on the rooftop. Our special place to escape from my crazy life—how ironic.

I tugged at my hands, which were bound to the brick wall high above my head. This was where the beautiful trellis had been. Austin had hidden my prison behind the gorgeous pink roses I loved. Next, I tried to move my feet, but they were chained to a metal ring clamped into the foot of the wall. I yanked and pulled, but nothing budged.

"Pulling on the chains will only make your skin more and more irritated," the familiar voice called out from the doorway. Austin walked over.

"What are you doing?" I asked, trying to find the boy who had told me he loved me only a few days ago.

"I, my dear, am getting my revenge," he said. He ran his fingernail down the side of my cheek, piercing it just enough to allow a bit of blood to drip down.

"Revenge for what my father did? The father I didn't even know? What's wrong with that picture?" I pulled at the chains again, trying to reach him. If I could get him locked in on my eyes, I could compel him to let me go.

"Naughty girl." He ran his fingernail down the other cheek, piercing that one as well. "I know you can use compulsion. I watched Jelena give you that book, and I was looking for a chance to take it. Your stroll outside was the perfect opportunity. By the way, it was irresponsible of you to leave it on your nightstand. No, I won't let you compel me. I'm going to have fun today. I'll make you suffer the way Madeline suffered, and I don't care if you have personal daddy issues. You'll pay for what he did to her, and when I'm done with you, it'll be your sister's turn."

I kicked my foot out as hard as I could, only to come up short and feel the shackle cut deep into my ankle. Wetness pooled in my shoe. The way this was going, I would end up committing suicide before he could torture me.

That's when I heard footsteps climbing the stairs. Another person was here. When he stepped onto the roof, I recognized him immediately.

"Cas, help me!" I yelled. The younger boy who had become so close to Emily had wandered up the stairs. When he saw me, his face turned pale.

"I thought you said she was unconscious." Cas's attention lay directly on Austin, almost as if he was too scared to look at me. He placed a large box on the floor across the way and sat on the bench.

"No, not you too," I said, squeezing my eyes shut. "Who else is in on this? Who else is stupid enough to risk helping you?" I stared out into the city. Was this how my life would end?

"Poor Tasi—she's still trying to get used to the fact that the guy she thought loved her is not too fond of her after all." The crazed look on Austin's face was back. He walked over closer to me and licked the blood off the side of my cheek. "Tasty. I may have to drink you before I rip you into pieces . . . finger by finger . . . hair by hair."

His shimmery black eyes grew hungry. He wet his lips and chuckled.

"You won't get away with this," I argued. My tongue got stuck in the dryness of my throat. "I'm going to kill you. I swear it, Austin, you will die."

Austin's laugh made my skin crawl.

"Cas, grab the scalpel. I want to show Tasi how much she means to me." His thumb caressed my cheek.

"Gladly," Cas said. "You know, Tasi, Austin said that if I help him with you, I'd have first dibs on your sister. I can't seem to get the amazing smell of dhampyr blood out of my mind ever since we found you in the alley. I'm going to enjoy her." He waggled his eyebrows, which boiled the blood inside me.

I jerked at the chains again, thrashing around as hard as I could. The pain in my wrists was excruciating, but the thought of these two hurting Emily made me push harder to get free.

Austin closed in on me, his lips touching my ear. The touch I once desired now made me feel dirty. The hairs on my neck stood on end.

"By the way, thanks for telling me you were leaving. I wasn't planning on doing this until I made you fall in love with me, so when I finally ripped your heart out, you would know what it was like for me."

I turned my head, and my teeth tore at his cheek, ripping flesh. He snapped back and punched me in my face. The impact made me gasp for air. Why did this keep happening to me? That's when I noticed the warm liquid running down my chest. My head fell forward. Austin had used the scalpel to cut me along my collarbone, and his eyes told me what to expect next.

It would be a matter of seconds before he pushed his mouth against my glistening red skin. He wanted to drink my blood, but I wouldn't die without a fight.

Before I could do anything, Austin flew backward.

"Ethan!"

I shook off the dizzy feeling and looked up to see Cas and Lizzie also fighting. I pulled on my chains again—but nothing. Ethan and Austin grappled, baring teeth and repeatedly slamming each other into the wall.

"Tasi!" screamed Emily. She ran to me and pulled on the chains.

"They won't budge," I said as I yanked at them again.

"Pull with me, Tasi. We can do it. One, two, three!" The chains loosened from the wall. "One more time—one, two, three!" They snapped off, and pieces of metal flew everywhere.

I was free. I was also still a little woozy from the blood loss, but that meant little to me right this second. Kick ass now, pass out later.

"Go help Lizzie, Em. I'll help Ethan."

I couldn't tell who was winning, Ethan or Austin. They both had multiple bruises forming on their faces, and Ethan had a cut on his cheek, probably from that damn scalpel. Austin grabbed Ethan and threw him against the wall next to where I now stood. Ethan fell to the floor.

Austin narrowed his eyes, trying hard to hide his surprise. Seeing me free from my shackles was definitely not in his plan. He went to backhand me, but I grabbed his arm and kneed him in the stomach. In one swift movement, I slammed him straight to the ground. My foot found his neck as I stood over him.

"Did I not tell you I was going to kill you?" I placed more pressure on his neck, but he grabbed my leg and twisted it, dropping me to the floor. He punched me in the mouth, and my head bounced off the cement. My eyes fluttered, and black spots invaded my sight. I blinked them away.

Ethan was now back up. He grabbed Austin, but Austin was too fast. He quickly snaked out of Ethan's grip and pressed Ethan's chest against the bricks, crushing him into the wall.

The scuffle that had been going on in the distance ended with a yelp. It distracted me for one moment to make sure Emily was okay.

"Tasi!" Emily yelled to me as I picked myself up off the ground. I watched as she pulled the stake from Cas's ashen body and tossed it to me.

Knowing Emily was safe made it easier to concentrate solely on my own fight. I had to save Ethan. Austin's back was to me—big mistake. Before Austin could stab, slice, or do anything else, I leaned into his ear and whispered, "Told you." Shoving my stake as far into his back as I could, I watched as he let go of Ethan. I pushed harder, finally making it through to his heart. He dropped to his knees before turning into a pile of ash.

I fell to the ground as the adrenaline left my body, replaced by pain and dizziness. Emily would always be there for me, but if it were not for Lizzie and Ethan, I wouldn't be alive right now. Emily would not be alive right now. These were the people I knew I could trust. They were my family.

Ethan scooped me into his arms. I leaned into his shoulder as he carried me down the stairs and into my room. None of us said much as the understanding of what we had done washed over us.

"I'm going to get a first aid kit," Lizzie said.

"I'll come." Emily followed.

Ethan sat with me on the bed, still cradling me as my tears soaked into his shirt. When I finally could look at him, my hand reached up to the cut on his cheek. He flinched but held me steady. My eyes, still blurry with tears, watched him. Pushing the hair from my eyes, he leaned in and kissed my lips.

"Twice in two days, Tasi," he said. "I wouldn't have been able to live with myself if something happened to you. Not after the way I left things last night."

"Don't take my hesitation last night as me not wanting you to come with me, Ethan. I hope you know that. If the decision were up to me, you would be with me always. I just . . . don't want to get my hopes up and then have you ripped away from me."

Lizzie and Emily came rushing back in. Lizzie pulled Ethan from me to clean up his cheek, and Emily sat beside me. "You're going to be okay, Tasi." She tilted my head to the side, getting a better look at the cut along my collarbone. "We don't even need to stitch this up. I'll just clean it. By tomorrow it should go away." She continued inspecting my wounds. "Your cheeks are healing, and your nose is fine. Wrists and ankles are okay as well, but between your fight with the Deity and Austin, I think you could use a break."

The corners of my mouth turned upward. "I can't believe how much you remind me of Mom. The more mature you get, the more like her you are." I reached around, squeezing her tight.

She squeezed me back.

"Sorry to break up the party," Sonya said as she entered the room. *Here we go*—it was the scolding that I knew was eventually going to come. I wondered if, because we were related, she would ground me too. Instead, she surprised me by lifting my chin, examining me with her eyes. "Are you girls okay? I knew Ethan, Lizzie, and Emily could take care of the . . . issue. I think it's best that we now leave immediately, so I finalized the arrangements." She turned to Ethan. "I considered your request to come with us when we leave. Normally, I wouldn't allow this, but I know you truly care about the Vasile girls. So, if you still want to come, I have cleared it."

"Yes, I still want to go," Ethan replied. "If you want me to come, Tasi."

"Yes. Oh my God, yes." All the pain I'd experienced in the past day washed away at the thought of Ethan by my side.

"Wait a minute." Lizzie took a step closer and placed her hands on her hips. "Where does this leave me? I'm not staying in this place while you guys are off trying to save the world or whatever you plan on doing."

Sonya's laugh was genuine. "I figured you were going to say something like that, so I cleared you too."

Lizzie ran into Sonya's arms, hugging her tight. "Thank you."

"You need to let me go if you plan on leaving with us." Lizzie, who hadn't realized what she was doing, backed off slowly, hands in the air. "We're leaving within the hour, so you two go get packed and meet back here in thirty minutes," Sonya said.

They raced out of the room, probably trying to leave before Sonya could change her mind.

"Tasia, I'm sorry. I didn't know about Austin." She sat down beside Emily and me.

"No one could have known," I said. "How could they? No one knew his past or his actual name. And if I'd been more careful and didn't tell him I was leaving, we would have just left, and none of this would have happened."

"Until he hunted you down and found you. Tasia, I saw the video. That fevered look in his eyes was like a rogue vampire's. He wouldn't have stopped looking for you or Emily."

"But Cas, he was so young," I said.

"And foolish to follow Austin. I don't know why he did it, but he chose his path," Sonya said.

"He craved dhampyr blood," I said. I remembered the first day I met him. How he had swooned over my blood as he bandaged my shoulder. His eyes had taken on the same glittery blackness as Austin's.

I looked over to see tears streaming down Emily's face. I pulled her into me.

"I just thought I finally found someone who understood me. Someone I could call my best friend," she mumbled.

"I know, Em, and I'm sorry. I can't say it enough," I said.

"No, Tasi, you did nothing wrong. This was all them." She pulled away, wiping the tears from her eyes. "Who knew that would be my first kill? Prepare for anything, I guess."

I smiled at her. "Prepare for anything."

Emily bounced off the bed, standing straighter than I had ever seen her. She was somehow glowing with pride, even in such a dark situation.

"Sonya, can I ask you something?" I asked.

"Of course." She cocked her head at me curiously.

"I knew you installed a camera on the rooftop, which, thankfully, I never told Austin about. But how did you guys know I was in trouble?" I asked.

She sat on the bed. "Ethan came to me, ranting about how we were leaving and I didn't ask him to come along." Her eyes narrowed at me. "I pulled him into my office to make sure no one heard us."

"And you saw the camera feeds," I added.

"Yes, I saw Austin cutting . . . something. You weren't in sight. But when Ethan walked around to see what I was looking at, he immediately knew," Sonya said.

"I've never been so thankful for cameras." A small smile crossed my face. "Is that why you are letting Ethan and Lizzie come along?"

"Lizzie coming along feels right. And after Ethan's rant about trust and loyalty, I realized how close you guys were and decided maybe he was right too. I trusted Lizzie for the way she saved Emily after Jelena's attack and didn't hesitate with helping Emily kill Cas, who I know she was longtime friends with."

"And Ethan?" I asked.

"I've trusted him longer." She studied my face for a moment. "When he protected you at the toy store and then lied to me about it, I knew I could trust him to always protect you, even if it would cost him his life. He knew the repercussions of lying to me typically lead to death."

"Wait—how did you know he lied?"

"When Austin came back alone, he was in a bad mood. I asked him where you guys were. He told me you'd insisted on going to Times Square, and Ethan was with you. So I sent Len to watch you guys in case you needed help."

"Oh," I said.

I remembered the kiss between Ethan and me in the toy store, and realized Sonya knew everything. My cheeks flushed.

Ethan strolled into the room with a backpack hung over his shoulder. The cut on his cheek was barely noticeable, and the black eye had already faded.

"Emily, do you want to help me hurry Lizzie along?" Sonya said.

"Sure do. She's probably packing up her entire room." Emily reached for Sonya's hand, the way she did when she wanted to feel safe. It took Sonya a moment, but she gave in to her, squeezing her hand around Emily's as if to tell her she would be okay.

Now alone with Ethan, I turned my attention to him. His chocolate-colored eyes were watching my mouth. He reached out and ran a thumb across my lips. My lungs were starving for air.

"Hi."

It was all I could breathe out. His touch left a current running through my body.

The corner of his mouth crooked up. "Hi." His face was so close to mine. When he spoke, his cool breath tickled my skin. He pulled back, running his hand through my hair and pushing it behind my ear.

"So, are you ready to tell me *I told you so* about Austin?"

"No, Tasi, I just eliminated the competition." He sat on the bed and pulled me into his lap.

"Ethan, you never had competition."

His lips crashed into my lips. The taste of vanilla filled my mouth and I melted into him. He pressed his tongue against mine, stroking it. He tugged at my lips before deepening the kiss and letting a low growl leave the back of his throat. If my heart stopped, Ethan and his sumptuous touch were to blame. There was no other way to describe it—the kiss was simply perfect.

There was a knock on the door. Ethan and I pulled apart.

"Coming in, so if you're naked, cover up," Lizzie said as she opened the door. "Oh well, better luck next time."

I stood up and gave Lizzie a big hug. "I'm so glad you're on the good side. I don't think I could have killed you. Hurt you, definitely—killed you, nope."

"Thanks, I think." I noticed the skin around Lizzie's eyes was pinkish and raw.

I touched her hand. "I'm sorry about Cas. I know you guys were close."

Her eyes met mine. "He chose poorly, but I should've known. It took him quite some time to stop drinking directly from humans. There was always a part of him fighting the bloodthirst. I never told anyone because it's been over fifteen years since he got it under control. Maybe if I had—"

"No, Lizzie, this is not your responsibility. If you ever want to talk . . ." I pulled her into a hug.

"Thanks." A glint of relief sparked in her eyes. She then turned to Ethan and dropped her huge duffel bag, which might have been able to fit two bodies in it. "I'll carry yours if you carry mine."

She grabbed his backpack and headed out. Ethan shook his head. "One day, Lizzie . . . one day, I'm going to get you back."

"Only if I can help," I said. "It's not fair for you to have all the fun."

"I heard that," Lizzie scoffed from down the hall. "Hurry—Sonya and Em pulled the Navi up out front. Don't want to leave them hanging."

Ethan and I sighed, then laughed as we headed out the door. I took one last glance at the place I'd called home and looked back at Ethan.

"To new beginnings," he said.

I kissed Ethan once more and said, "To new beginnings."

36

We put everything into the Navigator and headed out of the city before the sun was fully up. The Navi had vampire-grade tinted windows and a limo divider so we could all sit in the back while Sonya's trusted driver took us to where the small coven was.

"Sonya?"

"Yes, Tasia?"

"Remember when you made me promise not to do anything stupid, like getting attacked by Jelena and the Deity, again?"

"I remember."

"I wanted to make that promise, but also ask for one in return." The car was silent for quite some time. Maybe Sonya needed time to mull over my request, or perhaps she was purposely not answering me, which would be rude.

"What would you like me to promise? Then I can tell you if it's possible."

"My whole life, I've been on the defensive. I want to change that and go after Jelena instead of waiting for her to strike again. Sitting back waiting is taking a toll on me, and I know we have the upper hand."

Sonya was focusing her attention out the window. Not

wanting to be impatient, I waited for her to sort out her thoughts.

"Tasia, do you remember that painting above the fireplace in my office?"

"The one with you standing over all those dead bodies?"

Even from the third-row seat, I could tell that made her smile. "I didn't know if you would pick up on that being me. Well, the painting is from the fourteen hundreds. Rogue vampires were at an all-time high. They were taking over villages and moving on to larger cities. Your father and I, and a few other vampires, decided we needed to exterminate them, for a couple reasons—what they were doing wasn't right, and they were severely limiting food resources."

"You mean people, right?" I asked. I tried my best not to sound judgmental.

"Correct. So we started a war. We recruited humans, other vampires, and anyone who believed in life and not destroying it. We won, and the rogue vampire numbers dwindled. That portrait captured the victory and remained a reminder to fight for what is right," she said. "You're right, Tasia—it's time to go on the offensive, but we cannot do so without proper planning, and only with people we trust."

"Thank you, Sonya. I made a promise to Jelena that I would kill her one day, and I want to make sure that is a promise I don't break."

"And you won't, Tasia. Not if I can help it," Sonya said.

There was silence in the car as I thought of Sonya supporting me instead of holding me back. I was ready for this fight. Jelena and the Deity wouldn't expect us to come for them.

"So what's the deal with Sonya coming along?" Lizzie leaned across Ethan, who was sitting in the middle seat. "I mean, it's cool and all, you know, strength in numbers, but it seems like an odd choice."

"Because . . ." I picked at my nails, unsure what to say as both

Ethan and Lizzie stared me down, waiting for me to say something.

Sonya turned to them. "Because I am her aunt, and by aunt, I mean their father and I share the same parents." Sonya gave me an appreciative glance before turning back around.

"Whoa, that's crazy! You're an original?" Lizzie said. "You guys really have one strange family tree going on there. Vampires, humans, and dhampyrs, oh my."

We laughed, except for Sonya. Emily—who was sitting next to her—picked up on it first.

"What's wrong, Sonya?" Emily asked.

"I need to tell you one more thing." Again, her eyes were fixed out the window. There was not even a glance toward Emily to acknowledge her. "Where we are going, there will be a mix of humans and vampires. They are loyal to the Vasile family. These humans have been working for us for a long time, all more than ten years. Their children have grown up with vampires and will continue the family legacy of helping us."

My face grew dark as I thought of all the new people I now needed to learn to trust again. Ethan's hand reached for mine, and he gave it a gentle squeeze.

"I received a call before we left," she said. "It was an . . . unexpected call."

"You're stalling, Sonya," I said.

"Right." She inhaled deeply and exhaled slowly. "Your mother is there. Part of your parents' plan was that your father would give her his blood when the Deity came for them. She escaped the fire, but was killed shortly after. Whoever killed her thought she was still human. She died with your father's blood in her."

ACKNOWLEDGMENTS

Thank you to my family for all the support you have given me along the way. A huge shout out to Jon, you are my rock and the voice of reason in my books. For that I will be forever grateful. Evelyn, you are the best sister ever and I love that you read my manuscripts with so much emotion.

To the three amazing editors—Courtney, Lara, and Liz—thank you for all the work you put in to making this story the best it could be. I am grateful for the opportunity to work with each of you and extremely excited to continue our journey in the future.

To my cover artist—Stefanie Saw at Seventhstar Art Services. Your covers are visually stunning. Thank you for taking my vision and turning it into a reality. I look forward to working with you on the rest of the series. To my character illustrator—Donata, thank you for bringing my characters to life.

A special thank you to Diane, you have been my number one fan—and an amazing beta reader—since day one. I will forever consider you a friend. One day I hope to meet over coffee.

Finally, thank you to my kids—Levi, William, and Kate. You are each unique in your own way and I love everything about you.

Dream big and strive for greatness. You each have a bit of magic inside of you, don't ever let anyone take that from you.

CPSIA information can be obtained
at www.ICGtesting.com
Printed in the USA
LVHW100932111222
734995LV00004B/139